ACROSS THE BRIDGE

Morag Joss

ALMA BOOKS

ALMA BOOKS LTD
London House
243–253 Lower Mortlake Road
Richmond
Surrey TW9 2LL
United Kingdom
www.almabooks.com

Across the Bridge first published in the United States by Delacorte Press, an imprint of
Random House USA, as *Among the Missing* in June 2011
First published in Great Britain by Alma Books Limited in September 2011
This mass-market edition first published by Alma Books Limited in 2012
Copyright © Morag Joss, 2011

Morag Joss asserts her moral right to be identified as the author of this work in
accordance with the Copyright, Designs and Patents Act 1988

Printed and bound by CPI Group (UK) Ltd, Croydon, CR0 4YY

ISBN: 978-1-84688-210-4

ACROSS THE BRIDGE

For the ones who are still missing

"Thousands of people are reported missing each year, yet very little is understood about who they are, why they disappear and what happens to them. It is known that most people go missing intentionally, to escape family or other problems. Adults most at risk of going missing are those going through a crisis or a difficult transition."

"The likelihood of missing adults being traced and possibly reunited with their loved ones decreases over time. Among those who are ever found alive, only one in five returns."

Extracts from: *Lost From View: A Study of Missing Persons in the UK* by Nina Biehal, Fiona Mitchell and Jim Wade (Bristol: Policy Press, 2003), *research undertaken by the University of York in partnership with the National Missing Persons Helpline*

Part One

Part One

When Ron was first released he discovered that prison had made him observant, as if he'd been reminded there, by its sudden absence, of the world's surfeit of objects, its over-abundance of things to look at. Not beautiful things. It wasn't a case of seeing the world's wonders anew or anything like that; rather, it was the opposite. Observation didn't sharpen his faculties, it stupefied them. He was dazed by the quantity and variety, the massive, compacted volume of it all; he noticed everything but had no idea what was worth his notice. People's faces and brick walls, town gutters and ploughed fields, church towers and shopfronts, all claimed his attention equally. He couldn't discriminate, nor could he find in himself a particular attitude to any of it beyond disorientation, sometimes mild alarm. He surveyed the burgeoning, seething material of other people's lives, and very little moved him.

After a while, his alarm grew. He began to think there must be some invisible force at work in the world, some unstoppable law of accretion filling up every surface and corner with streets, office blocks, rivers, factories, houses. Only he seemed to see it, this chaotic, impossible density, all this hoarding and flowing over; was nobody else concerned? If it went on like this, some day the whole planet would clog up and there would not be enough room in the sky for all the criss-crossing exhaust trails of planes, or on the sea for the countless interweaving, frothy wakes of ships. Swirling lines of traffic would spill off the teeming highways. Already there was no such thing as an unfilled space; it was impossible to see *nothing*. However deserted or arbitrarily spacious, every inch of the world was a place taken up and touched in some way, claimed for one purpose or another, even if it was, as he found in Scotland, to be left bare so that people could see it empty. But there was no true emptiness, no real nothingness, no *desert stillness*, a phrase that came into his mind and he now wished were more than a phrase. Everywhere – crowded and disorderly, or deliberately pristine – was somewhere, laden with the paraphernalia and expectation of some human design, and in not one of these places was his presence relevant. He tried not to think about it. He tried not to panic, and to concentrate instead on tiny things, one at a time.

He practised on people. In cafés and checkout queues he would study them and take in only physical details: the curve of an ear, a ridged fingernail, the asymmetric lift of one eyebrow. Every feature was odd in some way, once he focused on it – not that this disappointed him at all, since he was not looking for perfection or hoping to find a special value in the unique. He simply noticed and remembered. He filed every detail in his mind disjointedly and without cross-reference, each alone for its isolated, particular, frangible self. He welcomed this dullness of perception in himself; it would have been unbearable to dwell on anything more than how precious and how breakable were these vulnerable, separate, flawed parts of other people's bodies. Sometimes he knew he was staring at a stranger too hard and should apologize, but he didn't know what to be sorry for. For not knowing how his own mind worked? For not being sure he bore more than a trivial surface resemblance to other human beings any more?

He would have liked someone to tell it all to. He called his sister. She told him it would be fine for him to come for a few days if it was up to her, but Derek wasn't ready to see him.

"Listen Ron, he accepts it was an accident," she said. "So do I. But he's just not ready, you know?"

Ron did know, but he said nothing.

"I mean, Ron, criminal negligence is, well, what it says. You know?"

"I know," he said.

"And as Derek says, six children died. Plus the pregnant woman. Give us a few months."

"I've been in prison over five years."

"And then he says, it just makes us look at our two and think, you know? Anyway, the extension's not finished."

He left her another couple of messages. Then she sent him a cheque with a note saying she trusted the enclosed would help him make a fresh start "somewhere new". She'd be in touch, she wrote.

He called his former neighbour Jeff and thanked him for the card. It had meant a lot, he said, on his first Christmas in prison.

"That'd be Lynne," Jeff said. "She sends cards to everybody."

He left the words *even you* unspoken, but Ron heard them nonetheless.

"How's Kathy? Has Lynne seen her?"

Jeff hesitated. "They're in touch, yeah. Doing better. Knocks you sideways, divorce, never mind everything else she's had to contend with."

Ron said it would be good to meet up for a drink. They agreed on a day the following week. The next day Jeff sent a text message to say he couldn't make it and he'd call soon, but he didn't.

They'd found him a room for the first month, and a social worker, and he worked the night shift for a while in a bakery, standing on a line wrapping buns and cakes in a warm, yellow-lit factory that smelled of sugar icing and machine oil. His fellow workers were all women who spoke rapidly to one another in their own language and ignored him except to pass on commands about cellophane or cardboard boxes.

To get away from all of that he cashed his sister's cheque, bought an old Land Rover and reverted to his life's previous pattern, the covering of distances. He knew how to measure a day or night in miles rather than in hours on a factory clock, and he found comfort in the old equation of roads travelled *versus* time spent *equals* a portion of his life somehow suspended in transit. As a boy he'd been fascinated by time zones, which he could hardly distinguish from time travel; if you went west crossing zone after zone, going always back in time, one day would you be a man of twenty-one in a high chair with a bib and a spoon? Or going always east and forward, would you find yourself stooped and white-haired and still ten years old? It couldn't be so, of course, but he had concluded then that the secret was to keep moving. Forget about direction and destination, just keep moving, and surely your life would never be able to catch you up with restrictions and obstacles and all its weighty boredom.

Now, amused by a childish hope that was, if foolish, at least familiar, he took again to the road, sleeping most nights in the Land Rover, parking at the end of the day within reach of a pub and whenever possible near a fast-running stream or a river, whose sound in the night was perhaps a lulling echo of the flow of the daytime traffic. Occasionally he stayed in cheap places when he needed to shave and shower and wash clothes in a hand basin, and sometimes he halted for a week or two here or there and took casual jobs: kitchen portering, labouring, hauling timber, loading and moving, anything physical; it was surprising how often he got a few days' work just by asking. But mainly he drove. As the first year passed, that was the task that kept him becalmed, though he had to get used to the absence of passengers. There could never be any more passengers.

* * *

There we were at breakfast in the Invermuir Lodge Hotel, on the last day when our distress was of a containable and ordinary kind. Colin was eating sausages at a table in the bay window, and I had gone to the sideboard for orange juice. The dining room was quiet, just us and a retired couple in hiking clothes, and a flat-footed teenage waitress going to and fro. I started to pour the juice, and suddenly the sugary scent of my shampoo as my hair fell over my face and the hot smell of the fried eggs the waitress was carrying past combined and attacked me, and I thought I was going to be sick. I had to put down the jug and steady myself with both hands and look away, and as I tried to swallow some air and breathe without drawing in more of the smell, I found myself concentrating on my reflection in the broad mirror fixed along the back of the sideboard. My face was not a good colour, but it did not reveal any disturbance, never mind dread. The hiking couple were squabbling about distances over a map unfolded across their table and did not look up. The waitress was waiting to set down their plates. So much is invisible.

My focus in the mirror lengthened across the empty tables to the window and the moving silhouette of my husband feeding himself, his head as solid and bony as a calf's, swaying down to the fork, his mouth opening and closing, working, emptying. I switched my gaze back to myself and saw all I expected to see: a nondescript woman over forty, her make-up slightly too determined and even a little clownish on a face sallow from sleep and perhaps also from some other cause – some new, active trouble. Then my attention flicked back as Col's knife tipped off his plate, clattered on the table and hit the floor. He picked it up, scrubbed at the cloth with his napkin and then he licked his index finger and scrubbed some more, sighing and wincing as if it were all the fault of a vague, absent someone who had failed to materialize in time to prevent this latest blunder by an overgrown, under-supervised child. I faced myself in the mirror in time to see the expression in my eyes turn thin and resigned. I was used to the idea that the someone was me.

I returned to my place as if nothing had happened, and maybe nothing had. We beamed at each other. Not even the briefest of dubious marriages foundered ultimately on a matter of dropped cutlery, did it? We smeared our toast from tiny unfolded packs of butter and miniature pots of jam, our faces puckered by the strain of being together on holiday at all, as well as in a worn-out hotel in mid-February. I'm sure we looked unremarkable, perhaps slightly formal, sitting up a little straighter than other couples about to enter a slow-moving middle age in a way that suggested they had never felt young or led rapid, excited lives. The hiking pair folded their maps and got up to leave, wishing us a good day as they went.

As their boots creaked across the floor, I thought well, maybe it could still be a good day or at least, like other days in the past five months, a good enough one, a day whose course would offer up to us any number of chances to overlook the disenchantment of our late and incongruous marriage. I poured my husband more coffee. We had already learnt to fill the place of love with an obscuring politeness; we observed the etiquette of keeping our disappointment quiet with upbeat conversations over practicalities, like optimistic gardeners keeping an unpromising surface raked and hoed in the hope that a flower might be growing underground. Above all, we extended to each other self-serving magnanimity in the granting of opportunities to spend time apart. On this off-season budget break in Scotland (which we were not calling a honeymoon, it being as near as we would ever come to one and yet nowhere near enough), we were keeping our voices bright, trading all the usual clichés to excuse ourselves from each other's company: not wanting to "get in each other's hair", we were each "doing our own thing". Col was doing "guys' stuff", I was "chilling out at my own pace". Col had rented a car, an expense he could barely afford, which made our separate agendas easier and perhaps almost natural. On this particular day he was "getting his money's worth" out of it by letting me drive myself up to Inverness to window-shop and visit the museum, while he went kayaking. We were, in fact, on two quite different holidays.

The hotel was built at the top of an incline, and the bay window looked down over the beer garden, still dank under dawn shadows, as the sun was not fully risen. Rain and melting frost dripped from a black monkey-puzzle tree onto the twiggy roof of a gazebo filled with stacks of empty bottle crates and drifts of dead leaves. Banks of chilly-looking cloud weighted the sky above the main road going north past the garden railings; beyond the road, the river flowed over rocks into glossy brown pools that spun with curls of froth.

"I'm afraid it'll rain on and off all day," I said. "I hope the weather won't spoil it for you."

"A bit more rain won't hurt," he said. "If it rains, it rains." He cleared his throat. "It might dry up in Inverness."

"It might. I won't mind," I said, my eyes still on the river. "That current's very fast. You wouldn't want to capsize in that."

"Well, if it's raining, I'll be wet anyway, won't I?" he said. "That would be quite funny."

I cast him too bright and grateful a smile, as if capsizing into rivers were some huge amusement I'd forgotten about. We went quiet again. Our table was crowded with white china and over-large spoons and knives that made too much noise, beneath which our silence seemed delicate and even meaningful, which it was not. But nor was it desolate, I thought. Incongruous it certainly was, after a year of Internet romance via an online chat room for housebound caregivers, finally to meet and within six weeks get married, all in a rush. But was it such a mistake to be in a hurry to ignore the undertow of something missing, to prove ourselves still marriageable before the notion of being

15

in love, fast receding, could vanish utterly? After all, no marriage was ever spontaneous, and most between people over forty were arranged, somehow or other and for any number of fragile reasons, among them a fear of loneliness. That was by no means a small thing. Col's parents had been dead for three years (he had kept up his membership in the caregivers' chat room, out of familiarity), and he stayed on alone in their house in Huddersfield; my father had just died, leaving me with no reason to stay in Portsmouth. These seemed good reasons, not bad ones, to chain ourselves to the mediocre but likeable real forms of each other that we encountered face to face, and put aside our hankering for the early, impossible, younger-seeming versions of ourselves we had come to know at our computer-aided distance.

His mobile phone burbled, and he took it out to read the message. "That's them telling us to bring waterproofs," he said. "We're in for a soaking. Time I was going."

"There's something I should tell you," I said, quickly. "I'm pregnant."

"*What*?" He flinched, then looked away.

"Aren't you going to say anything?"

"Oh, God," he said, blowing out his cheeks. He pushed himself back as far as he could get without moving out of his chair, and then, of course, the first thing that would spring to anyone's mind sprang to his.

"God. I mean, but aren't you—"

"I thought I was too old, too! It is a surprise. A mum at forty-two!"

"But you're supposed to be getting a job in Huddersfield."

"Well, and I will, when I can. Is that all you're going to say?"

He looked at me hard, as if searching for something to admire. "You know we both need to work. It's not my fault I don't bring in enough."

"Col, I know, but I can't help it. It's happened."

"I don't make enough for two, never mind three. You're supposed to be looking for a job." He gulped from his coffee cup and crossed his arms. "Anyway, I don't want kids. I told you from the start. I told you, for God's sake."

"Yes," I said, "but that was before. Ages ago, online. Before we'd even met."

He tipped his head and gazed at the ceiling for a while. His face was just as it had been when he was rubbing at the tablecloth. Was this the same to him as a dropped, greasy knife – an accidental mess, not much to do with him? Another blunder?

"It is a shock, I didn't expect it, either! But I didn't do it on my own. Please don't act as if I should say sorry or something!" I said, trying to sound light. "It must happen all the time. Other people manage it."

"I said I didn't want kids. I said so. I said so right from the start, when we were getting to know each other."

But we didn't get to know each other, I wanted to say. That wasn't knowing each other. This is.

"We said lots of things then. We hadn't really met, that was just online chatting. It was the Internet, it wasn't real."

"It was real!" he said. "It was real as far as I was concerned. I meant what I said. I don't want kids. They ruin your lifestyle."

"*Lifestyle*? Have we got a lifestyle?"

He glowered at me. "I don't want kids."

"But why not?"

"Why *not*? Because I don't. For a start we can't afford it. Anyway, it's not why I don't, it's why all of a sudden I've got to want a kid just because you've changed your tune. Why should I change my mind just because you have?"

"Why? Because I'm having one! And because... well, because most people have them. They aren't all miserable about it, are they? They manage!"

He shook his head from side to side and glanced out of the window.

"OK, so, money. Have you got money?" He placed his fingertips on the edge of the table as if he were changing the subject.

"Money? For today? Oh, yes. I'll be fine, I don't need much, just enough for lunch and the museum. I'm not planning on buying anything. And there's plenty of petrol."

"That's not what I mean. I mean for this. I haven't got the money, and neither have you."

"But it'll be fine, we'll manage! Because people do. You'll see!"

"Even suppose you live off me for the next nine months, what about after? You haven't got any money."

"Babies don't need all that much to begin with," I said, arranging my ideas about it on the spot, allowing pictures from the back of my head to press forwards. "People might give us things. I bet we can get good stuff second-hand. On eBay." There was a silence. "I'll knit!" I said, happily.

"The bit you got when your dad died. That's gone, isn't it?"

"More or less. But look, Col, please."

I had less even than he thought I had. Back when I never dreamed it could matter, I'd told him I would inherit my father's house when he died; it was the only thing I could say to the Internet Col, lest he think me a gold-digger and vanish. I didn't tell him until later that I'd remortgaged and remortgaged the house so my father and I could go on living in it. When it was sold, it had paid off the debt and left a little that I'd spent on getting married and small expenses since then. If I'd had even a little put by, I could surely have persuaded him it would be enough to see us through until the baby was born.

"Well, then. Even if you went back to work after, we'd be shelling out for the rest of our lives. Kids don't live on air. I'm nearly fifty, I don't want to work my backside off for the next twenty years. I can't afford it."

Why do we assume that ponderous, plain, clumsy people are more loving than everyone else, that what slows them down is a hidden burden of tenderness that does not encumber those who are quick and thin? I stared at him, this man who was now my husband, with his sullen voice and broad, shiny face and the bulky body I knew so well now. But I knew nothing, I realized, of these reserves of hostility – that they existed in him at all, never mind that they were so easily tapped, so available to be sent spilling into his dealings with me.

"Look, Col, it's a shock, of course it is. But when you said you didn't want kids, that must've been the *idea* of kids. Of course you didn't want them when you were single, on your own. Now it's different. OK, we didn't plan it, but it's real, it's actually happening. A real baby." I couldn't stop my face breaking out in a smile. "I thought you might have noticed something."

He looked at me blankly.

"It's for real," I said, encouragingly. "This isn't the Internet now."

"Don't I know it," he said.

"I've been feeling pretty sick. But that's normal."

"Look. Are you really sure? It's not like it shows," he said.

Just then his phone burbled again. He read the new message and then stretched back and stabbed in a reply.

"They're waiting for me," he said, standing up and pocketing the phone. "So, how far gone are you?"

"Oh, there's bags of time to get used to it," I said. "It's not due till the beginning of October."

"No, I mean, *how* far gone?"

"Only about five weeks. Did you really not notice anything? I probably haven't been all that much fun to be with!"

He shrugged.

"Don't worry, it doesn't last long, the sick stage. I'll be right as rain in a few weeks," I said.

He hesitated, his hands on the back of his chair, then jammed it in under the table. "Listen. How many ways do I have to say it? I don't want a kid. You can't spring this on me. I'm not prepared to have a kid. So you'll just have to do what you have to do. Deal with it."

"Deal with it? What are you saying?"

"I'm saying if you want to make a go of it with me, fine, I'll make a go of it with you. But not with a kid. A kid was never in the plan, there's no way we can afford it. If you get rid of it, fine. If you keep it, also fine, but you're on your own."

"You're telling me to get rid of a healthy baby? To have an abortion?"

"I'm telling you I don't want a kid. I'm not telling you what to do, it's up to you. I'm not forcing you."

He left before I could say any more. A few moments after he had gone, the waitress padded forwards to remove our breakfast dishes. "Take your time," she said to me. "No rush."

I did take my time. For several minutes I stared out of the window. The waitress returned and began wiping the sideboard. I closed my eyes, and when I opened them again it was like arriving back in the room after an absence to find it bigger, or at least empty of something it had contained before. The yellow electric globe lights on the walls shone with an old, dusty warmth. The sun was rising higher, burning proud of the horizon and casting streaks of silver light across the garden and in over the windowsill. The waitress set to work with a vacuum cleaner. I fancied she started at the farthest corner of the room so as to disturb me least – that was sweet of her. She smiled as she finished up and left, trailing the vacuum behind her on squeaky casters. Then a different waitress came with trays of glasses and cutlery wrapped in paper napkins and began to set tables for lunch.

I had no idea what I was going to do. When the sun was shining small and high and pale through a veil of rain above the river, I got up and walked away.

He missed the passengers, not for their company but for giving his journeys purpose. Alone, his travelling was just driving. That was why, summoning all his courage, he stopped outside Doncaster one rainy day in early September for two hitch-hikers, Canadian students heading for Scotland. They were trying to get to Edinburgh in time for some festival whose name they couldn't pronounce but which, they assured him, was an ancient Celtic celebration of the end of summer.

"It's her that really wants to go. She's really into folklore, aren't you, sweetheart?" the boy said adoringly, and wrote down the name of it – *Samhraidhreadh* – on the back of his girlfriend's hand while she laughed because the pen was tickly. He pulled her wrist forwards to show Ron, and Ron had never heard of it and couldn't pronounce it either. But something about their journey touched him – its pilgrim zeal, its pointlessness – and in a demonstration of goodwill that he did not really feel he took them all the way to Edinburgh, thinking that to perform, however disinterestedly, an act of kindness might bring flooding back a former true impulse to be kind, the way he might swing a numbed limb to and fro hoping that movement would restore sensation.

So began a habit of stopping for hitch-hikers and offering to take them wherever they were heading, since the direction or distance didn't affect him much. That winter, drifting farther north on the main tourist routes, he came across more of them than he expected,

and once or twice in bad weather he slowed down and offered lifts when none was being asked, until he realized how that might look. He told himself it was a way of meeting people – people distinct in his mind from fellow prisoners – though it was really only practice at being in proximity to them again.

Their company was easy because, he soon discovered, young people were curious only about themselves. He just had to keep quiet, as he was anyway inclined to do, and within minutes his youthful passengers would launch into an account of themselves that kept them chirping on for miles, as if Ron had demanded some justification for their being where they were at that precise point in their lives. Unless the journey was very short, Ron would soon know pretty much all there was to know about whole extended families: the birthday parties, the funerals, the divorces, the day the dog had puppies. A hundred personal philosophies were explained to him in all their complexity and variation; he learned of ambitious and intricate life plans based on a faith in something or other or on recovery from the loss of it, and all of it was offered to him, he sensed, as barter, a diligent trading of autobiography for transportation. Not that that made them real *passengers*, certainly not. It was a symbolic reckoning only, a token proffered for safe passage. So he listened quietly, intending his silence to convey that his side of the bargain was that he would not trouble his companions to pretend they were in the least interested in him. For the most part they honoured the transaction, measuring out their disclosures like shining coins counted from palm to palm and expecting none in return.

But on the rare occasions anyone asked, he was always ready to say that he was just taking time out, he liked Scotland, and it suited him not to stay in one place for long. Sometimes he was tempted to volunteer a remark or two about himself beyond that, just to hear his own words cross the air between himself and his passenger, to test the link between that person's life and his own. But when he rehearsed in his mind what those words would have to be, the temptation vanished.

I used to be a coach driver. Seven summers ago I took a party of schoolchildren to Portugal. We were late for the ferry going back, and during the ninth hour of driving, in torrential rain, I must have fallen asleep. We came off the motorway. Six children and a teacher, who was pregnant, were killed. I went to prison.

What link could there possibly be, after that, between him and, say, a happy young Canadian couple who were really into folklore?

During the evenings, and when he woke in the night, his passengers' words would come back to him as intermittent phrases in a dozen accents, the sounds fragmenting in his head like the scrapbook of images of the small physical details he recalled: the back of a hand sore from an insect bite, a damp space where a tooth was missing, an ear lobe punctured decoratively in three places. He would remember the smells they brought into the car, of the ferny, rain-soaked hills and their sour trainers and wet nylon clothes, and he'd recall how secretly and greedily he had inhaled, once they got talking, their cigarette and bubblegum-scented breath. As he lay awake in the night, it made him gasp, the fear he had felt for them at journey's end, setting them down blithe and undefended to fare again for themselves in this world crowded with dangers. He had no interpretation for any of these things.

Towards the end of the second winter, he noticed that most days he thought about stopping. He was still in the north, mainly because nothing was drawing him in any other direction, but he was running out of places to go. The landscape was beautiful, he could see that, but he had had his fill of the more or less stultifying succession of glimpses taken from the road, the amassing of the same mental snapshots over and over. On the night of his fiftieth birthday, he washed and shaved in the Gents of a pub called The Highlander's Rest, ate the mixed grill and chips alone in the bar, and slept parked in a lay-by. He woke tired. He wanted a spell of quiet away from the engine drone and diesel warmth of the Land Rover, to be in one place for a while. He had no idea where or how it was to be found, but he longed for somewhere to stay.

Silva, the geese are back, you said as you stepped into the trailer. Hundreds of them. You can see their shapes but not their colours yet, it's too misty. They're downstream over on the far side of the river on that long black rock you can see at low tide, just down from that old ruin you like, the cabin with the little jetty.

You left the door open. It was still early, and you let in the cold.

They must have found a whole family of fish down there, you said, waving your hands. All around the rock where the water's glassy, they're feasting. You should see them, they're landing and diving and dipping their necks and sending ripples all the way across, beautiful slow ripples lapping all the way over onto our side. You can hear them. Listen, can you hear the water?

I whispered to you to shut the door. Anna had kicked her covers off, and I was afraid the chill on her legs might wake her up. Then I listened and shook my head.

No, Stefan, I don't hear anything.

Well, of course you don't, not with the door shut, you said, coming over and sitting down. But it's a nice noise when you're outside. Want to come out, lazybones?

I hushed you with a finger placed on your lips.

What's the time? I whispered. She's still asleep. We've got a little time, haven't we?

You glanced over at Anna and back at me, pretending to be puzzled. You're awake, I'm awake, why would we want Anna to stay asleep? Then you rose and quietly drew the blanket back over Anna's curled little body and tucked her giraffe in beside her. You came towards me, smiling. I still remember precisely how the mattress tilted as you clambered onto it. We didn't have a lot of time. When you entered me, I wanted to cry out, but I trapped the sound in my throat and pressed my mouth against your neck.

Not long afterwards it was Anna who broke the silence with her creaky, waking-up noise that was not exactly crying but a test of her voice, a call of emergence. Although she was nearly two, when she fell asleep it really was still a fall, a sheer drop into that fathomless well of baby sleep; it turned her body solid, so her chest hardly rose and fell and her eyelids did not even flicker. It seems fantastic to me now that I could watch her like that without feeling panic at how far away from me she went in her sleep. I loved her waking-up noises, like the snuffling of a small creature returning from the lost, clambering back up through undergrowth from a foray a little too far from the nest. The real crying would start a few moments later, when she was awake enough to know she was hungry.

You tried to ease yourself away from me, but I caught hold of the chain around your neck and pulled you back for a kiss.

Oh, you've got me on the end of a chain, you said. Haven't you? A chain that I'll never take off.

Good. That's why I gave it to you, I said, as I let you go.

You stepped back into your jeans and went to her, laughing softly. You lifted her up high and crooned – *oh, Anna, Anna, Anna* – and the crying stopped at once. You carried her outside, sending me a single look over her head that signalled you were giving me some time, a moment or two to shake off the thought of any more of you for now, to get out of bed and dressed and ready to balance myself against the day. I sat up and watched you through the trailer window. You put her down on her feet in front of you and walked her along, holding both her hands. Her arms were raised and outstretched and you were edging her along on her wobbly, sleepy legs, her bare feet curling on the cold stones. You were asking too much of her. Sometimes you did that, forgetting she was so little. You wanted to show her the geese, but she had other ideas, she wanted her breakfast.

Look, Anna, look, you said, lifting her up again and pointing across the water. You made the *wark wark* noise of the geese against her cheek, and she laughed and twisted away, patting the stubble on your chin with both hands. I pulled on clothes and walked down to the end of the trailer and set out bowls and cereal and milk on the table. I put a pan of water on to heat for coffee. I got out spoons, juice, cups. I stood in the trailer doorway for a few minutes longer, watching you before I called you in.

You never knew I did this. Every day I watched you together, keeping myself apart while you were absorbed in each other and busy with this or that little thing around the place. I liked to study you, your resemblance to each other, with that identical tangle of dark hair, so different from mine. I liked that simple evidence of how much you belonged to each other, the everyday fact of it. The mother is blonde and the father dark, the child inherited her father's colouring – it's the kind of remark that gets made about families. It helped me pretend our life was like other people's, easy and regular.

I tried to keep them all in my mind, these pictures I made of you then. You feeding Anna, carrying her about talking nonsense, drawing pictures and singing songs. She gazing so seriously with her giraffe in her mouth and then chuckling back, reaching for your hands, tugging your hair. She left the wet trails of her kisses all over your face. Each of these pictures had to stand for something, a sign that our life would go on being possible, so I could say to myself, look at this life we have, so natural and loving, we are not defeated, we are not despairing.

That day I watched you. You dipped her hand in the river and waggled her wrist, sprinkling water drops from her fingers all over your face. You spluttered and screwed up your eyes, she laughed and laughed. You turned her hand and sprinkled her own face, too. I memorized you both for later that day, to bring you to mind when I was at work at Vi's general store over the bridge on the other side of the river. I needed to save you up like this, it was the only way I could spend the day away from you.

When I had put my hair in a ponytail and brushed my teeth, I still had some time before I had to set off to get the bus.

Silva, come on out, you called.

Anna was sitting on the ground with an old spoon in her hand, digging into tufts of grass that sprang up between the sand and stones of the shoreline. You led me a little farther down so I could see the geese bobbing on the river. The sun was up by then and still bright through a mist of cloud. I had to shade my eyes to see. On the far side, the old wooden cabin looked silvery-grey as if it were made out of water rather than from pine trees like the ones that grew steeply all around it. It shimmered like something wet, scooped out of the current and set up on the bank, solid but made of water all the same, shining in the sun just like the sheeny membrane of the gliding river. The white rowing boat moored at the little jetty sat as it had always sat. It hadn't moved in all the time we'd been there.

Stefan, see? That cabin, it's still empty. Nobody's even been there in over a year, that boat never moves. It's deserted. We could find the way down to it through the trees on the other side. Why don't we? It would be great to live there. At least for the summer.

You tugged on my hair. And then what? you asked. You think next winter we'll be better off there? First storm that comes, the roof blows off, then what? We'll have nowhere at all.

But the trailer leaks anyway. And the roof doesn't look so bad, it looks OK. We could do repairs. It's bigger than the trailer.

Don't keep going on about it, you said, tugging again on my ponytail. You can't even tell if there's glass in the windows. And it's not that much bigger.

I caught hold of your hand and pulled your arm around my neck, wrapping myself within a circle of you. You curled your other arm around my waist, and we stood swaying together, gazing across the river. Behind us Anna was talking to herself in a singsong and scrabbling with her spoon in the shingle.

Anyway, you said in my ear, it must belong to somebody. Any day they could just show up. We'd go to jail.

I know, I said. Worse. They'd send us back.

Then what about Anna?

Oh, I know. Don't talk about it.

I raised your hand to my mouth and kissed it, then I nipped at your fingertips. I didn't want you to start on again about borrowing money to get us out of our trouble. We'd been over and over it. You drew away, cupped your hands around your mouth, and hallooed, and the call rolled across and startled the geese off the rock in the river, all in a flurry. This was our way. We kept ourselves restless on purpose, distracting each other with these innocuous forms of disturbance: making love, sudden bursts of song and silly games, scaring geese into the sky. Anything that kept us from talking about it too often, about living in a leaking trailer hidden from the road, never having enough money to change anything. Being illegal in a foreign country, such a beautiful country but one that could give us no resting point, one we occupied like flies on the surface of a painting.

The geese were gliding back down to the rock. I clapped my hands, and they rose up again, flapping their wings.

Silva, I've had an idea, about the car.

I wouldn't let you speak. I shook my head and clapped and hollered across the river, and then I walked over to Anna and picked her up. I didn't want to hear it again. No jobs for illegals that pay enough, you kept saying, we should get a car, run a cab, you knew guys who'd lend cash and do false papers, you'd work nights. You'd pay the loan back, we'd get a proper place to live. And I kept saying, the kind of people we'd have to borrow from, the amount they charge, you don't get out of trouble that way. I kept saying we had to be patient and save up the proper way, owing nothing, we already had just over three thousand, I'd remind you, and then you'd lose your temper and tell me that way it would take ten years to get enough. We never got anywhere, did we?

So we would chuck pebbles and call across the river to the birds, we'd make childish jokes, make love, pull on each other's hair, play clap-hands with our daughter. Sometimes I was afraid our whole life was getting to be like a silly guessing game we were both secretly sick of. But still I hoped it could last. We needed it to keep going long enough for an answer to come.

The bus will be along soon, I said. Give me your phone. Here's mine.

Just another of our little survival rituals, swapping phones so I could plug each of them in, every few days, under the counter at Vi's, and that morning also a way back from the dangerous subject of how to go on living.

You walked me up the track to the road and a bit of the way along, until Anna got heavy. After you turned back, I watched you for a while, walking away. The noise of the road and the bridge traffic was too loud for me to shout out to you, and so I turned, too, and set off to the bus stop at the service station.

We'd got another day started, I thought. And if in ten hours or so I got off the bus and walked back along the road and down the track, my long shadow cast behind me, carrying a bag of groceries from Vi's past their sell-by date, and if I heard your voices as the rumble of evening traffic on the bridge died away, I would be able to count this one as another day that had let us stay together. Another day done and it still hadn't all come to an end, a day that would let the same day, with luck, come again tomorrow. A good day was one when nothing got worse.

I didn't go as far as Inverness.

The road from the hotel followed the river for several miles. I switched on the car radio and drove, singing along raucously with one song after another, refusing to cry, trying to drown out Col's words in my head. From time to time rain fell, not in spiky drips like English town rain but in milky currents that wet the air with cold, gusting sprays. Between showers, and seeming more liquid than the rain, sunlight poured down through gaps in the clouds onto the rocks and larch and pine trees across the steel-bright river. When my throat was so tired I could hardly make a sound, I turned the radio off and kept driving. Just as, when my father was dying, I used to absorb trivial details while waiting for bad news – every stem and leaf on the wallpaper in the doctor's surgery, every scratch on the floor by his hospital bed – I concentrated now on the sunlight, how it spilled over the landscape into refracting pools of sharp, unfiltered silvers and russets and greens. This was not my country, and I was glad I could numb myself with touristic gawping; I felt no tug of ancestral pride, found nothing revelatory or significant in its beauty. Each bend in the road and new angle of the landscape consoled me with a distracting kind of *un*-belonging; I travelled with the lulling detachment I might have felt thumbing through racks of postcards.

There were dozens of places to pull the car off the road and admire the views, and I stopped often. In some of them there were souvenir vans festooned with tartan flags and pennants, blaring out disheartening bagpipe music over the roofs of parked cars and caravans and food stalls. Sometimes I loitered, reading billboard warnings about forest fires and litter and threats to wildlife, watching people come and go, all of them in pairs or groups, never alone. I saw a family of seven disgorge themselves from a camper van and claim a damp picnic table; the mother and grandma spread plastic bags over the benches, the dog crawled underneath and lay down. The last of the four lanky children ran back to the van for a football, and a loud, hazardous game began at the side of the car park. The father got in the queue at the burger van and began a long relay of shouts to the others. He brought an armful of boxes back to the table, and the children darted into place, mauling the packaging, snapping open cans of explosive drinks, pushing torn-off lumps of pizza and burgers in their mouths, feeding the dog from their fingers. I made my way back to the car. I wanted to get away from them, from my envy of their messy, uncomplicated pleasure and from the shame they aroused in me. I had married a man who shunned the very idea of that noisy, easygoing acceptance within families; surely I must be at heart the same kind of person. I was at the very least someone who would consider aborting a child rather than be abandoned by its father.

But I have no choice, I said to myself, as if the family at their picnic were challenging me. I have to stay married to him. He is all I have.

After that I stopped only in deserted places. I would turn the car onto verges choked with scrubby thickets of undergrowth, and into lay-bys filled with sagging piles of gravel and sand heaped there for highway repairs. I parked and wandered for a while in the rubble-strewn forecourt of a boarded-up and derelict filling station until from an outbuilding came a hissing, spiteful-looking cat and two scraggy kittens.

Still some way before Inverness, I felt sick again and pulled over. I got out of the car to feel the rain on my face and breathe in its cold-water scent; there on the roadside, at the top of a bank of fields sloping down to the river, the air was mixed with a sharp, shelly, salt wind blowing in from the coast. Below me, the estuary flowed along white-flecked and bright under a sudden patch of clear sky. To the east about a mile downriver, a bridge arched across from the city to the north shore, black and permanent against the smoky, distant blues and greys of the horizon where water and sky melded at the start of open sea.

The nausea passed, and to stop myself thinking about the baby, I unfolded the road atlas over the boot of the car and began to trace the contours and place names dotted along the route I had followed, incredulous that the mountains, and swathes of forest, the concrete and steel bridge and the river running beneath it could have transmuted from the actual, touchable, physical vastnesses before me into printed words and shapes on a map. I stared at the page now softening under spattering drops of rain and felt, strangely, that it should have been the other way round, that really their first existence must have been as scribbles and marks in ink on paper and, only then abstracted and set down, had the land risen up and taken form out of nothing more than the idea of itself, to amass and flow and come alive with air and light, and sprout crops and trees and bridges, and teem with creatures. And I longed to apply the same sense of impossibility to the surely still notional little lump of ectoplasm growing inside my body; if I disallowed any connection between that act of cellular multiplication and a real baby, maybe it wouldn't become one, a terrifying, wondrous, real one. Maybe an abortion wouldn't be necessary, maybe I wouldn't have to make a decision at all. Maybe by the simple force of its mother's incredulity, a putative human being could be so belittled and denied as to be fatally discouraged from coming into existence. Suddenly I was filled with horror that this might be so.

I folded the map up and got back in the car. I waited for a while, observing time flickering along by the numbers on the dashboard clock and wondering how long I could stay like this, enclosed and contained, halted. I wanted to arrest any further forward momentum in time or space; although stranded on the edge of a road with traffic thundering by and looking down on a river flowing fast and deep towards the sea, I was, however improbably, in the only place of safety and stillness I had. As long as I remained there, I could put off my next move which, whenever it came and wherever it led, would take me nearer to my decision, whatever that was to be. For the future must have its location; if I refused it that, if I just *didn't* turn the key in the ignition and go forwards, if with every thought and breath I reduced the baby inside me to less than baby, to mereness, to nothing, perhaps I could will it not to be. I wanted its end to be painless and unknowing and without violence, and afterwards I wanted to be left quiet and unnoticed. I wanted to be left alone to carry on living as before. How could it be that I would afterwards suffer the loss of something I had never quite had?

But I gazed at the bridge and saw in the span of it over the water an inevitability, as if the points on each opposing bank had cried out to be joined, as if the flow of the river beneath the bridge was dependent upon each side's throwing out its great black steel arch to connect across it. Events must reach forwards to meet their consequences, consequences must throw backwards in time bridges linking themselves to causes; where else is the meaning of all the things that happen in the world to come from, if not from connection with what happened before and what will happen next? How unbearable otherwise, if human activity were no more than a succession of haphazard little incidents exploding at random all the time over the planet, arising from and leading to nothing. The commission of even a single action surely sets in motion somewhere a yearning, distant and reluctant maybe, for its outcome eventually to have a point. However oblique or delusory the link with past or future, the connection must be attempted, for one thing must be seen to lead from or to another; we prefer a rickety and unreliable bridge between events, if that is all we can have, to none at all. I started the engine and drove on. Even after all that has happened, I do not believe anyone can behold a bridge and not feel a compulsion to find out what lies on the other side of it.

Yet I would not go across. I parked at a service station a short distance further on, just before a large roundabout where one road led off left to the bridge approach and another went straight on towards the outer edge of Inverness. I went into the café and sat there for a long time under the swimmy piped music, sipping water, pushing my finger into a little mound of crumbs on my opened biscuit wrapper and pressing them onto my tongue. It was quiet, the flow of customers sporadic: one or two truck drivers with deliveries for the city, I supposed, and a few people in suits, slightly self-important, travelling on business. Occasionally families came in; usually the men paid for fuel while the women hauled little children to the bathrooms. Between customers, two waitresses in striped conical hats conversed in a clipped, private lexicon of phrases and low murmurs, and exchanged looks full of knowing. They could have been telling each other secrets, or complaining about the boss, or speculating about me.

I hadn't until that moment felt conspicuous, but I realized then how intently I must look as if I were waiting for something, perhaps for a purpose either to stay or to leave. A person with nowhere to go could go anywhere, of course, but this was not the freedom I might have supposed. I still had to be *somewhere*, and this seemed to bring with it an obligation either to explain my remaining where I was or to keep moving. Apologetically I bought a cup of tea and took it back to my table.

The fact was I did not have to sit here in this way, as if under some vague suspicion, wondering where to go. There was a place on this earth where someone would be waiting for me this evening. Albeit on his terms, after his fashion, my husband wanted me. Not everybody had that. I had waited so long for it, and I need not lose it. Why *should* I lose him, for the sake of a child I never thought I would have and that he, to be fair to him, had never led me to imagine he would want? If we had money, it would be different, but we didn't. Col was just being honest and probably more realistic than I was. And since I hadn't been expecting to have a baby, if I didn't have it, I wouldn't be continuing without anything I had been hoping for.

But I had set out in married life hoping to stay married, and if I did not, I could not shrink back into my old life. When I sold the house near Portsmouth and moved to Huddersfield, I disposed of every trace of it – not a difficult thing to do, in fact, with a life so small as to have gone almost undetected. In any case, I had grown so tired of it, tired of myself, tired of getting on my own nerves, tired of the thoughtless, overlapping, blurred accretion of years going nowhere; I had been desperate for greater distance from it, in any direction, even towards a mirage. If a mirage was what marrying Col turned out to be, it was still the first attempt I'd ever made to escape the person I had let myself become.

And escape her I had, so successfully that, except as Col's wife, I no longer really existed. My dutiful care of my father (though I loved him) had arisen not from goodness but from a lack of vitality and imagination about myself; I stayed at home because I was diffident and unadventurous. I had not, as I had told Col, sacrificed a promising career in local government. I had been made redundant at twenty-five from a dull administrative job in Traffic and Highways in a restructuring simultaneous with my father's first stroke, while three colleagues, including my fiancé Barry, were kept on and retrained.

Within six months Barry was my ex-fiancé and engaged to somebody in Payroll. I may then have "devoted" myself to my father for sixteen years, denying myself the chance to meet someone else, but for most of that time I had been too isolated and easily discouraged to imagine any such thing, anyway. I did not, as I had also told Col, "enjoy my life", and if he left me I would spend the rest of it mourning the expense of my error and trying not to think too much about what it had displaced. It would be incalculable.

I would have to get rid of the baby. I could make arrangements as soon as I got back. A month from now, it would be over. As soon as I thought this I felt sick, and suddenly wanted my tea sweet, though I didn't usually. I reached into the sugar bowl and noticed a folded slip of paper, crammed among the packets. It read, in handwritten letters,

Cash for 4 door saloon in gc. Private Text CAR to 07883 684512
Discretion guaranteed

I drank my tea. I fingered the piece of paper, turning it over and over. Practicalities flooded into my mind: all the reasons why this was an outrageous thing to contemplate. What its consequences would be in the next hour, the next twelve hours, in a day's time. I thought of a month from now, a year, ten years. I thought how simple the next step would be. Merely texting one word to a telephone number, such an insignificant thing to do. How could a thing so small affect very much? I thought of my baby and the decision I had just reached. I thought of the need to make this effort to survive. I could settle the matter quickly. I drained my cup and went outside.

I texted the word CAR to the number. My telephone rang, and a man's voice, foreign, harsh and breathless, asked me where I was calling from. When I told him, he demanded I call him back in exactly half an hour. I hung around shivering and then I did so, and when he began to interrogate me, my voice shook. I realized I didn't know anything about the rental car except that it was a Vauxhall. I read him the registration written on the key tab.

"I don't know the exact model or the mileage. It's pretty new, I think," I told him. There was a silence. "It's silver," I added.

"Yes, I see it's silver," he said. "You sell or not? You waste my time?"

I stared round at the car park, the fuel pumps, the café windows, the scrub and farmland beyond, but I couldn't see anyone.

"You sell or not?"

"It's just, the car... I don't know if you ... if you..." I said. "I mean, I haven't done this before. The thing is, I need money. The car doesn't actually—"

"That's none of my business. You need money, I need car. You got a car, if I want it, I pay you cash. No papers. That's it. OK?"

"OK. But I don't even know who—"

"No names! No documents, you understand? No papers. That way it's all private, OK?"

"Yes, but how much—"

"Listen. You come back here tomorrow. Just you. You understand?"

Just then I heard the cry of a young child in the background. "Wait," he said. He spoke a few words in another language. A pause, then I heard him speak in English. "Ssh, hey, hey, Anna? It's all right, wait just a minute, Papa's busy..."

I caught my breath. His voice had grown musical and soft.

There were some noises of movement and murmuring from the child and then, "Good girl, Anna. Papa's baby..."

He would think me insane if I began to cry.

"OK, listen," he said to me. "So you come back tomorrow. Exactly same place. Then you call me again, same time, I tell you where you bring me the car. If car OK, we agree price, I pay, you get cash, we both get discretion. We don't say to nobody."

His voice was changed, young and rounded and cadenced. I was certain this gentler, slightly shy voice belonged to the person he really was.

"I'll be here tomorrow," I said.

Since last year, a certain mood would come over me at nightfall. When night masked the trees around the trailer and turned the river water to ink and the far bank was a steep black hulk against the softer dark of the sky, I couldn't tell what country this was, or what season or century. Time and place were unnamed, it was night and it was anywhere and any year, and that was all. The moon made me feel smaller and safer than the sun. If it was a fine evening, I would go outside alone. I liked to walk with my head thrown back, following the moon. I could go in any direction I chose along the shore, and often I missed my footing and nearly fell, but somehow I would still always be following the moon. Wherever it led I followed, until my neck felt stiff or I finally stumbled. I must have looked so silly. Then I would do it all over again but imagine this time the moon was following me, and it always did. Dreamy and drunk on moonlight, I needed a while afterwards to steady myself and get used to being back on the river shore by the trailer, for it really did feel as if I'd been a long way away. *Moonbathing* was how I thought of it.

I didn't speak of it to you. I knew you would have found it amusing. You'd have snatched it away and held it out of my reach while you scrutinized it, you would have tossed it around for fun and handed it back to me a little spoilt. Though you never meant to be unkind.

And though it was funny, I didn't do it for amusement. Though I was soothed by it, it wasn't for relaxation. It was surrender. I gave myself up to it long, long before it was dark. Even when Vi wasn't being difficult, I would be looking forward to the day at work being over. Part of me would yearn all day long for the coming reward, to be absorbed and lost in the moon. You knew that much, I think. You would gather wood while it was still light and stack it around the circle of rocks we'd built on the ground between the trailer and the riverbank, and you would bring out chairs for us and a blanket for when the evening got colder. You'd light the fire while I was settling Anna in bed, so I would be guided down to you by the orange glow and the crackle of burning sticks. At night the noise of traffic passing on the bridge far away downriver settled to the occasional whirring rise and fall as cars in twos and threes approached and crossed over. That was soothing, too.

I liked it best when you found silvery, fallen tree branches for the fire, which burned with the baking smell of old, sun-parched timber. Sometimes we had to burn scrap wood that people had dumped along the verge at the top of the track: bits of old furniture, broken doors – once, nearly the whole side of a garden shed – and then the fumes would be harsh and toxic and the fire would flare with blistering paint and melting glue.

That night the flames were different, a sulky, wavering yellow giving off greenish clouds of smoke with a sharp, rotten smell.

These sticks are damp. They must have been lying in the water, I said, poking at one with my foot. Did you pick them out of the water? The smoke smells of weeds. And dead fish.

You grunted. It's all I could get, I didn't have time to go getting dry stuff. We've used up all there is round here, the only dry stuff's a mile down the shore. Anna was too tired.

You didn't have time? What else did you do today?

Nothing much. Went up to the service station to fill the water cans. Anna ate nearly a whole muffin.

That's a long walk for her. No wonder she was tired.

Well anyway, after that I didn't want to take her along the shore. I can't carry her *and* drag wood back all this way. It's enough just getting the water.

You need to get something to fetch it in. Maybe you could make something. You could get some old wheels from somewhere, make a little cart. You could give her rides in it, she'd love it. You could pretend—

I saw your face and stopped speaking. You glared into the fire, then you got up and kicked a sticking-out branch farther into the flames.

Little rides for Anna? Little rides in a little cart? Yeah, let's pretend. Let's make Stefan play fucking games all day. But we won't let him do any proper work, will we? Not for money.

Stefan, don't. You can't—

You turned and stood away, out of the circle of warmth.

You treat me like a kid! he said. I should be making proper money so we can get out of here. But you don't want that, do you? You want things as they are, you want me wasting my time making little fucking carts!

Of course I don't. You know I hate us being like this.

No, you *like* it. You like us right here, living like this. Well, I don't, I've had enough. I'm going to change things.

Don't be stupid! Somebody's got to look after Anna. OK, I'm the one with the job, is that my fault? Tell me what I'm supposed to do. Give up a job to let you borrow money we'll never pay back? So you can drive people around all day in a cab that'll never belong to you?

I'll get a cab some other way.

What other way is there? Everybody needs a loan to get started, and we are not borrowing money from those bastards. We'd never get away from them. I'm not stopping you making things better, I'm stopping you being stupid, I'm stopping you walking into trouble.

I have to get a car! Can't you see? As soon as I'm getting fares we can pay rent, get a proper place, and we're out of here!

Stefan, if you borrow from the kind of people who'd lend to you, the car will never, ever be yours. You can't own your own car in this country. You don't even *exist* in this country.

Loads of people do it! Tell me how else we get out of here!

You haven't been talking to them, have you? Is that where you were today, in the city? You haven't talked to them, have you? Stefan!

Listen, in two years, maybe three, we'd have good money. We'd owe nobody.

Suppose it goes wrong? Suppose you're on somebody else's patch or the car's stolen? Suppose there isn't enough business? Those bastards, you think they're going to say, Oh, Stefan, you're a nice guy, that's OK? They'll burn the car, that's the least they'll do. They could burn it with you in it.

Oh, come on, those are fucking scare stories!

No, Stefan, they're not. And you know what else? They take the woman and sell her to get back at him, they sell her to other men. Children, too, even children.

OK, what do you want me to do? You want my balls on a fucking plate?

Stefan, stop it. You'll wake up Anna.

No, go on, tell me what to do! We can't go back home, we don't exist here, we can't go anywhere else. So what's the big plan, Silva? We go to your magic fucking cabin across the water, live in a fairy story, is that it? Is that the big plan?

You strode down the shingle to the river edge and started chucking stones into the water. We'd had this fight so many times, I knew enough to leave you for a while. I shivered inside the blanket and stared up at the stars. There were many sounds: the hiss of damp wood burning and the scrape of your feet on the shore, the *plock* of stones going into the river and the burr of traffic under the sky. I said your name, but you didn't come back. I called out again, into the dark.

Stefan? Maybe I can get an extra job. Get more hours. We'd save that way. I might find something where I could take Anna, and then you could work too. And anyway when the season starts you can work in the bar again, like last year, at the White Hart.

The noise of stones hitting the water stopped. You trudged back to me and sat down by the fire.

You can't do any more hours. If we got the car, I could work every night. There's loads of cabs in Inverness without licences, they never check. I'd work the airport, clubs.

We were silent for a while, imagining it.

The weekends, guys coming off the rigs, they drink hard, they always need cabs. It's good money. You could stay with Anna instead of working for that cow.

Oh, Vi's all right. When she's sober.

Your voice was very quiet, as it was when you were either really angry, or lost in a dream. I knew it very well, the way you withdrew into yourself. You had begun to shrink a little, rubbing your face and sighing as though the rage in your brain was rising from the surface of your skin like a sort of dangerous, flammable vapour that had to be wiped away and expelled in slow, careful gusts. I took your hand and started to say something. I didn't think you were really listening, so I stopped speaking, but you didn't snatch your hand away. We sat like that in silence for a long time, moving only to put more wood on the fire. From time to time you looked at me as if you wanted to speak.

Suddenly you sat up very straight. Sssh, you said, and you stared through the darkness towards the river, cupping your free hand to your ear. Listen!

What? I squeezed your fingers tight. What is it? What's wrong?

My heart started to bump. We'd heard about them, homeless vagrants wandering out from the shelters they'd made under the bridge, high on drugs, in gangs. We were at least a mile away and there was no easy path along the riverbank, but it had happened a couple of times about three years ago, a couple of old caravans in a field near the service station had been set on fire. That was why you wouldn't leave Anna and me alone at night last summer. You'd stayed on working in the bar, refused when they offered you the night-porter job. If anyone found the track down from the road we'd be OK, you always said, because you'd be there. We'd hear anyone in plenty of time to get away and hide. They wouldn't know the riverbank as we did and they'd be too stoned to think of staying quiet. We'd be OK.

But what if you were wrong? What if they'd been watching for hours from the darkness beyond the fire? I clutched at you. I was trying not to scream.

Stefan! Somebody's there! Get Anna! Oh, God, Stefan, get Anna!

No, no, just listen. Anna's fine. Listen to the geese, Silva, you whispered. Can you hear them? The geese?

I listened hard, waiting for any sound, the slightest sound, coming off the water. My eyes were watering from the smoke. All I could hear were the sounds of the fire and the traffic on the bridge.

The geese? No. I can't hear anything.

Well now, you said in my ear, pulling me closer to you. Well now... That'll be because they're all fast asleep. As you should be, silly girl.

I pushed away from you, bashing at your shoulders, and you grabbed my hands and kissed them and started gnawing on my fingers, growling and mumbling. Just then there was a wail from the trailer. You looked round but I got up at once, pulling the blanket with me.

I'll go. Don't stay out long.

I left you poking a long branch into the fire. I was glad she'd woken up, and to the sound of laughter. In a moment you'd come into the trailer to see that she was settling again and the sight of her, asleep or not, would be almost the last stage of your restoration to yourself, and to me. At such moments I would often see tears on your face. That night, your love for her flooded your eyes.

The very last stage came later, after she was asleep again. It came like this. In the way I might casually happen to be first to reach a door and open it for both of us, I told you that I was sorry. It didn't matter to me at all that I didn't believe anything I'd said was untrue or that I didn't think I had anything to apologize for. The assumption of blame wasn't important, that wasn't the purpose of it. It was a way of saying I knew that you wanted to forgive me, but much more to forgive yourself, for the way we were forced to live. It was a way of letting you do both. Because then you took me in your arms and wrapped me in close against you, and with no more words we made love, fitting ourselves to each other's bodies for each other's consolation and for the glad familiarity of it, our slow, deep rocking together in the dark.

I was having a bath when Col returned from his kayaking, and he shouted through the door that he would wait for me in the bar. When I came down, he offered me a drink and declared with a little bravado that he would "join me" and ordered the same for himself, tonic without the gin, though usually he drank beer. He meant it as a kind of compliment, symbolically rejecting the notion of our incompatibility by rejecting a different drink, but the gesture was slightly too big for him. He sat and sipped his tonic, cowed by the formality between us. We had to be so careful. We exchanged tight remarks and little smiles, until I ordered him a pint, which he drank as if released from some test or other. I watched him, not sure what I loved. But whatever it was in me he wanted, I did not want him to stop wanting it.

We ate early. Over dinner he drank a bottle of wine, which helped him, and we talked a little about his day on the river and about mine, supposedly in Inverness. We pared our stories down to safe generalities. I barely had to lie; I said I'd had an interesting time and had enjoyed seeing new places, and he didn't ask any more of me than that. His lack of interest in my day was a courtesy, an offer to me to talk free in the knowledge I would not really be listened to, so it was easy to reel off inane remarks about a day of vague impressions without being specific about locations or – the courtesy reciprocated – endanger him by bringing him anywhere near the orbit of my real thoughts. In return, when I asked him about the kayaking, I showed satisfaction with answers that were neither engaged nor precise. We ate in small mouthfuls, and every one was taken slowly, as an opportunity to push a little more of the evening behind us. But still, when we had finished I was appalled at how much time was left. Our bedroom, smelling of carpet cleaner and hot electric light, lay above us at the end of a musty hotel corridor. I had imagined, all through dinner, the hours of the coming night, cramming themselves into its emptiness, lying in wait.

I suggested we have coffee in the lounge. The couple from the morning were already there, drinking whisky and yawning over the papers. The waitress brought in our tray and made her exit, saying she hoped we would enjoy the rest of our evening.

But there was so much of it. While Col glowered over a book of aerial photographs, I browsed the bookcases on the other side of the room and wandered around studying the prints on the walls, of stags and mountains, Highland crofts and cattle. I sat down again on the sofa and examined the china minutely, as if I might discover in it something about cups and saucers that had so far eluded me. The couple got up to leave, and invited us to join them in the bar when we had finished. Col looked longingly after them. I took up the newspaper they had left behind and completed a couple of crossword clues, then folded the paper back up as neatly as I had found it. Col drank his coffee. I drank my herb tea.

"Col, if it's about money, if there wasn't a problem about money, do you think—"

"There's no point discussing it," he said. "We haven't got the money. I'm not discussing it."

"But suppose we had, suppose—"

"Stop. Just – stop," he said. "There is nothing to say."

I got up again and studied a rack of leaflets and maps. It was no good. No task took long enough. I found myself looking at a pamphlet about salmon-fishing, wondering how long I would be able to keep this up, listening to my life pass along in thudding little ticks of my heart. I was forty-two years old and I knew it was finite, this bright, regular tapping in my chest, but I also knew that for every few seconds I aged, the baby grew a little; it became a larger, livelier thing to kill. I wanted to blurt out my feelings; I feared my impatience for the next day would somehow break out of me and declare itself. I returned to the sofa.

"By the way, I'm going kayaking again tomorrow," Col said. "You'll be all right, will you?"

"Yes, I'll be fine," I lied.

I couldn't think of anything else to say. The air of the lounge grew dense with our hoarded silence; the clock ticked and ticked with a sound like seconds snapping off in small splinters, only to reassemble maliciously behind us, ready to come round again. The hours yet to come thronged around us with all their awful availability for no other purpose than to keep a vigil against marital disintegration. Eventually a drift of laughter came from the bar. My husband raised his head.

"I'm tired," I told him. "You go on and enjoy yourself. I think I'll have an early night."

The rain fell all night, clattering on the roof and cascading off into the ground around the trailer as if it was being poured from a jug. The place would be a mud bath in the morning. I would have to fish out Anna's boots from the storage space under the mattress. Would they still fit her? As I lay thinking in the dark, working out that if she needed new boots I wouldn't be able to get them before Friday, the day Vi usually paid me, I heard a different dripping noise. It was inside. It was coming from over near the door. I slipped out of bed and immediately knew that we were unsheltered. I felt a chill on my skin as if nothing protected us properly any more. Either the door was open or the roof was leaking. Rain or night air had entered the trailer. Anything could enter. In a couple of steps I had reached the door. It was shut and locked, but my feet were wet. I touched the wall. It was running with water, seeping in through the join between the trailer's side and the roof. Reaching up, I discovered that it was dripping from farther along, where the seam turned at a right angle. From there it was plocking down on the shelf where I had left bread for our breakfast in a paper bag, now soaking wet.

You were asleep. I fumbled my way back to Anna's bed. She was asleep, too, but her covers were pushed up against the wall, and they were already damp. I lifted her up gently out of her nest, hoping the sudden cold breath of air wouldn't wake her, and clasped her against me, willing my arms and the palms of my hands to project all my body's warmth into her through her back. Without waking, she curled her legs and arms around me and pushed her head in under my jaw, snuffling against my neck. I settled her in against you and got back into bed. I wouldn't be able to sleep perched on the narrow edge of the bed that was left now, but I could lie calmly enough, knowing she was warm. I dreaded the morning, so I spent the rest of the night waiting for it, trying to work out what to do.

First thing, you would climb onto the top of the trailer, which would be slippery, and wonder how to repair it this time. You'd sealed it before, which only worked for a while; if you could get hold of some plastic sheeting or tarpaulin you could cover the roof and weight it with rocks from the shore. That might work for a bit longer. Then we'd have to dry the trailer out, but if it kept raining that would take days. The ground would be soaked, and the mud and damp would cling to us, we'd bring it into the trailer and make matters worse. Anna couldn't be left outside so she would have to be kept in the trailer, and she hated that, and the floor would be filthy. You would have to get a fire lit somehow to dry out our clothes and bedding, never mind wash off the mud, and I didn't know how you were going to manage that if the rain poured down all day, and with only soaked wood to burn. There was the propane heater to keep Anna a bit warmer but it cost so much, and the cartridge was low and I wouldn't be able to get back with a new one until the evening. How would you manage? You'd need hot food. It took nearly an hour to get up to the service station for hot chocolate and muffins, soup maybe, and nearly an hour back, probably longer if it was muddy, and you'd get so wet coming and going it might not be worth it.

I was glad you were asleep.

I did manage to doze off towards dawn. When I woke again a soft pale light was replacing the grey inside the trailer. I was aware of an absence, but for a moment couldn't work out what it was. You and

Anna were still beside me; Anna had a few strands of my hair clutched in her hand and had pulled them into her mouth, and you were just beginning to wake but in that eyes-shut way of yours, convincing yourself you were still asleep. You turned and draped your arm across me. I started to prepare in my mind how I would tell you about the weather and the leaking trailer and the horrible day ahead. That was when I realized what was missing. It was quiet, because the rain had stopped. All I could hear was the traffic on the bridge. I drew my hair gently out of Anna's grip and raised myself on my elbows. The trailer was set too far back from the bank of the river for me to see the horizon at the end of the estuary, but from that direction, over from the east, a few fringes of sunlight were beginning to sparkle on the pewtery, dark reaches of the water. That meant there was about to be a proper, unclouded sunrise, and if the sun shone bright for even a few hours today, we'd have a chance.

You would be awake in a minute, and soon you'd be outside clapping your hands at the geese and laughing at me for worrying. You'd fix the trailer, you always managed to fix it. By tonight we would be all right again. Maybe if the mini-mart wasn't too busy or I got a minute when Vi went to lunch or dozed off, I might be able to raid the freezer and bring back some steaks for us. I'd seen some lying in the bottom nobody would want to buy, anyway. I could lift a bag of charcoal from round the back on my way home, and if the rain stayed off we could cook on the old barbecue you picked up that time from the verge at the top of the track.

But when we were awake and up and dressed, you didn't say anything to that idea. You swore a few times and stared at the trailer and then didn't seem to care about it any more. You set your mouth in a grim, thin line, and I didn't get a happy word or a smile from you before I had to leave for work. You had been that way before, impatient to make it all different, angry about things you couldn't change, furious with yourself for not giving us a regular life. But you had been getting angry more and more often, and for longer, and it was harder each time to bring you round. I didn't really see that that was because what made you angry had changed. By then it was me you were angry with.

That day you wouldn't walk me even part of the way up to the bus. You didn't take Anna to say good morning to the geese, though they were lovely with the sun on their wings and they landed so beautifully on the black rock in the river, hooting that low, rounded noise over and over like a thousand wheezy old organs in a fairground, so funny and also so sad a sound it was, like home, and sweet and faraway.

I slept badly and got up long before Col was awake. I didn't want to speak to him, about the baby or anything else, so I left quietly and drove east from the hotel, as I had done the day before. That early in the morning there was frost on the ground and the grip of ice in the air, as if during the night winter had crept down from the mountains, pushing back the spring. A white fog obscured the hills and shoreline of the north bank of the river. I drove into swirls of it ahead of me on the road, and on either side it hung in freezing clouds under the bare trees and along the hedges.

I had meant to take a different route, striking north at Netherloch across the river at the small stone bridge there and continuing eastwards up into the mountains above Netherloch Falls. I had been studying my map and had worked out a route following the road down through the forest on the north bank of the estuary, eventually crossing back to its south side over the City Bridge and entering Inverness. After a couple of hours wandering about in the city, it would not take me long to drive back westwards to the service station.

But I didn't cross the river. Overcome with weariness and nausea and fear, I stopped in a little car park on the south side of Netherloch, before the stone bridge. I had got up far too early, trying, I suppose, to bring the day's transaction nearer, because although I was a little shocked by how swiftly my mind had worked out all the details of what I was going to do, I was still very afraid. I was anxious to have it over with, one way or another, both dreading and hoping that it would all come to nothing. Maybe the man wouldn't answer the phone. Maybe he wouldn't show up, or I could take fright myself and reconsider the whole idea. Or I might not have to go through with it at all; my telephone could ring at any moment and it would be Col saying he was sorry, he'd made a terrible mistake. Please come back, he might say. Come back right this minute, we'll spend the whole day together. I'll look after you.

That was when I began to cry. The car park was one of those places for tourists, with green areas planted up with bushes and dotted with picnic tables, and there was nobody there. I sat in the car weeping noisily, tears pouring down my cheeks. With the engine turned off, the air was soon stuffy with the peppery, acrylic smell of car upholstery, and to stop myself feeling any sicker, I wound the window down. Cold, foggy air rushed in, and still I could not stop crying. I sank my face into my hands and rested my head on the steering wheel and cried, and cried.

When I raised my head several minutes later, feeling a bit calmer, there was a man watching me. The fog was clearing under the trees and he was sitting at one of the picnic tables a few yards away, looking at me. He didn't avert his gaze when he saw I had noticed him. Instead he slowly got to his feet and, with a sympathetic nod of his head, walked away. I wanted to be angry, and I should have felt foolish, but all I felt was that I had been not watched, but watched over. I stared after him. I couldn't have described his face except for his eyes, which even from a distance had conveyed something light and clear. His head was heavy and square and covered with greying stubble, he was powerfully built and dressed in jeans and a black sweater. He climbed into a Land Rover parked in a space on the far side of some bushes and drove away.

I wound the window up and got the car warm, then I tipped back the seat and slept.

Later, I drove on from Netherloch, staying on the south side, retracing exactly my path of the day before. As before, I kept pulling off the road and loitering along the river, for I had decided against going to Inverness at all. The stopping places were quiet, and because of the fog there was much less to see.

I went again to the café at the service station and sat at the window. Across some fields to the east, near where the squat concrete pillars of the bridge approach studded the ground towards the river, lay a patch of industrial wasteland. Beyond it I could see cold spangles of light on the water. There was a strong breeze blowing across it, and the breeze was also rocking the bushes and bracken in the fields and lifting the fog out from the trees. I waited until it was time for me to call.

I waited, staring at my phone, until after it was time. When it rang, I didn't answer. It rang a second time, and on the third ring I picked up.

"You're supposed to call, you got a problem? Listen, you want to sell the car you call me in next half hour, OK? That's all the time you got. You don't call me back, I got other clients, OK? I pay cash, remember, good deal. You call me back."

I had expected that the man would tell me to drive into Inverness, but when I dialled the number, and once I had assured him I was alone, he gave me instructions to drive back towards Netherloch.

"Go west along the river road. There's a lay-by a mile on the right. Slow down when you see it. Go past it two hundred metres more and there's a gap in the trees and a gate. On the right, the river side. Pull off the road and stop at the gate. Wait there."

I did as he said. I followed the road until I saw the lay-by. It was where I'd stopped the day before. I bumped the car to a halt over stones and deep ruts on the verge opposite the gate. I was glad he'd told me not to go any farther. The gate was rusted and skewed and off its hinges, and a track stretching behind it was barely a track at all, just a narrow scree of stones and crushed branches dipping sharply down through undergrowth in the direction of the river. I waited, my heart thumping, with all the doors locked. Traffic rushed past, buffeting the car. Then I noticed a movement, and from the undergrowth at the edge of the track a figure appeared, a young man in jeans and a short jacket. His arms were clasped around a well-wrapped and heavy-looking bundle: the child. He was wearing a hat but no gloves, and as he came up to the fence I saw his hands were raw and red. With some difficulty he hoisted the bundle higher up on his shoulder and motioned at me to approach. I started to get out of the car, but he shook his head and waved me back. Then he put the child down at the side of the track and beckoned to me again, and I understood that he wanted me to bring the car forwards. He freed the gate and hauled it back, keeping hold of the child's hand. I started the engine and turned the car, and he waved me on past him. When he'd closed the gate, he gestured at me to keep going, and I did, slowly and carefully, but scraping the car sides against branches as I went, sinking into ruts, skidding on the stones. He followed with the child in his arms. I had no idea where the track led or how I might get back up it again, with the car or not. But I had glimpsed his face and I had seen how he held his child, and though those were hardly reasons enough to trust him, I kept going, edging the car forwards at barely more than walking pace.

A long way down, the ground levelled out into an area of water pools and grimy rock and reeds strewn with jetsam and river debris. Ice lay in patches under fallen trees. The tide was out; the river ran along some distance away, and upriver, almost out of sight, was a disused jetty sticking up from a shining field of mud.

Set on a patch of cleared ground under some trees a long way from the river was an old trailer with plastic sheeting over its roof. Amid the encroaching dereliction it was still clearly a home; it looked tidy and well kept. Laundry swayed on a washing line fixed between one corner of the trailer and a tree. A bucket and broom, a plastic bath and picnic chairs, some large plastic toys and water containers were stacked neatly along the side. Nearby was an ashy fire pit set inside a circle of rocks.

I got out of the car and waited in the freezing wind for him to make his way down. We were quite a long way from the road now and well below it, hidden by a thicket of frost-bound undergrowth. On the far side of the river the thickly wooded land sloped steeply all the way to the shore. It was hard to tell how wide the river was until I saw a frail-looking wooden hut set into a curve in the bank and a white rowing boat moored to a little jetty nearby, both standing out brightly against the silvery whorls and eddies of the tide. All at once I understood what I was seeing on a human scale, and then I saw that the wind in the pine woods around the hut was restless and quick; branches jerked and trembled with none of the dreamy enchantment of swaying trees seen from a distance. And I thought, if someone were to appear from the door and walk down the jetty to the boat, I would be close enough to call out. I looked downriver to the bridge, maybe a mile away, arching over from the city to the forest side. I walked a few yards down the shore and closer, until I could hear above the shirring of the water a stately, faint thrum from the traffic crossing over it, and carried by the breeze that blew across, there came an eerie, soft booming that I supposed had to do with the disturbance of air through the steel spans stretching up into the windy sky.

Suddenly there was a rattle of stones and a shout behind me. I turned in time to see the man struggling to keep his balance, sliding sideways on the slope of loose rocks and puddles. Falling, he let go of the child, pushing her away from him so as not to squash her under his weight as he toppled. I ran towards them. The child was a rolling bundle of unravelling clothes and wrappings, and I reached her just as she began to scream. The man tumbled several feet and landed heavily, letting out a long cry just as the child screamed again. She wasn't hurt, but she was frightened, and when I picked her up she was so puzzled she abruptly stopped crying to stare at my face. I saw her eyes register that she didn't know me, and then she writhed in my arms and took a deep breath, ready to roar her head off. I jounced her up and down and smiled and chuckled, and turned her around so she could see her father getting to his feet.

"There, there, little one, there's Papa, ooh, look, oops-a-daisy! Silly Papa! Look!" I crooned, and the child gave me another assessing look, before she burst out wailing, stretching her arms out to her father. He came towards us breathless, unsmiling. I handed the child over, but he had hurt his arm or shoulder and winced under the weight of her.

"Oh, here, I'll hold her for you," I offered, and tried to draw her to me again, but she curled up crying into his chest and he took two long steps back. He spoke a few words to her in a foreign language I couldn't identify, then cast me a pained look and nodded towards the trailer. "I can manage that far," he said.

At the trailer door the child scrambled down without a word, plonked herself on the bottom step and lifted up first one foot and then the other to her father, holding on to her socks while he pulled off her boots. Inside, he unwrapped her from her layers while she craned round, staring at me. She clambered up onto the window seat and settled herself into a nest of soft toys, pulling a rubbery-looking giraffe onto her lap, and the end of its tail into her mouth. The wall above her head was covered with pictures in crayon, some wild, col-oured scribbles that had torn the paper, and some done by an adult for a child, of cats and houses, flowers and boats and birds. She kept watching me, no less suspiciously. She was beautifully and magically the image of her father: the same curly, slaty-blue-black hair, the intense gaze from strikingly clear blue eyes, long, fragile hands. The man, nursing his wrist, nodded to me to sit down, and as I took the place beside her, she raised her eyes and smiled at me. I looked away. She made me nervous, more nervous than he did. Her beauty was close to overwhelming, but it wasn't so much her beauty as her physical, breathing existence that moved me. I was sitting close enough to reach and touch her hair, and a few hours ago I had been almost ready to rob myself of even that small gesture towards my own child.

"Hello," I said, turning to her. "And what's your name?"

"No names," the man said. We both looked at him. "Better we have no names, OK?" he said, a little more gently.

The child poked one finger at her chest and said, "Anna." She beamed at me and then pointed at her father. "Papa!"

There was a pause, and then Anna declared her name again, and then the man laughed, and he shook his head. Anna and I laughed, too. I hesitated, and then I said, "And what's Papa's name?"

I saw at once I had made a mistake. There was another pause, tighter than before; the man looked suddenly terrified, and angry enough to hit me. Then Anna stretched out her giraffe towards me and said carefully, "*Jee-raff.* Anna, Papa, Jee-raff..."

He took the giraffe and waggled it at her, then thrust its head at her and cuddled it into her neck so it tickled. She tried to grab it, giggling and squealing.

"OK, OK, Anna," he said, letting it go and looking at her, and then at me. "OK, so what. I'm Stefan."

Whatever it was that had caused him to be so tense, his daughter released him from it as if she had let go of a bird trapped in her hands. She was sucking again on the fronded tail of the giraffe, and staring at her father. She already knew something about adoration,

61

but she didn't have an inkling of her power. She didn't understand that just the sight of her fingers flexing and pointing at a stranger's face and her voice experimenting with a stranger's name could do this. She made him believe that nothing else mattered, that he could handle anything. He sank down on the seat on the other side of the trailer, leaning gingerly on the table.

"You hurt your arm," I said. "Let me see."

When I asked him to make a circle with his wrist, he hissed with pain.

"Can you move your fingers?" I asked. "Can you bend your elbow?" He could, but when he tried to turn his forearm, the pain shot up and down between elbow and wrist. The redness of his hands had got worse since we came inside the trailer, and they were now mottled with blue, and he was shivering. He might have been quite ill; at the very least he was frozen, and probably shocked by the fall.

"You need a hot drink," I said.

He wiped his uninjured hand across his face and didn't reply. I got up and moved to the other end of the trailer, where there was a double gas burner. I filled a small saucepan with water from a plastic canister, lit the burner using a box of matches from a shelf, and set the pan on it. I opened cupboards and found grassy-smelling herbal tea bags of some kind. I decided that he needed sugar but there didn't seem to be any, so when the water was poured I stirred some honey into it. As he drank, the trailer filled with balmy, hay-scented steam, like when the sun warms leaves and wild flowers after rain. The fumes reminded me of the kind of summer day almost impossible to imagine looking at his sore, pinched hands, while a few feet away outside the trailer the air splintered with cold and the river ran past swollen by the wintery, dark flow of melted ice.

He saw me glance past him through the window. As if remembering what I was there for, he pushed his cup aside and looked at his watch.

He said, "There isn't much time. Come outside. Anna, stay here a minute and be a good girl."

He stepped down from the trailer; I followed. He was in a hurry now, but Anna scrambled after us to the door and wailed to be lifted down and kept near him. He got her boots on again and buttoned her into her coat.

We walked all around the car. He kicked at the tyres and peered in the windows, and he tried all the doors and inspected the boot. When he asked to see the engine we had to fish out the manual and look up how to release the catch under the bonnet. I could tell he knew no more about car engines than I did.

When he'd finished looking, he said, quietly and without surprise, "Rental car. You steal it? You come to sell me a car that's not yours?"

"I need some money, that's all. You said no questions." I turned away, pretending to cough, so he wouldn't know that my voice trembled and my eyes were filling with tears.

"OK, you didn't steal it. You rent it. And this," – he tapped with his foot on the licence plate – "this is the real number?"

"Yes."

He blew out his cheeks. "OK," he said. "So. If you sell, you have to tell them car was stolen. Because you are a thief."

"No. Yes. I know."

"So if I buy, I need to change the plates, maybe change the colour. So I pay less for car."

"I need three thousand," I said, without thinking. I was guessing; it sounded like enough to ask, enough to change Col's mind about the baby.

"Maybe. Maybe not so much. It drives good? I need to drive it. If it drives good, I pay. No receipt, no documents."

"How much?" I asked. "How do I know you've even got any money?"

He glanced at Anna, who was absorbed, digging a pebble out of the tread of one of the tyres. Turning from her, he produced an envelope from inside his jacket. He drew out just enough for me to see the top edge of a wad of banknotes.

"I got money." He stood watching my face as I tried to control another wave of tears. I had begun to tremble. I was horrified at myself, bartering a car that wasn't mine for money to keep a baby. How flimsy it was proving to be, the border between the kind of person I was before this, whose life had never strayed off the path of the conventionally law-abiding, and the kind of person I was turning into; it was terrifying to learn how irresistible, how effortless was my descent. Could I have offered in mitigation of my wrongdoing the plea that I had no choice? Of course I had a choice. Having taken it upon myself to judge that the legal destruction of my baby was the greater and truly unacceptable wrong, I was choosing to break the law. But I was not acting out of principle in pursuit of a finer moral good. My reasons, circumstantial, quite possibly hormonal, were a clumsy, misshapen clump of love, need, fear and, in the end, self-interest. I was going about getting what I wanted.

"OK, listen. You're selling me rental car, you need money that bad. I need a car. For my wife. For a surprise, big surprise for her, big difference for her life." He gave me a hard grin. "So, smart lady? You need the money, you owe it somebody?"

"I just need it."

"OK, right. No questions. We go now to drive car around. If car OK, we agree price, I pay."

I shivered. "OK."

He went back inside the trailer and brought out a heap of bedding. He arranged it in a mound on the back seat, then lifted Anna on top of it and began to fiddle with the seat belt.

"That's not very safe," I said. "Small children are supposed to have those proper car seats when they go in cars."

He clicked the seat belt in place and straightened. "Do I ask you for help? What can I do about it right now?"

Anna started to wail. "Jee-raff! Papa, Jee-raff!" she said and burst into tears. Stefan returned to the trailer and brought back her giraffe.

"You will get her a car seat, won't you?" I didn't care that I was making him angry. "You've got to get her a car seat so she'll be safe."

"You drive it back up the track," he said, getting in on the passenger side. "Any damage then you don't blame me."

I drove very carefully up the track and stopped at the top, and we swapped places. He turned the car towards Inverness, nudging it back onto the road nervously, unused to having the controls on the right and possibly to driving at all. Anna dropped her giraffe and began to bounce and squirm on top of her heap of bedding in the back seat, and he spoke to her sharply, in their own language. I retrieved the giraffe for her, and she pushed it into her mouth; her eyes began to close. In silence Stefan drove us past the service station and on to the roundabout as if to turn left across the bridge, then reconsidered and swerved round to go straight ahead, to the outskirts of Inverness. The traffic grew heavier, and it unnerved him. A couple of miles farther, cursing under his breath, he made a complete circuit at another roundabout and headed back the way we had come. At the bridge roundabout, he took us back onto the Inverness road, where he picked up speed. Then he turned back in the same place as before.

"Car OK?" I asked, and he nodded.

"I go back to service station now," he said.

But when he pulled in, he shook his head and inched past the rows of parked cars. "Too many cars, too many people," he said. "I don't stop here."

At the far end of the car park, just at the start of the slip road back up to the road, a disused track jutted off to the left towards the derelict ground near the bridge, the wrecked and abandoned place I'd seen from the window of the café.

"More quiet here," he said, turning the wheel. The track crossed an empty field and then opened out onto a vast stretch of cracked concrete where factories or warehouses had once stood. He stopped the car. We got out into a terrain of piled-up rubbish: lumps of masonry, rusted metal spars and guttering and old window frames, warped board sheeting, buckled machinery, shattered glass and heaps of what looked like sodden old clothes. In the distance a man shuffled out from a broken shed clasping a piece of carpet around his shoulders like a cloak. Without seeing us, he wandered away in the direction of three or four plumes of smoke rising from behind a half-demolished wall.

"Bad place. Junkies," Stefan said, glancing in at Anna asleep on the back seat. "Hurry up. Bad place."

"Do you want it or not? If you want the car, you have to pay me. Now."

"First I need promise. I need favour," he said. "No, not a favour. For both of us." His eyes were anxious. "I have to change licence plates. It's OK, I can do, there's a guy I know. So you don't tell police the car is stolen straight away. You report the car later, OK? Wait till I got new plates. Wait till six o'clock." He looked at his watch, then pointed back to the service station. "Up there you can get the bus. You go in bus to Netherloch, you say you left the car in Netherloch. The bus comes there soon, fifteen minutes."

"It's too cold to wait for a bus. I'm not feeling well. Can't you drive me to Netherloch?"

"No," he said, looking back to his daughter. "You can get bus easy, plenty of time. Bus is warm. Listen, when you get to Netherloch, there is car park behind the school."

I nodded.

"So cars get taken from there. Stay in town a while, you can get coffee, food. Wait till six, then I will have new plates. At six o'clock you go to car park, you call police, you say you left the car there all day. Tell them this morning you went to walk, you go along by the water and in the forest and then you get back and car is not there. OK? You got no car, you have to tell story, explain them something. It's for both of us. You understand?"

"OK."

He pulled out the envelope from his jacket. "Two thousand," he said.

"Three," I insisted, numbly. I had no idea what the car was worth, no idea what I was talking about.

"Two thousand five hundred," he said, counting it through his fingertips, note by note, before I could argue.

"All right," I said.

He handed it over, and pointed to the service station again. "Just up there."

He smiled. He was anxious for me to go. But some natural courtesy – maybe even a little gratitude because I liked his daughter – prevented him from showing it.

"All right. Goodbye."

In absolute misery, I zipped the money into an inside pocket of my shoulder bag. Just as I was turning to go, I glanced in at the child, lying aslant across the collapsed wad of bedding and beginning to stir from sleep. Seeing her father outside, she pulled herself up and patted on the window with the palms of both hands, about to cry. Stefan and I looked at each other; we both wanted to say something else, and we both started to speak at once. He tried to laugh.

"OK. What?"

"You will remember to get her a car seat, won't you? Today?"

He smiled and reached out and gave my shoulder a little shake. "Sure, sure, lady. Today. I will."

"What were you going to say?"

"Nothing," he said. He pulled out his envelope again, just as Anna began to sob, pressing her face up to the glass. "Only, here. Three thousand. Here, take," he said, pushing more bills into my hands. Then he turned quickly to the car and I started walking away, towards the service station. I heard him open the car door and speak gently, but I kept walking. I could not bear to see her hands outstretched for him as he lifted her into his arms.

I didn't want to wait for the bus. It was too cold to stand in the shelter, and I wanted to get away and keep moving, putting distance between myself and what I had just done. I kept walking. Soon I had reached the bridge, and I could see that the pathway for pedestrians was a separate narrow carriageway, built lower than the steel deck that carried cars; once on it I would be almost invisible except to anyone I might meet walking across from the other side. I strode along fast with my collar up against the roar of traffic and the estuary wind. I liked the thought of being hidden. After a few minutes, the bus rumbled on past me.

Looking inland, I could see all the way to the point where the river emerged from the neck of the loch, and turning eastwards, I saw as far as it ran, past the docks and the city, and widened into the sea. As I walked, in each direction the views hit my eyes like old, stuttering film as the black spars of the bridge flickered past between me and the landscape.

At the first junction on the far side, where nearly all the traffic bore right to go north and up the coast, I turned left and followed a much narrower road that rose and curved inland. The signs pointed towards Netherloch Falls and Netherloch. The paved walkway from the bridge came to an end, and I continued along the side of the road, suspended in wintery afternoon darkness; the way was canopied by overhanging trees, through which blinding slashes of daylight cut until they stood too densely planted for light to penetrate. After a while I could only sense but not see the river, a long way beyond the trees and below me. One or two cars passed, leaving hollow echoes of engine noise. As the road rose ahead of me I could tell I was going higher; soon I heard a faraway rushing in the treetops and the air was cold with pine resin and raw mountain winds that carried none of the green, reedy damp of the river. I came upon the remains of a clearing where trees had been felled in an apparently disordered kind of order: straight rows of sawn stumps poked up between tractor ruts and receded back into the line of the forest. Everywhere the ground was scattered with shards and chips of torn wood and the scabs of stripped bark. Dozens of tree trunks lay stacked horizontally, and around them were stiff, feathery heaps of smaller pine cuttings alongside dried out branches and twigs, grey and tangled like wires.

I had been walking for nearly an hour and had a stitch in my side, and I stopped to rest against a mound of logs, digging my foot into a mulchy carpet of pine needles and moss. I was scared and cold, and sick with disgust at myself; I stared into the darkness of the trees and wanted to escape into it. Just then I heard another bus. Without thinking, I ran back to the road and waved it down. I climbed on breathless and shivering and wondered if I was getting flu. By the time we reached Netherloch I ached with tiredness and the afternoon had turned cloudy and raw. It was only a quarter past two. I knew I could not bear nearly four hours loitering in the streets, going from one café to another. I had to get into a quiet room and lie down, I had to sleep.

The sign on the front of the bus said Wester Muir/Fort Augustus, which I knew were some miles west, beyond our hotel, so I clambered down to the driver and paid the extra to go on to Invermuir where, he told me, the bus stopped at the postbox on the far side of the village from the hotel. Col would not be back before six o'clock. I could hide in our room for at least two hours, and later I would get back somehow to Netherloch. If there wasn't another bus I could get a taxi, and if I didn't get there until after six it wouldn't matter; in fact it would help, it would give Stefan even more time. We would be safe. But I didn't know what safe meant any more. I opened my bag and flicked the money through my fingertips, powdery soft paper amounting to three thousand pounds. Just paper, after all, but I was trusting to it to buy me my safety.

I stared through the bus window and tried to distract myself by identifying the plants along the road. Gorse, bracken, patches of rushes, and spongy, brownish pads of decaying nettles and saturated moss. I was collecting observations that I could array before Col one by one, to fill our evening before I mentioned the baby and the money. Then I would tell him that I had solved the problem, that there was now plenty of money, so there was no need to worry. He would love his child when it arrived, and anyway, I would take care of everything. Soon I found myself in a pitiful daydream in which kindness and remorse and enlightenment washed over his face, and henceforth we moved on together towards a sweetly melancholic, poetic future as Mummy and Daddy. I modified the daydream; at some later date, next year maybe, I would be pregnant again. If it happened at forty-two, it could surely happen at forty-three, and it would be different next time, because making the best of one accidental baby was one thing, having a second quite another, undertaken only by devoted and deliberate parents. By then I would, as a mother, be well acquainted with anxiety about the world at a level previously unimaginable, but I would be watchful and capable, too, and our happy children would – I whispered the very words – make our happiness complete. This was a manageable and familiar dream to me, set in a future in which I was altered, having blossomed in my husband's eyes and acquired proper, wifely value as a person whose wisdom and clarity about life were necessary to him. I concentrated on it for the rest of the journey.

The store wasn't busy; lunchtimes never are. A few campers from the Lochside Holiday Cabins were coming in at the weekends now, but still hardly any during the week, and they usually stocked up early in the day. The bus stopped outside at two o'clock, on time. Nobody got off. Around the same time some fishermen came in to fill up their flasks from the vending machine. They told me again we should be selling soup and hot pies. Get a microwave and you could do it easy, you'd make a fortune this weather, they said.

I nodded over at Vi, who was sleeping behind the counter with dribble going on her cardigan.

Tell her, it's her place, I said. She says she's not running a bloody restaurant.

There was stuff from the Cash & Carry to price and put out, so when the fishermen left, I woke Vi up and told her I was going to the back room, not that she really heard. It was just cans and cotton wool and firelighters and tinfoil, plus one of Vi's impulse buys, a bag of soccer shirts, so there was no hurry. I took a sandwich past its sell-by from the chiller and made my tea, and when I'd had my lunch, I sent a message to you, but you didn't answer. I thought you must be out of range, along the shore or getting water from the car-wash tap at the service station. Then I went back with a cup of tea for Vi and made her go across to the house. I told her to have a lie-down and I'd see her later, but I knew she'd have another bottle in there and I'd be locking up tonight. She wouldn't go at first, she said the house would be cold. So I went over, and it was and also dirty, as always. I switched on the gas fires and her electric blanket and bedside light and then went back for her. I led her all the way to her bedroom door, and I promised her I'd look after everything. I hoped she'd fall asleep before she could start crying.

Soon after that a family came in. They'd been to the Netherloch Falls. There was a sulky girl chewing on a leaflet from there, and their feet were muddy. I didn't like them. It was a weekday, so the children should have been in school. I made the man go outside with his cigarette even though it was only in his mouth and not lit. The woman asked if we had Internet access, and I told her no because I'd seen her wiping her nose with her hands. She said what's that then, pointing at the sign outside, and I said it wasn't working. For all I knew it wasn't. Nobody had logged on for a couple of weeks. Then she shook out a rail of tartan scarves and tried them all on, even though there was no mirror and they were only scarves. After that she took a basket and went up and down the shelves helping herself, digging in the deep-freeze and handing ice creams to her children before she'd paid for them. I told them there was no eating in the shop, so they hung around staring at me and sucking and tugging at their ice-cream wrappers and fingering the chocolate bars and playing with the key rings in the "Under £3" tray. I'm sure they took some. The eldest one kept whining to her mother about why wasn't there a toilet and when could she get on Facebook.

After they'd gone, I sent you another message and told you what they were like, but you were still out of range.

Then it was quiet again for a while. A man came in, someone I remembered seeing before. He came in now and then, always in outdoor clothes like the men who ran the angling weekends or worked in the forest, but he was always by himself and he was older than most of them. Not that I could really guess his age. He had cropped hair that I thought would be silvery-grey if it were longer. When he brought his things to the till he smiled as if he knew me. I noticed the colour of his eyes again, a bluish-grey like the colour of water in winter, and there was a brightness in them, almost a flashing, as if he had just caught sight of something startling, not in me but in the air surrounding me. But he was friendly. I remember thinking he was the first person I'd seen smiling since Anna waved me goodbye that morning, and my face felt a little unaccustomed to smiling back. I forgot how it showed, worrying all the time. He said something I didn't hear.

"Sorry, what did you say?"

"Nothing, doesn't matter. You were miles away," he said, still smiling.

I laughed and started to ring up his shopping. "Yes, I was. Sorry."

"Good place to be, sometimes. I think so, anyway."

The radio was on as usual, and I also remember there had just been a commercial break and a time check. That was how I was sure exactly when it happened. Two forty-five. He'd bought milk, a can of beans, cheese and tomatoes and bread, I remember that as well.

"You're not Polish, are you?" he asked. "Where are you from, then?"

"Me? I'm from miles away," I said, and rang the till.

"Well, that's two of us," he said, and we laughed in the way people laugh when they want to show something doesn't matter, but it does.

Then the first sound of it came. It rolled at us like a shape, a dark colour, a giant boulder. Other sounds were squashed under it: the radio, the *ting* of the register, my voice counting out change. I stopped trying to count, and we stood staring at each other, then I began to feel the noise as well as hear it; it came from underground and rumbled up through my legs and into my throat, and rattled the words I was trying to say against my teeth as if my mouth was full of buttons. The man was trying to speak too, but his lips just opened and closed.

Then this underground roaring rose and grew into a jagged crashing and breaking over our heads. Vi came hurrying in from the house, through the back of the shop and heading straight for the doors.

"Oh, Jesus!" she was shouting. "Jesus, what is it? Is it a plane? Jesus, it's a plane crashed at Inverness!"

We all went outside, our faces raised to the sky.

It wasn't a plane, but the noise was coming from the direction of Inverness. Faraway sirens started to wail. A couple of cars stopped dead on their way up the road, and people got out of them shouting, and two or three of them ran back, eastwards, towards the noise. A moment later a car coming down the other side from Netherloch braked suddenly and swerved in at the side of the road just past the turn-off and our parking area; two bikes on the roof shuddered and slipped forwards onto the bonnet. The door swung open, and the driver stumbled in our direction with his phone at his ear.

"Oh, my God! The bridge? The bridge, fuck! It's going down, the bridge is going down!" His voice was squealing and jerky. "Oh, my God! Are you OK, are you OK? Yes, yes all right. Oh, my God! You stay there. You stay where you are. Don't move, OK? Oh, my God!" He ended the call and for a moment stood rooted, staring at the phone and pulling his hair. More cars were stopping, more people were swarming on the road. He came towards us, waving his arms. "The bridge! Hey, it's the bridge! Something's happened to the bridge! It's going down!"

His voice pulled other people in a circle around him. "It's the bridge! She saw it! My wife, she saw it! She's in her office, they're on the twelfth floor, riverside, they all saw it! It's gone down, the bridge is down, they can't leave the building. It could be a bomb!"

From here there was nothing to see but the road and the forest that grew right to its edges. From Vi's place you had to cross the road and climb in through the pines and go right up to the head of the waterfall to get a sight of the other side, the town and the falls tumbling down and the river stretching away from the east corner of the loch, and on towards the bridge and beyond, Inverness docks and the ocean. There was a moment of disappointment while we all stood listening. The noises around us were changing. The roar lessened to a low rumble under the screams of more sirens. Everyone had turned in the direction of the city. Then a man in a checked shirt tugged at his wife's arm. "Come on! Come on, then!" he said, and ran towards the trees. His wife glanced at us, then followed him.

It was all the rest of them needed. The excitement returned. Of course they had to see for themselves. Suddenly it was all right to run after a glimpse of it. People headed for the trees. Cars were still pulling up and stopping, and soon there were ten or twelve banked up in both directions. Some drivers wanted to move on but the road was too narrow for them to get around the cars blocking them. They leaned on their horns and got out and stood with their hands on their hips or went striding up to the vehicles in front. Other people fished around in their cars for boots and cameras and followed the others making for the trees. One couple quickly unhitched their bikes from the back of their car and set off down the road, weaving through the line of stopped traffic. Even though she had no coat, Vi pitched forwards and joined the flow of people disappearing into the woods. She turned back once and shouted something at me, but I didn't hear what. Probably something about minding the store, which she knew I would do anyway. When I looked round, the man had gone, too. He had left his bag of food on the bench outside.

In the space of the next minute, everyone vanished. I sat down on the damp bench and tried to call you, but I couldn't get through. Two miles farther up the river and on the south side, you were much nearer to what was happening than I was. I wanted to know that Anna wasn't scared.

I couldn't always predict what Anna would understand, what would frighten or delight her. Sometimes she would stare at me for a long, long time and sometimes she looked away into such a far-off, sad place in her mind that I could believe she saw every sorrow there has been and is yet to come in this world. At other times, she was brave and bold. Do you remember one time when she was crawling, last summer, and you and I both thought the other one was watching her? It was only for a moment, but she set off on her hands and knees across those sharp stones towards the river, and I'll never be sure she wouldn't have kept on until the water was over her head if you hadn't yelled and dashed down and scooped her away from the edge. You lifted her up high to show me she was fine, and she was laughing and kicking, her legs were dripping. She laughed as if it was funny I might think she was anything other than immortal. She was laughing at me for being afraid she'd do anything as stupid as get herself drowned.

I tried you again, but still I couldn't get through. Then I felt guilty, remembering that phone signals get overloaded at such times with callers trying to find people they fear are caught up in the danger. There would be hundreds of people frantic for news, not just a little anxious, as I was, that a child might have seen something frightening from a distance. I thought of you coming down the trailer steps and hurrying to the water's edge with Anna in your arms. You wouldn't be able *not* to watch the bridge, but you'd make sure she wasn't scared. You'd hold her tight, shield her eyes, comfort her. She might not even know what it meant, it might be simply exciting to her, a spectacle. She might be clapping her hands. I flicked through the photos I kept on my phone of the two of you. Shivering on the bench and with the sirens wailing far away but all around me, I sat smiling and looking at pictures.

After another while the sirens faded, as if all the panic were somehow being placed at a distance. The cars on the road were empty. I decided I would go in and make some tea and see if I could fiddle with the radio dial and get the news. I picked up the man's bag of groceries and took it inside to keep safe for him in case he came back.

Soon afterwards Vi returned. She was sober now, and scorched-looking, as if what she'd seen had radiated a kind of blast that had burnt off the drink in her. Her sandy, dry hair had frizzed up in corkscrews, and her eyes were small and hot under her stiff eyebrows. She'd been up to the top of the falls, she told me, high enough to see down the estuary to the ruined bridge.

"There's a whole bit gone right out of the middle," she said, talking fast, bringing her hands together and opening them wide again. "Disappeared. Torn right away and in the river. And there's loads of cars went with it, they don't know how many. Cars with folk still in them."

I had never heard her talk so much. Disaster had made her lively. The river was choked with wreckage: girders, concrete, tarmac. She had seen the roofs of cars and an upended truck in the water. She hadn't seen any corpses, but people were dead, people were missing. The roads on both sides were closed. Up at the falls the man in the checked shirt had been getting news and police reports on his phone, and he'd told her that on this side of the river the police would be stopping all the traffic coming down from the north to Inverness and diverting it past the broken bridge. Everyone would have to come all the way along here on our little road, seven miles inland, and cross the river by the little stone bridge at Netherloch. Then from Netherloch the traffic would have to travel the seven miles back again, right down the riverbank on the other side to the end of the estuary at Inverness.

"Oh, think of the people," I said. I realized I was crying. "Those poor people."

"It'll be pandemonium," Vi said. "Pandemonium. Detours from here to Inverness, it'll add hours, you wait and see." Her voice was greedy. She was thinking of all those cars crawling past outside, all those drivers, bored and hungry and thirsty. She was trying not to look pleased.

"I mean the people in the water," I said. "The drowned people."

"Aye, right enough, but now what? That wee bridge at Netherloch'll never cope, it couldn't even take two wee vans going past each other, never mind thay great big trucks."

I remembered the first time we went there. I remembered the little bridge, made of dark-grey stone like the rest of Netherloch town. It had a shallow arch and curved recesses on each side. For people to step out of the way of carts and horses, you told me. It must have been built hundreds of years ago. Or to stand fishing, I said. Or set up stalls, selling things. People set up markets on bridges, don't they? It's where you can wait and catch customers, while they're going across. We stood there a little longer but I don't remember what we said after that. It was one of those conversations that did or didn't have an ending, like seeing a puff of smoke in the sky that drifted away and you weren't sure if you saw it go or just noticed later it had gone. It didn't matter.

Just then more sirens started up, and we went to watch at the window. The sound came nearer. Three or four police cars with blue flashing lights swept past in the direction of Netherloch.

"See?" Vi said. "That's them going in to set up the diversions. Pan-de-bloody-monium."

It was getting dark and soon from down the road another blue flashing light appeared and drew nearer, travelling slowly. Behind it a pair of white headlamps followed, growing round and glaring. More headlamps flickered behind in a long, moving necklace of lights winding up from the Inverness bridge. Soon the traffic was juddering nose to tail all along the road outside. We waited.

"I might have kenned," Vi sighed. "Nobody's stopping. Once you're in a queue like that, you stay in it. Nobody's going to pull off just for sweeties and a drink and lose their place."

She went over to the counter and rummaged underneath it. She poured out the dregs from her bottle and raised the glass towards the window. "Pandemonium. Break your bloody heart." She tipped her drink down her throat and swaying a little turned to watch the traffic again. "It'll be a different story in Netherloch. Folk pouring into a wee place like that, oh, they'll do fine, ta very much. Mind you, it'll bring in all sorts."

"I like Netherloch," I said.

Vi turned her gaze from the window. "Your lot don't go to Netherloch. It's for holiday folk."

"I've been once or twice."

"There's nobody in Netherloch these days. It's for holiday folk now," she said firmly. "None of your lot there." She made it sound as if Netherloch had escaped a pestilence. I felt my eyes fill with tears again and I moved away to the door, where all the tourist stuff was laid out, and began tidying up the shelf with the pottery Loch Ness Monsters and bookmarks. Over my shoulder I could feel her thinking about what she'd said, wanting to balance it with something less unkind. I saw that in her, sometimes, and a look that told me she was sorry for the way she was.

"Well, anyway. Where is it you stay again? Over the other side, isn't it? You'll be a while getting back tonight," she said. "All that traffic all the way up to the wee bridge and all back down the other side."

"There's still the stock at the back to put out," I reminded her, and got the pricing gun and the order sheet from under the counter. Vi looked at the clock.

"No, on you go," she said, taking them from me. "You get going. Walk down to Netherloch and there'll be police there, they'll help you out. There'll be other folk needing lifts most likely. I doubt there'll be a bus tonight."

As I went to get my bag and jacket, I heard her ring the till open. When I came back she was leaning over it, gripping the sides with her hands.

"There'll be nobody in this weekend. I can't be paying out to mind an empty shop." She looked up. "Don't come in till Monday, OK? You'd struggle to get here anyway, all that bloody big detour."

She started thumbing through the few notes in the till drawer. It was Thursday. Maybe she'd forgotten she was due to pay me on Friday. I had less than five pounds in my bag. I didn't know how we'd manage the weekend, never mind that I was supposed to work Sunday and now she didn't want me in, so I'd lose that money as well.

"I could make it. I could get here," I told her. I stood there for a while, hoping at least she'd pay me what I was owed.

"Not worth it. Could be we won't get a summer season at all," Vi said, banging the drawer shut again. Then she gave me a kind of wave and lurched back to her place by the paraffin stove. I think she meant it partly as an apology, but mainly she wanted rid of me.

"Come in Monday. I'll pay you Monday," she said and closed her eyes.

That made me feel a little better. If she wasn't settling up now, it must mean she really did want me on Monday. She wasn't telling me I hadn't got a job any more.

"See you then, Vi," I said. "Take care."

Just at that moment I had an idea. I reached under the counter and picked up the bag of stuff I'd kept for the man who hadn't come back. We'd manage through the weekend all right. Probably you would want to get us some fish as well. Those times we were down to nothing, you always tried fishing. Hours and hours you spent at it, without the proper lines or anything, and usually you got nothing.

Mainly you did it because you liked it – not the fishing itself, the try-ing. But I'd stop you this time. I couldn't eat fish from the river now.

I turned and walked out into the night air. Cars trickled past me, their headlamps shining in a silvery curve out of the trees bordering the road, their beams sparkling ahead into blackness. The night was damp and cold. Suddenly I felt I was down there at the bottom of the dark river with the fish, their thick, flat, muscular sides quivering past me, swimming right past those poor drowned people and flicking their dead faces, sending pulses of dark water into their open mouths and pulling silky fins through their waving, frondy hair.

On the day the bridge collapsed he'd been standing in a shop, a dingy roadside place called the Highland Bounty Mini-Mart, where he'd stopped a number of times before. It was run by a pathetic old drunk and a skinny blonde woman, foreign, who as far as he could see did all the work. He wasn't good at small talk, but he'd found out gradually he was better at it than the blonde woman, and she seemed always sad, and that made him want to speak to her. He would have liked to cheer her up a little. He was taking his change when the roaring and crashing began, and they rushed outside and a moment later someone was shouting about the bridge, and without wanting to be, he was swept along in a group of people all racing up through the forest to the head of Netherloch Falls.

Long before they got there his heart was hammering in his chest, partly from the noise and shock and the physical exertion of climbing up the dark, rooty path between the trees, but also partly from a rush of excitement. Here he was, talking away to people unknown to him, all of them struggling through the forest together, helping one another, listening to breathless theories and speculations about causes and casualties. The others seemed to assume he was somebody just like them. Even in the wake of a catastrophe, perhaps because of it, they accepted him without question.

At the top, the ground opened onto a flat patch of smooth rocks and clumps of bracken and heather, and the group halted by a low wall at the tourists' lookout point. Conversation dropped away to silence as they gazed at the stark, fractured bridge ends, already sparkling with emergency lights and divided now by the torrent of the river. For a long time nobody moved; a kind of an impotent acceptance, a subdued awe at the sight of the wreckage, weighed upon them all. Then two or three who stood close by Ron began to cry quietly. The rest moved to and fro, talking softly again or just looking; some took photographs, some gathered round a man who was picking up live news on his mobile phone. Slowly, most drifted away. Ron stood apart and wept, his whole body shaking. His companions, if they were taken aback by his sobbing, did not show it, and one of the women squeezed his arm as she turned to go.

He lingered for a long time after everyone else had left, sitting on a low rock and watching the white sky deepen to grey. Down at the bridge, the lights sharpened and winked brightly through the dusk, and as he watched he became calmer. It sank into his mind slowly that the blame for this was not his to bear. This was greater destruction even than that he had caused seven years ago, and although the enormity of that would never lessen, before his eyes those seven and a fraction deaths were multiplying. He felt grievously helpless, but out of his distress was arising a gratitude that he was not, he really was *not* to blame for this suffering, too. He was innocent; for that he was both relieved and ashamed of his relief.

And it filled him with an urge to do something to help, as if he were being granted permission at last to make amends, to involve himself somehow in the righting of this calamity as a way of uncoupling himself from the dragging guilt of the last one. There must be work he could do that would bring about some little good; he could volunteer. They would be setting up assistance for casualties and families, there would be people down there now, stranded and needing help. He would go and make himself available to do whatever was needed. There would be, at the very least, people wanting lifts home.

While there was still enough light to see by, he made his way down through the forest path and back across to the Highland Bounty Mini-Mart. When he saw that the place was dark and closed up he remembered about his bag of shopping, but he didn't care about that now. Outside the shop, the road was now choked with barely moving traffic in both directions. There would be chaos at the bridge; in the Land Rover he would not get near it. He would have to forget about driving anywhere tonight and see what he might do in other ways. He thought for a moment about waiting until morning, but the urge to act at once was too strong. He set off, walking towards the bridge against an oncoming line of vehicles. It was the nearest to happy he had felt for seven years.

When I got back to the Invermuir Lodge it was that dead time of afternoon in small hotels, after lunch and before the bar opens, when all the staff disappear. I went straight upstairs and lay down to rest but when I closed my eyes, pictures from the day loomed at me, a day of brightness and darkness and of distant views of the wilderness of the forest seen from the city side of the river.

Soon I was wandering along a path of linked half-dreams where fog curled through unrecognizable trees and lifted across a mirrored loch and sunlight snapped between the spans of a bridge, and I stood within the imprisoning mesh of a forest, waiting for something. To be found, I thought, or maybe just to be seen; if by some magic twist I were able to be in two places at once, to be standing where I was and also seeing myself in the place I was looking towards, would I behold a less shabby me, transformed, reinvented, valid? It came to me, as I fell asleep, that that was what I was waiting for, and that I had always gone about my life this way, looking with yearning across distances. I had reached from my father's sickness-bound house in Portsmouth towards a far-off, more authentic self as Col's wife; now I was reaching from the flatness of our marriage for the distant picture of us as parents. I heard again the cry and the scrape of rocks as Stefan stumbled and fell, casting Anna away from him towards her safe, soft landing. I saw them as they had sat in the trailer, looking at each other, and when they turned to me, their faces wore frayed smiles, full of sadness because they knew I was incomplete in some way, lacking something specific, like money or an important fact, but something they didn't have a word for. And for all they could not say quite what it was, it was something definitive and tremendous, and they were regretful that by not having it I was excluded and set apart from them. I pulled a pillow across the bed and held it in my arms against my stomach. I watched the red numbers of the clock alarm at the bedside wink in the gloom, and I fell asleep again.

I was awakened by a text message from Col.

Soaking freezing. Going for drink their hotel F Aug. Back at 7.

I turned and stretched out on my back, relieved. I was still groggy, and the square of light from the window showed a sky silvery with cold and fading towards evening. Fort Augustus was twelve miles farther west of Invermuir. It was just after four o'clock. Now I could stay warm and rest for at least another hour, which would be time enough to get used to the thought of going out again.

I got up to make a cup of tea. Instead of switching on a lamp, I turned on the television, for its flickering light rather than the actual pictures, and I kept the volume off. It wasn't until after I had filled the little kettle from the bathroom tap and come back to plug it in that I took any notice of what was happening on the screen.

I was watching trembly pictures of a man with a fishing rod standing by a river. He was showing off and smiling. He turned to the water to cast, concentrating for a moment or two, sideways from the camera. The picture swung up to the top of the rod and back down, the man grinned and cast again. It was an amateur video; it must have been one of those programmes of supposedly hilarious home-video clips and in a minute there would be a mishap: he'd fall in the river, a gull would land on his head, something like that. But in the instant before I turned away, the man's body jolted and his knees buckled. He turned abruptly upriver and dropped the rod. When he spun round a second later to look at the camera, his face was frightened and bewildered. Then he was shouting and waving his arms, and he ran off, out of the frame. The camera swung away; the picture tilted up, zigzagged and hit darkness, and then it began to jerk irregularly and very fast, up and down. Black bars broke across the image; the person with the camera was running through trees. When the picture settled, it was trained on the water. It focused in, silently, on the distant bridge.

The bridge I had crossed that day was untying itself from the earth. Its taut steel curves were loosening, its angles unfolding and turning slack. Cables were swaying and bending out of the sky, curling down and inwards and falling in cast-off tangles into the water. Around and underneath them, across the river, cars careered off the tilting road and sent up white explosions of foam as they hit the surface. I turned up the sound and now the cries of the man with the fishing rod mingled with creaks and a hollow roaring from the bridge and the coming-and-going groan of the wind, or perhaps it was not the wind but the breathless rasps from the man who kept hold of the shaking camera when all he must have wanted to do was turn his eyes away and weep. But he held on, and then came the high squealing and tearing of tons of breaking masonry and steel. The uprights supporting the bridge spans tottered stiffly towards and away from one another. With awful slowness they, too, crashed into the river, one by one, and the road, tipping and sagging some more, in a slow, rolling twist disappeared under the water.

Then the image froze. From the bridge's severed ends, girders hung suspended in space and in time, not yet lethally collapsed. A car arrested in a nosedive towards the water hovered in mid-air, its occupants not yet trapped and drowned. There was a digital whirring.

For a second or two, the video ran backwards and speeded up like some ludicrously cruel comic caper; the car reeled back from disaster and jumped up onto the road. Then the screen went blank except for numbers racing in one corner. There was a flicker, and there again was the man larking about with the fishing rod, his face untouched by what was about to happen. Again he twice cast his line, started, turned, dropped the rod, shouted, ran. Again the stumbling camera followed until it broke through the undergrowth and fixed on the collapsing giant of the bridge, the breaking concrete, the buckled spans, ripped lengths of roadway, and falling cars, the river boiling with debris.

And again. Unable to move, I stood and watched with the kettle in my hand. There he was, a man about to cast a line on a riverbank in early spring. And again, what happened instead. What happened next. This time the footage came with commentary from a news anchor in the studio, but of course it didn't alter anything; the fisherman started, turned, dropped the rod, shouted, ran. The juddering camera followed. Voices cried out, the wind howled, cables snapped, concrete and steel tore, and the bridge went down. But I was finding out what I suddenly realized I needed to know, because this time the commentary gave a chronology, minute by minute, of what happened. I put down the kettle, scrabbled in my bag for a scrap of paper, and wrote down all the figures I could. When the pictures stopped, suddenly the strength went out of my legs and I sank onto the bed. With my hand shaking, I checked the timings and worked out the arithmetic.

Right up until a quarter to three that afternoon, traffic had been flowing as normal in both directions over the bridge. I had left Stefan and Anna at the service station before one o'clock. Stefan hadn't said so, but the man changing the licence plates would be sure to be in Inverness. There was no reason for Stefan to have crossed the bridge. They would have been driving into the city within minutes of my leaving them. There was no cause for them to have been near the bridge at all.

I kept watching. The amateur cameraman was in the studio now. The young man and his father-in-law, after a pub lunch in Inverness, had crossed the bridge themselves soon after two o'clock. They had parked and gone down to the riverbank on the north side to record the first try-out with the new rod, a birthday present. The bridge began to creak and lurch at two forty-six, as his father-in-law watched in terror, turned, dropped the fishing rod, shouted and ran. The young man followed and his camera was on it within thirty seconds. By two forty-eight, three of the central bridge spans and the stretch of road between them, measuring two hundred and seventy feet and bearing, the young man estimated, about twenty vehicles, had collapsed into the water. He contacted the news channel straight away, and his video, "probably the only eyewitness record of the disaster", was broadcast for the first time at ten minutes past four. Then they asked him what he had felt as he watched it all happen, and the young man broke down in tears.

I found myself crying, too, with a strange sorrow that was both impersonal and personal. I cried for the strangers who were lost, but also with relief for Stefan and Anna. They would be safe. By now the new licence plates would be on the car, and all I had to do was get back to Netherloch and pretend I had just discovered that it had been stolen from the car park behind the school. But would anyone care, now? A bridge had collapsed and people were dead and missing; it was impossible to believe that the lies I was going to tell about the car could be of any real importance. Yet I had to go. Stefan was relying on me.

But Netherloch was only about seven miles inland from the estuary bridge, and the narrow stone bridge in the town was the next crossing place over the river. There was bound to be disruption on the roads. For the next hour I kept the television on for traffic news. The video of the catastrophe was replayed endlessly. At a quarter to six I had another text message:

In nothr bar! Going for curry. Eat without me ok sorry

I lay back on the bed in the dark room. Reflections from the screen danced in muzzy patterns over my hands, folded across my stomach. In the next half-hour the video was run another four times, with slight variations in the commentary as a range of people gathered in the studio to give their viewpoints. Then live footage appeared. Rescue teams with boats and helicopters and ambulances were scrambled under emergency lighting. A reporter in an overcoat stood on a roadside with a microphone and said that the number of vehicles believed lost in the water continued to rise. It was feared that it might never be known for certain how many, for in such strong tides and deep water, cars and bodies could be swept out to sea and never found. But, on a more optimistic note, nobody was giving up hope, the reporter said. Some people had made it out of their cars and swum through the freezing water to the riverbanks, where they were being treated on the spot for shock, exposure and injuries. There was severe road congestion, and police were urging people to keep away. Anyone concerned for a loved one should stay by the telephone and not attempt to come to the bridge.

Then the screen filled with different images, dark and grainy. I was looking at more video footage which, said the news anchor (relieved to have something new to show) had just been made available. Another, more solemn voice said that what was about to be shown captured the moments before the collapse. It might provide evidence as to the cause and help with identification of fatalities. Some viewers might find the images disturbing, and at this stage police were not confirming the identities of any of the vehicles shown. In silence the new pictures rolled, blurred and grey like old newspaper photographs suddenly animated, but lit by a kind of innocuous afternoon light. The vantage point was a fixed, bird's-eye view of a road whose broken white line stretched away in the tarmac through the centre of the image. This was the vital footage, said the voice, from the traffic camera at the top of one of the arches of the approach on the southern side, only a hundred metres from the start of the bridge. The back view of a blue car swelled into the picture and receded, leaving the road empty again. The commentator remarked that the time, mid-afternoon and midweek in low season, meant that traffic on the bridge had been relatively light. A van and another car appeared, slowed, moved beyond the reach of the camera. For a few moments there was silence again, and the empty road. Softly, the voice said that viewers were witnessing the procession of the last vehicles known to have passed under the arch when the bridge was still standing. The timing of the footage and the recorded moment of the collapse meant that these cars could not have made it all the way across; seconds after these images were caught they would have been on the bridge. Moments later, they must have been plunged into the river. Two more cars emerged into the picture, paused, and drove on. Then speckles of grey and white invaded the screen, it turned black, and the video wound back to the start, with the bird's-eye view of the empty road.

The footage ran again; cars came into view, moved across the screen and out. This time the video was stopped, trapping each vehicle for a moment in a fuzzy blizzard in the centre of the screen. The studio voice stressed that the police were not releasing any details. Anyone concerned for a relative was urged to stay by the telephone. Emergency information lines would be operational soon. Slowly each car came forwards, and each time the camera froze. And there, a few seconds after a black four-wheel drive and in front of a white van, was my car, the silver Vauxhall with the car-rental company logo along the edge of the boot. It edged its way on and out of the picture.

My telephone blinked with another message:

Come if u want. Jewel of Raj in F. Aug. Feet soaked bring other trainers ok?

I listened again to the voice from the television saying emergency lines would be open soon. Another message came through.

No transport back l8r unless u come with car.

I switched off the television and sat in the dark. I didn't move at all. I didn't dare move, for fear the least flutter of my hand or blink of an eye would alert someone to my continued presence in the world. I ought not to be here. It was through some error of fate I was still here; it was a mistake. Someone else instead of me had driven my car onto the breaking bridge and straight into the force that had twisted the road away from under its wheels and flung it into the river. I tried to control my shaking. It was essential I remain still. I ought not to be here.

I switched on the television again. In silence, the bridge camera video ran once more. The numbers for emergency information lines flashed on the screen between cars crawling sporadically up the approach road. Again, my car passed under the arch and on towards the bridge. Along the flat lower edge of the muzzy rectangle of the back window I saw the merest soft, dark curve: the dome of Anna's head.

The next pictures were from a village hall on the north side of the bridge, where a shelter had been set up for casualties. A pale, young, shivering face peered from the hood of a blanket and spoke to the camera.

"Suddenly there's no road, there's nothing in front of me and then I'm going down and I'm thinking this is it I'm going to die, but I got myself out I don't know how next thing I'm in the water, it's cold it's really freezing but I get to the surface and then I'm trying to swim and I'm just thinking keep going, keep going. I saw people in the water, there was all this wreckage and cars and stuff then I couldn't see them any more, you just keep swimming and keep your head above water and hope for the best and I hope they made it." His face crumpled; he looked five years old. "I'm lucky to be alive."

I scanned the people in the background for Stefan and Anna. They must be there. He and Anna could not have died that way. What was the use of it, a love like that, unless it achieved at least the keeping alive of the beloved? I thought of them in the car together and of the money in my bag and why it was there, and I felt sick. Could it be that I had bought my own child's life at the cost of theirs? I thought of my mother and the price she believed had been exacted from her, and paid, for her child. Did nothing change?

Another text message came.

Heard it on news re bridge. Weird u were there y'day! Raj ok? Call me when u get here. Don't 4get trainers

The light from the television flickered across the leg of the dressing table and over one of Col's trainers lying against it with the laces tied and a wad of dead leaves trapped in the sole. On the chair in the corner I could make out the outline of his heap of clothes, big overstitched things with copious pockets and zips and gadgety little clips and features to meet a couple of dozen Boy-Scoutishly anticipated variants of weather and carrying requirements. On his bedside table were a baseball cap, his phone charger and a book of word puzzles.

Tonight, sooner or later, he would come back here and look round and see that this room contained everything he needed. Sooner or later, maybe not until tomorrow if he collapsed in bed too drunk to find out where I was, he would learn that our rental car had been on the bridge. If I had died in the river, this room would still contain everything he needed. If I got up now and just left, this room would still contain everything he needed.

He would probably spend some time feeling numb, even sad. He would spend some time (to his private surprise, rather little) adjusting his expectations back to those of a single man, gaining a touch of celebrity among people who knew him for the improbably lurid bad luck of losing his bride in a freak accident. He would let them describe it as tragic. He would allow them to think he minded that there couldn't be a proper funeral; he'd go along with a modest memorial service of some kind. He would never tell a soul that I had been pregnant, and soon he would not mention me at all. Within a few months he would look back on being married as a botched experiment in becoming somebody else. Relieved, mildly ashamed, he would go back to the chat room on the Internet, but he'd be careful never to get caught out that way again.

I straightened the bed so it looked untouched, emptied the kettle and switched off the television. I deleted all my text messages and voicemails and turned my phone off. I put it in the bag I had left the hotel with that morning and walked from the room. I slipped downstairs. Everyone was in the bar or the restaurant. I let myself out of the door into the garden and made my way towards the road.

I walked away, not just from Col but from my failure to become a wife he wanted to keep. I walked away from having to justify wanting my baby. And for my baby's sake as well as mine, I walked away from the humiliation of counting out money to its father as if this or that sum were an opening offer in a haggle for its life. I wasn't just walking away; I was also bearing my baby, hidden in the warm, fleshy pod of my body, to safety. I was saving both our lives, and we were together.

Nearly a mile out from the collapsed bridge, men in fluorescent jackets milled around the ROAD CLOSED signs, directing cars back to the bridge at Netherloch. Ron moved quietly into the stricken, displaced little bands of people roaming around on the verges and among the trees, like mourners or refugees. A bright moon in a silky, deep-violet sky shone above the road, but in the distance arc lights lit the river ominously, as if illuminating a stage for more spectacle and greater violence; the limbs of the bridge, jagged and black against flashing orange and blue emergency lights, jutted out above the water. Helicopters roamed overhead, sending down vapoury cones of light, hovering low enough for gusts of air from the propellers to blow trembling circles of flecks across the impenetrable, mercury-dark river.

The drift of people carried Ron along into a denser crowd at the forest's edge, where spectators stood facing a television crew, and a spotlight under which a journalist was shouting into a microphone. An exhausted-looking man in a safety helmet was led forwards to be interviewed. The crowd began solemnly to applaud him, and as he started to speak, Ron stepped away from the throng and slipped under the barrier tape. Expecting to be stopped at any moment, he passed quickly into the pines that covered the sloping land between the river and the road. So close to the forest edge, there was no path; keeping within the darkness of the trees, he scrambled down through a prickly mesh of branches until he was almost at the water.

When he emerged from the trees he saw that crowd barriers now separated the forest from the site of the collapse. He could have climbed them quite easily, but he remained outside, watching. There seemed surprisingly few people at work on the riverbank; about a dozen who looked like paramedics and rescue workers came and went around a tent that had been set up, as far as Ron could tell, as a first-aid station for casualties; he saw two men carry a stretcher from the tent and up the uneven bank towards a helicopter standing on the last strip of the bridge approach road. Ron had learnt first aid when he became a driver, but he did not dare go forwards and present himself. He would be ejected at once as *unauthorized.* There was no place here for simple willing hands; this was not a neighbourly effort. The operation was professional and, for all he knew, efficient. He drew farther back into the trees. Once he was more familiar with what was going on, once it was daylight again, he would find the courage to ask if he could help.

As the night wore on, the rescue settled into a regular rhythm, determined and unspectacular. Under the arc lights, boats and helicopters made their forays to the river in droning, dogged circles. Ron hunkered against a damp tree trunk and grew drowsy. He dozed until the cold woke him. Then he got up and moved back farther into the trees, where the wind did not cut so keenly. He didn't want to spend the night in the open, but he was reluctant to walk all the way back to the Land Rover; without knowing where he was going, he slipped deeper still into the forest's shelter. He was afraid of losing his way, and remembering that the road above him followed its path, he kept the river always in sight on his left, shining through the fringe of pine branches. He was still cold. After a while he came upon an area where trees had been felled, but not recently; years of hard weather on the rutted ground had left it almost impassable with dank troughs and exposed, torn-up roots. From here the bank rose steeply to his right;

there was no clear path up to the road. So he made his way instead down to the gleaming river, and when he reached it he saw he must be almost a mile from the bridge. The sharp arc lights had softened to a glow in the night sky. That was when, almost at the water's edge, he came across the derelict prefabricated cabin. The door on the river side was padlocked, but at the back he found a small, warped door, locked and jammed tight with damp. It was soft with rot and sagged against his shoulder when he pushed at it. After several heaves, the lower of its two hinges split from the frame, and he was able to squeeze through. The place was unfurnished and comfortless, cold and dirty, but it was a roof for the night and out of the wind. By the moonlight through the smeared windows he saw there was a stove and some fuel, but he had no matches. He curled up on the floor and lay listening to the sounds from the bridge; the motors and sirens had faded to remote purrs and squeals that mingled with the river flowing softly by outside. Yet the fright and injury of the day reached into him – or maybe he had brought it with him – and suddenly his heart, a berg of ice, seemed to shatter and burn within his chest. He began to shiver violently, and he curled tighter, trying to tell himself this was physical stress, nothing more. A fragment of his first-aid training came back to him: *When people experience trauma, one of the first things to go is the ability to fend for themselves.* It calmed him to realize that he *was* fending for himself, to a degree; at least he had found shelter. But why, he thought, was he steeling himself at all against the disintegration of his heart? Let it burn, let it melt. Let it even break again, if only he might no longer be alone.

It was cold, so I hurried. In Invermuir village the main road was jammed with traffic bound for Netherloch and Inverness, but the other side, heading west to Fort Augustus, was choked, too. I don't know why I set off in the direction of the bridge, but I walked eastwards along the roadside into the night, at a pace hardly slower than the crawling line of cars. There were emergency vehicles stationed here and there with their lights flashing and policemen standing in the middle of the traffic, attempting to keep it moving. Drivers were sounding their horns and turning around, manoeuvring back and forth in the road and sending up plumes of exhaust, headlamps looming and criss-crossing the darkness with restless beams of light.

I kept away from the glare as much as I could and moved on through the smoky drifts of petrol fumes, my head down. Knots of stranded people had gathered at the village bus stops and cars were stopping to give them lifts, but I couldn't risk joining them, looking lost and in need of help. I had watched my car go into the river, I had seen myself die; I ought to be gone, invisible for evermore. Until I had had time to think and re-establish myself, somewhere and somehow, as another person, I had to learn how to have no presence at all, to move among people with the stealth of a ghost. I must be alive to no one.

Soon I no longer noticed the cold. I felt newly light and unhindered, exhilarated by having accomplished so conclusively and tidily the bringing to an end of my life with Col. But I also felt left behind, as if my true fate had gone forwards and was enacting itself in advance of me, somewhere up ahead. I had to rejoin my life, or rather meet up with myself again and make another life. This was another reason to hurry.

I took a pathway off the road that led down to a walkers' trail along the river, where it was leafy and quiet. I had no torch, but the road ran parallel above and the lights of cars washed through the trees, showing me my way. From time to time the traffic thinned and the way cleared for wailing emergency vehicles. A few miles before Netherloch the riverside path fizzled out, so I joined the road again.

I walked on, still not knowing why I was going in the direction of the bridge, but walking with purpose. Was I seeking out the broken gate in the hedge that led down to Stefan's trailer? Not consciously. I was keeping disconnected in my mind any daytime memory of the road and the murky, illogical contours of the night landscape.

But it was getting late. More and more cars drove on past me, and I grew tired. Netherloch was still some miles away, and I had to spend the night somewhere. I pulled my hat down over my ears, tucked my chin into my scarf and waited at the next bus stop I came to. Within a minute a car stopped. It was driven by a woman about my age who had two teenage girls with her. They were doing their best to get to Inverness, and I was welcome, she said, to go with them. I was looking a bit shocked, was I all right? And wasn't it a terrible thing that had happened?

I thanked her and got in the back. I was just cold and tired, I assured her, and gave her some story about my car breaking down and leaving it at the roadside because I preferred to walk rather than wait for rescue with the roads so jammed, but I'd underestimated the distance to Netherloch. She told me I had no chance of getting a room there for the night, the radio said the town was heaving. I'd do better to go on to Inverness with her, however long it took. We crawled along; the two girls fell asleep, and to avoid conversation I pretended to also, turning my face to the window and keeping my eyes half-closed.

It was only when I saw the lights of the service station up ahead that I realized I was returning to the trailer. All the hours I had been walking, I had been holding tight to myself a belief that Stefan and Anna were among the people who'd got out of the river alive. But I had to make sure they were safe. I had to talk to Stefan. He had lost the car that had cost him all the money he had, and I couldn't alter that, but I had to divide the money with him. I would explain why I couldn't part with all of it; as a father, he would understand. But I wanted to give him half of it back, to ease his loss. I made excuses to the woman about needing a bathroom, and got out at the service station.

I walked back to the broken gate and down the track. The trailer was dark and shut up. There was nothing strange about that, I told myself. They might not be back yet; they could be still in one of the temporary first-aid stations near the bridge. Or they might be in hospital, as a matter of routine. Of course they wouldn't be here. I felt foolish, staring through the dark across the shingle at the closed door. I imagined it opening and Stefan appearing at the top of the steps, looking suspicious and puzzled until he recognized me, and then I realized what an odd sort of rescuer I must look. Sweat was running down my body and through my hair, and I was shivering. Nausea swept over me again, as it often did when I was hungry. But my hand thrust in my pocket was clutching the envelope with the money; pleasure was welling up inside me as if I had already seen the relief on Stefan's face. Of course there couldn't be anyone inside the trailer, but I walked carefully across the stones, up the steps and knocked on the door.

Nobody came. I waited, and the nausea grew worse. I tried the door handle. It opened into blackness and silence, and I was afraid, yet I wanted to go in. The night outside was suddenly no place to be; I needed walls and a roof, I needed shelter even if only this: precarious, thin, leaking. I stepped up into the doorway and peered inside. I could smell the soapy, vinyl smell from yesterday and also the bitter tang of cigarettes. Nothing moved, but in the darkness I knew there was something warm and alive. My heart was thumping like knuckles into the back of my ribs, bone against bone, and I took a breath to say something but I doubled over and retched. My mouth filled with bitter saliva. Without intending to, I spat on the floor, and as I was trying to stand up straight again, a torch snapped on. Instantly its beam lurched away and upwards, and I felt it come down hard on my head and shoulders, and then a hand was hauling me upright by the hair. A woman's screaming filled the trailer, the torch fell with a clunk, and its beam played jaggedly on her kicking feet and jerked over the ceiling and walls. I was trapped. I couldn't get out of the trailer or away from the screaming. Then the slapping and punching started.

I couldn't speak. Even if I could have explained, or got any words out at all, she wouldn't have heard. Fists and arms and feet were flying in a rolling beam of light, and through the screams she was spitting out words over and over, telling me to get out, go away, leave her alone. I held her off as best as I could until, shielding my head, I managed at last to stand up straight and face her. I was taller than she was. I stopped her next blow by grasping her wrists.

"Stop! Please stop! I didn't mean any harm," I said. "I'm sorry. It's OK. Please! Please—"

My voice cracked suddenly. The woman stopped screaming and stared at me, and then she burst into tears. I wanted to say more but I couldn't. Keeping hold of one of her wrists, I scooped up the torch at my feet and shone it at her. In the shaking light, her face was colour-less and stricken, the long blond hair sticky and matted to her scalp.

How could I comfort her? How could I dare offer comfort?

"Please, don't. Please. I'm sorry," I said.

We were stock-still for an instant. My grip on her wrist loosened. Suddenly she wrenched her arm free and backed away. The foldaway table and pull-out bed behind her, the blankets dragged to the floor, a heap of clothes, were now caught in the glow of the torch. She was alone. Part of the ceiling had curled away, exposing a web of saturated fibrous stuff from which water was seeping into a bucket on the floor.

"You tramp! You filthy tramp! Get out of here, get out now! Get out!"

She lunged forwards, shoving me towards the door so hard I stumbled and fell. Then she sank back into the dark mass of bedding and hid her face in another burst of weeping. I scrambled to my feet and ran from the trailer.

I climbed as fast as I could up the track, and when I reached the top I collapsed on the ground, coughing and fighting for breath. After a while I managed to sit up, and I stayed there, trying to drag in a proper lungful of air and stop the shaking in my legs. I was exhausted and sick from lack of food. I had nowhere to spend the night. I had no name. Which terror should I face first: being hungry, pregnant, homeless, or nameless?

But the worst terror was that Stefan and his daughter hadn't come back. They hadn't come back, and the woman in the trailer didn't know why, and I had not been able to tell her. I had sold him the car and now I had money to keep my child, but where was hers? I turned towards the lights of the service station.

It was thronged with people, but hunger forced me inside. I had to hope that although my face might appear in the papers and on televi-sion as one of the dead, it would be an old wedding photograph, the only pictures Col had of me. My hair had been curled and adorned with ludicrous turquoise feathers on the day I got married; now it was shorter and darker, and most of it was hidden under a flat woollen hat. Nobody would link a smiling photograph with this wretched woman, her face stung with cold, shuffling along in a cafeteria queue. I bought what was available, coffee and a muffin, and took them over to a table, which I had to share. There was a television suspended from the ceiling tuned soundlessly to the bridge news, and I ate and drank with my eyes raised to it, avoiding contact with the three other people at the table. I kept my cup up close to my face and let the coffee steam rise and warm my skin in between sips.

By now the service station should have closed for the night, but it was staying open for the people who were stranded. Extra plastic chairs had appeared, and people were bedding down on car blankets and jackets and coats all over the floor. Some appeared to be sleeping, others were talking and drinking doggedly, doing puzzles or playing cards, trying to control children. From the games arcade came ceaseless zooming and firing sounds and the unfettered, giddy yelps of teenage boys. A woman dozed in a wheelchair near the door to the Ladies, half hidden by the fronds of a huge artificial fern. Every table in the cafeteria was full, although the serving counter was down to tea and coffee in polystyrene cups. In the shop, people were buying up the last of the chocolate and sweets and magazines, but the queues had lessened because there was nothing of much use left; untouched stands of Frisbees and celebrity autobiographies stood out among the emptied shelves and racks. Although the place was thronged, there was a pall of numb, anxious quiet that perhaps hangs over all refugees.

I was wondering what to do, hoping I might find a space on the floor somewhere away from others and out of the freezing gusts from the doors, when four police officers came in, two men and two women. They didn't seem to have any particular task in mind; there was no disorder to bring under control. The manager and a younger sidekick joined them, and after a few minutes of talk, swinging on their heels and looking around, they drifted off, patrolling the mass of sprawling bodies. Several people went up to talk to them, with questions or complaints, I supposed. I watched all this from behind a bookrack in the shop. When it began to look as if the police were settled in for the night, I knew I couldn't stay.

Outside, the temperature had dropped further. I needed to find shelter somewhere. I made my way around the back and followed the fence into the darkness at the far corner of the car park, where I found again the opening to the abandoned track I'd driven down with Stefan and Anna twelve hours before. Only twelve hours? It seemed – in a way it was – a lifetime ago. Ahead of me I could see the flames of several small fires burning among the wrecked buildings on the wasteland; to my right I could see the glow of arc lights over the bridge abutments and the flicker of helicopters in the sky. I walked past the first straggly piles of debris at the sides of the track towards the fires, on through broken glass and old cans, mounds of rubble and discarded tyres, piles of ripped roofing felt, wiring and perished cable. Parts of wrecked cars rose in heaps around me; broken office furniture and rotten carpet jutted up from buckled and vandalized skips. I was far enough from the traffic and the service station to catch the cold tang of the estuary, mixed with the smell of damp fields and rust and a sullen overlay of smoke. I reached the corner of a derelict brick shed and edged my way along the wall to the next corner until I could see a barren stretch of cracked concrete that must once have been the floor of a factory or warehouse. At its far edges I could make out the jagged remains of half-demolished walls. There burned several bonfires in whose cloudy yellow light the stooping silhouettes of people moved to and fro, passing bottles, lifting sticks into the flames, collecting from the ground anything that might make shelters for the night. Beyond them the black estuary glittered with the sweeping lights of the helicopters, the air thudded and shrieked with propeller noise and sirens. Under the gleaming sky there was a great, desperate agitation, but here the faraway wails were an unreal music, part of the rushing-by of a world miles from this encampment among the scrub and banks of litter, where human beings hunkered down to get through the night, staring into dying fires.

I crouched down and watched. About a dozen people squatted or lay in aloof, solitary hovels of cardboard and rags, arranged in a haphazard outer ring as close to the warmth and light as they could get, but several feet from one another and a safe distance from the elite little groupings of twos and threes nearest the fires. Among these, proprietorial squalls would break out over a swig from a bottle, a cigarette, a package of food. From time to time the air fell silent as if everyone had fallen asleep or retired to his own thoughts, and then there would be cries and scuffles again, sometimes the sound of breaking glass or a hallucinatory insult or misunderstanding, for sly demons came and went among these people. To some of them, the smoky sky was alive with spectres that could enter through the space between blinks of their eyes and whisper tormenting messages inside their skulls, goading them into outbreaks of itching or howling or whimpering fear. One man sat upright, staring round with crazed vigilance, batting away phantom attackers with his empty bottle.

I got up carefully and foraged at the margins of the firelight. No one turned from the flames to look at me. I found some plastic and cardboard in a heap against a ruined wall, and I dragged an armful across the concrete and set it down where I could feel a little warmth but would not be presumptuously close to the fire. The dark mounds around me shifted from time to time through the smoke, coughing, rearranging their coverings. I saw the smooth lifting of the burning dots of cigarettes, the red flares as they were inhaled. Nobody spoke. I went back, found some frayed sheets of bubble wrap, brought them to my place on the ground. I arranged a kind of sleeve of cardboard, and pulled the bubble wrap around myself. There I lay, my hand clasping the money in my pocket, my body wrapped as china is against the breakages that occur in transit through this world. I fell asleep.

I dreamed of a man who was taking me in the silver car on a hazardous journey. We drove through puddles that turned into lakes, we splashed miraculously out of them again and lost the road under a blizzard of snow, but on we went, because our destination was a place where I was to give a performance of some kind in front of a lot of people. I allowed myself to be taken, keeping silent about the only thing I was sure of, which was that I had nothing to give the audience, nothing to merit their attention or applause. I walked to the centre of the stage and waited for their disappointment. Then I was standing under a tree and I had no excuse for my reticence to offer all the reproachful people walking by, save the one I spoke as they went past. I can't give you anything, because I am going to have a baby, I said, and although they kept on walking, they knew this was the truth and they forgave me.

You weren't at the trailer when I got there, but I knew you were coming back. You were stranded somewhere, like everyone else that night, and you must have lost your phone. You took perfect care of Anna, always. I knew you were coming back.

First I told myself you had taken her out for a bus ride somewhere and got stuck in the traffic. When it got past nine o'clock that evening I knew you would be trudging towards me along the road, cold and tired, with her asleep against your back, her hair tickling your neck. I didn't like to leave the trailer, but I climbed up the track to meet you, going quietly so I would hear the scrape of your feet or the rattle of the gate, your voice calling from up ahead that you were home at last. I didn't go as far as the road, just to where I could hear the cars and see their headlights splitting the dark. I stayed back in the trees and waited and waited.

The traffic was moving almost as slowly as before. It was four hours since I'd walked from the shop down to Netherloch and got a lift with an elderly couple trying to get back to Inverness. They'd been to see his sister in a nursing home in Fort Augustus. The man had said nothing and the woman had tried to be nice, but I pretended I couldn't speak English because I couldn't have told her much that was true about me and I didn't want to lie. They weren't big talkers anyway. In two and a half hours we travelled six miles in silence except for the radio news and their soft remarks of despair, about the tragedy and the inconvenience, equally. I got out at the service station and walked back so they wouldn't see me set off down the track. It didn't look like a suitable place for people to live.

I waited for you at the gate until I was so cold I either had to lie down where I was and burrow under leaves like an animal, or go back, and when I turned away and thought of the empty trailer I began to cry, and I couldn't stop. When I got back I threw myself onto the bed and lay sobbing, and after a while I lit a candle, as if it could make me feel less alone, and in a strange way it did. I think that's why we light candles when we think of the people we really have lost, supposedly to God; we need to fill the emptiness of churches and the space their absence makes with small flames. By then I was warm again, and I managed to fall asleep. It must have been hours later I heard noises outside, feet on the stones and then on the trailer steps. I was up and nearly crying out for joy before I realized there was something wrong about it. If it had been you, you would have been calling to me long before you got to the trailer. For a moment I wondered if it was a deer. Then there was a knock on the door. My throat went dry. I tried to speak, but my voice wouldn't work. Then the door opened. Everything it is possible to feel at once – rage that it was some dirty, crazy stranger and not you and Anna, terror that this person could just knock and walk in like that, relief that it was a woman and not a gang of men with knives – everything surged into hatred, and I attacked her.

I remember thinking in the seconds after I'd scared her off that she hadn't really threatened me at all. She was pathetic, not dangerous. She must have wanted something, because she left behind an achy feeling about herself, some powerlessness. I felt almost guilty. I never saw her face clearly, but if I had seen her eyes I think they would have been saturated with want. But I thought these things only after enough time had passed for me to be sure she wasn't coming back.

I felt calmer, even though I was weary and confused. It was nearly two o'clock in the morning and I was wide awake.

I found the number of the hospital in Inverness and called it again and again. When I got through I was given another number for enquiries about the bridge victims. I kept calling that number until finally somebody answered. I asked, quite calmly, because it was of course foolish to worry, if any buses had been on the bridge. No, the man said. Or, I asked, were there people killed or injured who had been crossing the bridge on foot? He asked for names, and although I was taking a risk I gave them your real ones, vowing to myself that I would never, ever tell you I did this. I had to wait a long time. Then he came back and said they did not have those names on any lists. I could hardly speak, I was crying so hard. But then, I thought, how stupid of me. Of course you would have given false names. So I asked was there any man of about twenty-five with a little girl – any man and child at all – injured or, I whispered, lost? He told me that three adult cyclists were in hospital and two had been killed, and all the other casualties had been in vehicles. So far. There were cars still unrecovered, he told me gently, and I should call back in the morning.

I didn't sleep again. But before daybreak I knew even more certainly you were coming back. It *was* foolish to worry. Something had happened to keep you from getting home, but you hadn't been on the bridge when it collapsed. You were safe, somewhere. You'd had to stay the night somewhere where there was no telephone signal, and you were coming back.

I went down to the river edge as soon as it was light, with half the bedding wrapped around me. From downstream, echoey metallic sounds dented the air above the water. In the distance, the arms of the bridge reached through the haze to each other, apart and still. I crouched down and picked up a handful of stones and started chucking them, sending them with short flicks of my wrist one by

111

one into the river, and humming some old tuneless thing along with the rhythm of their little splashes.

It was very cold, but I kept sitting there, hugging the blankets around myself and humming and tossing stones and remembering what the man in the hospital had told me about the casualties. I was also keeping a tight grip on something else I knew. You had never taken Anna near the bridge, not once. It was over a mile along the busy road from here to the start of it, too far for her to walk, and anyway, yesterday had been much too cold. Oh, you did get sudden ideas, but even if you'd had the thought of taking her along the bridge to stand and look at the river and out to the sea, you would have been turning it into a plan for a summer day. You would have come to me with your eyes shining, and the whole thing worked out. We would wait for fine weather and get the bus as far as the southern end of the bridge. We could walk all the way across because Anna would be a few months older and a bit more able to manage. It would be windy whatever the time of year, but never mind. We would find a way down through the pine trees on the opposite bank and have a picnic at the water's edge, almost under the bridge. We'd be able to see our trailer way over on the other side! You would fish, and Anna would splash in the water and I would doze in the sun. I chucked more and more stones in the river and thought of this, and as I gazed, the bridge ends began to soften and float against a watery yellow sky and the far bank wavered and sparkled with light. I could see us, little figures in summer clothes clambering down through the dark pine trees to the shore, our shoulders skinny and bare and warmed by the sun. I could hear Anna playing in the water and squealing, our voices calling out to her. I could hardly tell if I was imagining it or remembering a day we'd actually spent. But we certainly would spend a day like that, I decided, when the summer came. I smiled, thinking that such a day was now my idea, not yours.

There was a sudden sound behind me, a low, human bellowing. I turned and saw the mad woman from last night throwing up on the ground, staggering away from the trailer. By the time I reached her, her stomach was empty and she was gasping, watching me through scared eyes. Her hat had slipped off, and she was using it to clean vomit out of her hair and wipe her steaming mouth. The poor thing looked terrified and half out of her mind, staring and dribbling and moaning apologies. I couldn't make out what she was trying to say. I didn't know what she wanted. Maybe she had people to find, too.

"Are you looking for somebody?" I said. "Have you lost somebody?"

She shook her head, then she nodded. "I think so."

She didn't say any more, because the nodding of her head had started up a violent shuddering in her whole body. I thought she was going to fall, so I took hold of her by the elbow. Her hand clutched my forearm and sent a shiver through me. Her fingers were hard and fleshless. She raised her other hand towards the trailer and tried to speak again, but all she could manage was *I'm sorry, I'm sorry, I'm sorry.*

I understood. She was saying sorry for last night. Maybe she had needed somewhere to take shelter and thought the trailer was empty. But she hadn't come back just to say sorry. She still needed a place to stay. Whatever had happened to her, she was in a worse state than I was. If I scared her off again, she'd never make it back to the road.

"Are you lost? Have you nowhere to go?"

She swallowed and gulped and looked me in the face, and nodded. She had sweet, frightened eyes. Suddenly I didn't want to watch her go. I didn't want to be left here alone again, maybe into another night. You would come back soon, you could come back at any moment, but until then we'd be safer together, this wretched woman and me. She looked too weak and ill to do me any harm, and by now I could see she didn't mean me any. My mind began to work properly at

113

last. She was English, and she was surely a nice person underneath all that roughness. In a few hours, when she felt better, she'd be able to talk to the police for me. She could find things out without me taking the risk of being caught. If you weren't already back – and you could come back at any moment – she would help me find you. If I helped her now, she would owe me that much.

"You're sick. You can stay and rest here for a while, if you want."

Her eyes darted over to the trailer.

"You can stay here for a while," I said. "I'm Silva."

She clutched my arm tighter. "Thank you."

"What's your name?"

I pulled the blanket away from my own shoulders and drew it around hers as well, and led her to the trailer.

"I'm... My name is Annabel."

The next day dragged me to its surface early, pricking my eyes open with a rush of chill air and making them water. The sky was white with dense, icy cloud, and full of noises; the sirens had stopped, but the drumming and clanking of engines and heavy machinery had started up at the bridge, and the road was already loud with traffic. It hadn't rained in the night, but the ground was damp and my clothes were sodden. I checked I still had my money, then I peeled the cardboard back and unwound myself from the plastic. Instantly the night's sweat froze on my body, and I felt the wind slipping between my bones as if there were nothing under my skin but cold, flowing air. All my joints and limbs hurt, and I started to shiver. The fires had died out but for a reed of smoke rising from one or two. A man was peeing into the scrub over at the far edge of the concrete, but nobody else had stirred. My stomach felt empty yet queasy; I had to get my body moving and I had to get warm.

I retraced my steps to the service station. Traffic was moving past on the road again, but the car park was still full. I saw no police vehicles and, when I paused at the entrance to look around, no police officers. Inside, the concourse dormitory was waking up to serene piped music and the smell of frying. People dazed with sleep were moving slowly here and there among those still sleeping, and cleaners quietly mopped floors and pushed trolleys and wiped surfaces, trancelike in the warm, stale air. The washroom was a mess, out of soap and paper and towels, but I managed to run some hot water in a basin, and I splashed some on my face, which warmed it without getting it much cleaner. When I came out, the café was open. I was relieved to see there had been a changeover of staff, and once I was quite sure I couldn't see anybody who had been there yesterday, I joined the others already lining up for food. New supplies had been found from somewhere. I ate a big plateful of sausages and beans, and I drank my tea so fast I scalded my mouth. Almost as soon as I'd finished I felt sick, and went outside to get some air. People were leaving in a steady stream now; I watched them as they walked past me, talking into phones, getting in their cars and driving away. They were all expected home.

I was not like them any more; the "I" I had been could never again be expected home, or call anyone to say how late she'd be. That woman was dead. Not one single person, not even the most primitive, empty shelter on the planet waited in anticipation of her presence. Nowhere in the world was there a cupboard or a shelf holding a single object of beauty or practicality belonging to her that she would ever see or use again. Even last night's cardboard, if it had dried out enough by nightfall, would tonight be drawn around another body or tipped onto the fire.

In Portsmouth there had been a man I sometimes saw in a particular spot in the shopping-centre car park, a stinking recess near the doors to the stairwell on Level C. Most days he was there hunched in a heap of rags, drinking or asleep; sometimes I saw him heaving himself up or down the stairways. He never begged, but I used to drop him a coin as I went past. I suppose he was moved on from time to time; he would disappear for a month or two, then drift back. And always, lying in his filthy nest or shuffling around the place, he would be guarding four dirty carrier bags. Always four. I suppose he replaced them as they wore out, but he always had four, clutched in both hands in a tangle of strings. What could be in them that was so precious, I used to wonder: spare shoes, a quarter bottle of booze, a lucky rabbit's foot? Now I thought I understood why he haunted the place and why he guarded his bags as if they contained gold bullion. He wasn't just afraid they would be stolen. In a life eked out on a patch of concrete, he was holding off the final shame of destitution, an existence that carried no trace of who he was; for as long as he occupied the *same* patch of concrete, and was custodian of four bagfuls of the talismans and gadgetry and keepsakes that made that life his, he was a person, not a stray animal. Though he no longer had his own roof or so much as a bed or a chair, he still had his place and his "things". He still owned a few of those nuggets of significance or usefulness or whimsy that accrue in even the poorest of lives.

But I no longer had even the poorest of lives. I had no life that I could lay claim to. In less than a day, I had discovered what perhaps should have been obvious: in ceasing to be the person I was, I had lost more than my life as Col's wife. I had lost something even more crucial than her home to go to, an enclosing place to be at night, her belongings; I had lost the possibility of journey's end. However meagre it might have been, the life I had discarded had been the nearest I had to a compass, a fixed point recognizable as mine that I could travel from or towards. All that lay ahead of me now was a wearying and arbitrary moving on, in perpetuity. Being no one, I had no reason to be anywhere, and I had not expected such a falling-off of purpose.

Had it not been for the baby I would have despaired, and for the baby's sake as well as my own I had to decide what the hell I thought I was doing. Twelve hours ago I had walked away from my life, yet I was still less than ten miles from it. What was wrong with me that I felt anchored here? Something had been overlooked, something had me in shackles. I was behaving as if I still had hopes of having the

117

baby with Colin, as if nothing he had said was real enough to have a bearing on what happened now. I had to get away before I started to consider asking him to forgive me. I had to start believing that, after what I had done yesterday, I even deserved my baby.

I watched her sleeping. I knew her exhaustion was real as soon as we were inside the trailer, because the first thing she did was pull off her boots. Nobody who's planning to attack and rob you would do that. She crawled onto the bed, and her eyes were closing even before she had shrunk herself away into the covers. Soon her shivering stopped, but she lay for a long time with her eyes closed before she fell asleep. So I watched her sleeping out of wariness, though I knew there was no real need for it. But by then caution was a habit with me.

She wasn't clean, but I also knew about that. I knew the hopeless filth of people accustomed to months without hot water and soap and a proper, safe space to be undressed and attend to themselves. I had seen plenty of that on the journey to here, and after a while that loss of pride doesn't wash off at all. It wasn't the same as the swift, dismaying layer of dirt on someone like her, unable to wash for a single day and a night.

And in fact there's a third way homeless people go, and that's the laboured cleanliness of people like me, encamped in run-down places, condemned buildings, damp trailers, people who will lug buckets and light fires to heat water and scrape their skin raw and wear their clothes out with scrubbing. We're the ones who are terrified that the dirt and shame that encroach on illegal lives might touch ours. She wasn't like that, either. She was used to keeping clean easily and had never thought that having the means to do so might be a luxury. She was stained by sudden and brief deprivation, and as I watched her sleeping, I wondered why.

My name isn't Annabel. But at that moment I needed a new name, and I hadn't until that instant thought what it would be. I still wasn't thinking when I blurted out *Anna*. My mouth opened in a panic and produced a sound almost involuntarily, and it was a natural pair of syllables to utter in those circumstances, I do believe that. I didn't choose to say it. But it was the obvious association to make, stumbling towards the trailer with Anna's mother's arm around my shoulder, her kind, sad face looking at me like that. And although it was also unthinking – and not a piece of deliberate and hasty disguise – to add the *-bel*, it was also necessary, for the time being, to conceal that I knew anything about her daughter and Stefan. I would have to go into it all later, but I knew I was about to collapse. I had to get inside and lie down, and I couldn't start to explain it then. But of course there was more to it than that.

My mother died of a particular sorrow, which was that she took the life of a child. In a drawer in our house there was a photograph of the child, a baby girl. In the photograph were also the child's mother, Marjorie Porter, holding a cup and saucer, and my mother Irene, with her teacup on her lap and one hand on the crucifix in the hollow of her throat. At the time Irene was forty-one, a year younger than I am, come to think of it. The women were in deck chairs on a patch of grass in a back garden; the ground around them was studded with floppy clumps of lettuce and lined by long fringes of carrot tops. In the background through a fence you could see the next-door garden sprouting the same rows of vegetables, the same pointed towers of bean plants climbing up bamboo frames; these were clearly the gardens of neighbours who shared packets of seed and swapped cuttings. A curl of smoke rose from a cigarette that rested in an ashtray on a kitchen chair beside the women. Next to the chair stood a man in braces holding a garden sieve up to his face and laughing through the mesh into the camera. His face couldn't be seen very well, but it was certainly my father.

What was also certain was that they were in the Porters' garden and not ours, for there on a rug in front of Marjorie was five-month-old Annabel, all baby jowls and bandy baby legs and puffy baby feet, wearing ballooning, frilly pants and a sundress and bonnet. Marjorie's face as she looked down at her child was weary, eternal, transparent; motherly love had opened her out, and had also laden her for ever with its ballast of implications: responsibility, fertility, continuity, and all their warm perplexing weight, their proud, dull glow. Even knowing what was about to befall her, I envied her that. (At the time I still had the photograph to look at, I believed I would never have a child myself.) The picture had captured her in new motherhood, before all this knowledge had reduced her to mereness, to that dumpy, overlooked category of numberless, undifferentiated mums. In fact, on that day, in her sleeveless dress and lacquered beehive hairdo, she looked less maternal as well as a whole generation, rather than the actual sixteen years, younger than my tightly permed and dirndl-skirted and still childless mother, whose sharp, wing-framed spectacles had caught a ray of sun and trapped her eyes as though behind small, blazing mirrors. Marjorie's husband, Mr Porter, whose first name I never knew, must have taken the picture. It was probably his cigarette in the ashtray.

The strangest thing about any old photograph is it is all containment, all innocence. My parents and Mrs Porter happy and joking on the second or third day of a heatwave: of course they had no idea what was coming, how could they? Their unawareness is the most tremendous thing in the picture. I used to scan their faces for a flicker of fear assailing any of them as they posed in the blinding sun; I searched for one of those slight, momentary twitches of dread that can descend on someone on a summer's day, the dread that nothing can last. I never found it. If only they could have remained there for ever, in their grainy, bordered ignorance, clicked and shuttered into rectangular place by Mr Porter's Box Brownie, trimmed and untouchable – if only they would not be propelled, in the coming days, into the imprisoning, defining series of events that would capture and frame them in their misery for as long as they lived. And of course, in that picture, they knew nothing whatsoever about me, for there was nothing yet to know, least of all that I was, in my way, in it with them. I thought that strange, too, that I could be conceived yet not conceived *of*, and this was not egotism on my part but a regret that I was powerless to turn them all in another direction altogether, even though I was *there*. I longed to shake them all alive again and make everything come out differently. But my wish was futile, and perhaps also paradoxical; my mother would have claimed that I could only have come alive to have such a wish because what happened *did* happen.

When Anna's mother put her blanket around my shoulders and drew me against her I was begging her silently to ask me nothing more than my name. She didn't. When I got into the trailer everything seemed very simple. I had no strength left, and I lay down. I knew I would sleep before long, but I lay with my eyes closed for a while, wondering about the name I had given myself – Annabel – and about the photograph.

I didn't have it any more. I had put it along with everything else on a bonfire in the back garden, the same garden beyond the fence in the background of the picture, though the fence had long since been replaced by an ornamental breeze-block wall. I had been in a hurry to be done with my father's things and get going; in three weeks I would be married. I had watched the trembling air above the flames suck the photograph upward, curl and blacken it into weightless fragments of ash, and I was impatient with myself for noticing at all that it was fragmenting away to nothing in the very place it depicted, our back garden captured in Kodachrome more than forty years before. But I hadn't let myself ponder any further on my strange *in utero* status in it, both invisible and present, or on the absence in it of any omen of the tragedy into whose tainted echoes and rhythms I would be born and grow up. I just watched it burn, and I trusted it to disappear.

I woke her in the early afternoon. Her face was puffy and white and not healthy-looking at all, and she would have gone on sleeping, but I'd had enough of waiting. I was curious. Also I needed something else to think about, because although I knew you would be back before dark, I was puzzled at what was keeping you. I could hear that the traffic was moving again up on the road. You must have taken her over to the other side of the bridge, I was hoping, or maybe even to Inverness. You knew I didn't like you doing that, and that would be why you hadn't called. Or your phone had run out of battery. You'd confess to it when you were back, and after a time you'd try to make me forgive you, and after a time I would, in our usual way. Or maybe you'd caught the bus to Netherloch, and got stuck there when the roads jammed up. Wherever you were you'd be trying to get back. You would both be home soon.

While she'd been asleep, to keep busy and warm I had wandered up the bank and brought back some wood and laid a fire, and I'd dragged over the old enamel bathtub and set it there on top of the circle of big stones. Then I hauled water up from the river in plastic canisters and filled the tub and lit the fire. When the water heated up, it sent off great clouds of steam into the cold air. All that took hours.

When her eyes opened, I expected her to be shocked to find herself there in our trailer. I thought she would immediately be ready to go. But she lay there drowsy and half-awake and watched me as if she was in no hurry while I sorted through a bundle of clothes. I wasn't sure if I liked or disliked that.

"You've been asleep. Are you feeling better now?"

She raised her head a few inches and shook it, then grunted and lay down again.

"I don't know." She rubbed her hands over her face, then sat up. "I'm still so tired."

I picked out some things of yours and Anna's for washing and went back outside to the fire. I drew off a few jugfuls of hot water into a basin, then I stirred in some washing soda and added a few grains of washing powder, for the scent. The soda is cheap and makes the powder go further. I dropped your clothes in and let the slippery bluish scum lap over the wet material. It always amazed me slightly, the chemically floral smell rising from a basin on the ground outside the trailer, where the real smells were of river mud and wood smoke and sometimes frying onions and the rain drying on stones. I loved it, that house-proud, indoors scent of laundry.

She came outside and stood watching while I swirled the things around, pressing Anna's little clothes against the sides of the basin.

"I was wondering... I mean, the bridge, if you knew," she said. "Yesterday – I mean, you can see it from here. Did you see it happen? Has anyone—"

"I was at work. I heard it."

"So you weren't here? But was there, I mean, was there anyone—"

"Look, who are you? What do you want?"

"Nothing! Nothing, honestly. That is, I wanted... Are you here on your own?"

"My husband is on his way back. With my daughter. Right now."

"On his way?" she said.

"Right now. I'm expecting them soon."

I turned back to the washing. Now it came to it, I didn't want her calling the hospital for me. Even asking her to would be like believing you and Anna weren't safe and already on your way back to me. I went on knead-knead-kneading your saturated things, lifting, rubbing, squeezing, submerging them, over and over and over. She didn't move. I looked up. She was staring at the basin of wet clothes. Tears running down her face.

"Oh, thank God. So it's all OK. Well. I should go."

But she didn't go. I stood up.

"Who *are* you? What do you want? What were you doing down here last night?"

"I'm sorry, I'll go. I just needed... I was tired, I feel so sick sometimes. I'll go."

"What's the matter? Are you ill?"

"I just wanted to make sure. Your husband, is he, I mean, where is he?"

"My husband is fine. What is it to you? We can take care of ourselves." I said.

She was looking at me with her frightened, watery eyes, and suddenly she turned away and doubled over, trying to catch and hold her breath. She was going to throw up again.

"Oh, for God's sake. Sit down. What's the matter with you? Sit down and get warm."

"Thanks. Just for a minute." She squatted by the fire and wiped her eyes, then pulled a ragged bit of tissue from her pocket and blew her nose. She stuffed the tissue into the fire and held her hands over the steam for a while to warm them, rubbing her fingers together. She looked hard at her palms, then rubbed them down her jacket. Her hands displeased her. There was disgust in her eyes at the way dirt and cold were starting to cling to her.

"Did you say your name was Annabel?"

She nodded. She was still rubbing her hands.

"Well, thanks. I'll be off in a minute," she said.

She lifted her head and looked out beyond the yellow ring of the fire and across the river into the raw afternoon. There were a few geese on the water, and the grey cabin stood lonely as always, the sky collapsing with the weight of low cloud into the sloping treeline above it. Sounds from the bridge and the road were muffled by cold and fog.

"Oh, for God's sake, look at you. You haven't got anywhere to go, have you?"

She looked surprised. "Oh, well, not really, not anywhere permanent... I suppose I'll get myself organized, find somewhere." Her eyes filled with tears again. "I didn't know it would be this hard. I didn't think I'd feel this bad."

"There's hot water." I nodded at the fire. "I need some of it for rinsing, but you can have a wash if you want."

She moved a bit closer, waving the steam away with her arm, and peered in. The river water is dark with peat, but the silt stays at the bottom. She probably didn't know the salt water that comes in on the flow tide is heavier than river water and runs underneath it.

"In there? Wash in that?"

"It's all right for washing. It's not seawater. You have to wait a while, though," I said. "I'll kick out the fire, and when the metal's cooled down you get in."

She looked round. "Get in? You mean here – out here? What about, I mean—"

"Where else? I do it all the time. You don't have to if you don't want to. I just thought you could do with a warm bath."

"What if somebody comes?"

"Don't be stupid. Who do you think's going to come down here?"

I laughed, thinking of you coming back and finding her standing naked and dripping. She tried to smile, but there was a genuinely shy look about her. I didn't think I had ever seen anyone older than me blushing before. How could she be embarrassed about her body, at her age?

I tipped out the clothes water from the basin on the ground and refilled it from the enamel bath.

"If Stefan comes I'll make sure he doesn't see you. I'm only offering. Of course you don't have to."

She managed to smile. "I'd love to get clean."

"You'll be OK," I said. "There's nobody here but us." I pushed the ashes of the fire with the end of my foot into the ground. "Wait till I've done this and then you can get in."

When I'd rinsed and wrung out your things and pegged them up, she pulled off her hat and ruffled her hair. It was thick and dyed reddish, and dark at the roots. She got up and dipped a hand in the water. "Have you got any shampoo?"

"I'll get it. You need to undress quick and get straight in. It cools down fast."

When I came back she was stepping into the bath and I saw I was right about her age. She was at least forty, maybe even old enough to be my mother. As she stooped and curled modestly into herself, her waist folded into a line just above her belly button, like a crease in a roll of dough, and the skin on her haunches looked dusty and neglected. She crouched and soaped herself, splashing water over her shoulders for the warmth, and her skin was wet and shining and bright-white.

"Come on," I said. "You have to be quick. My husband will be back soon."

She stood up again and took the jug while I waited with the shampoo.

"Keep your mouth closed," I said. "It's not drinking water."

She filled the jug and lifted it high in both hands to wet her hair, and as she raised her arms, her breasts swelled out, surprisingly firm and large and high. Her belly was rounded, as it would be at her age, but it looked hard, not soft. She tipped back her head and closed her eyes, and the water poured down, soaking her hair and face and neck. I watched it run in tiny, branching trickles down her breasts, I saw beads form and hang and drop from her nipples, which stuck out like little carvings in polished red stone, the way they do. She was pregnant.

I handed her the shampoo and took the jug. She stood with her hands folded protectively over her stomach, and I rinsed the suds from her head with jugful after jugful of water, until it began to go tepid. By then she was starting to shiver, so I made her step into the towel I had brought, and I sent her inside to get dry. And just as I did every time after Anna's bath, I tipped out the water, picked up the jug and soap and shampoo and the pile of clothes, and followed wet footprints across the stones to the trailer. The poor woman needed looking after.

Another day passed before Ron returned to the bridge.

Very early the first morning, he'd awakened in the cabin exhausted and cold, his mind stunned and somehow also stale from the shock of all that had happened. He knew he would barely be able to talk that day, let alone convince anyone he was strong and fit for work, and the floor was dirtier than he'd judged it to be in the dark; his clothes were heavy with damp and grime. He needed to steady himself and also get good and clean, he decided, before he went asking for work. So he made his way back along the river's edge and struck up the steep slope into the forest; across the patch of cleared ground he was now able to make out on the far side the remains of a track that took him, after another climb, up to the road. No traffic passed him, but the roadside was crowded with vehicles parked in all directions, abandoned the night before. From the Highland Bounty Mini-Mart he set off in the Land Rover, travelling inland.

By eight o'clock he had driven nearly forty miles, far enough from the bridge, he hoped, for the usual tourist places to be unaffected by scores of stranded people seeking rooms. In a village called Aberarder he knocked on the door of a bungalow with a "Vacancies" board swinging from the sign that read "Glendarroch Bed and Breakfast", and explained to the landlady that his plans had been disrupted, he'd been turned back from going farther north and had been on the road nearly all night. He even managed to make a joke of asking, if it could be managed, for breakfast and bed, in that order. She was sympathetic; she'd been up half the night herself, watching the news. He ate ravenously, showered, and fell asleep in an overheated, immaculately floral bedroom. In the afternoon he went out and found a camping and outdoor-supplies shop, where he bought new jeans and work shirts, T-shirts and socks, a jacket and boots. He ate early in a pub and returned to the Glendarroch, where he watched football on the tiny wall-mounted television, lying naked on the glassy, nylon lilac quilt. Before he fell asleep he realized that his face was tired and tight, because he had been smiling.

The next day he drove back up through Netherloch. He parked the Land Rover at the Highland Bounty Mini-Mart again, noticing and thinking it odd that the store was closed on a Saturday. As before, he walked the three miles to the bridge. The area around it was still crowded with spectators, and there were now several radio cars and two TV mobile-broadcast vans parked just beyond the barricades on the road. He could see that down by the bridge approach a pontoon holding winching gear now reached from the bank almost a quarter of the way across the river. Men were walking up and down on it, directing the lifting of twisted, dripping hunks of steel and concrete onto a salvage barge moored alongside. Some dinghies and a couple of boats were tied up at the pontoon, close to the bank. Farther out he saw two pairs of divers flipping into the water from two launches mid-stream, and he could see that work was underway across the river, too. A smaller pontoon had appeared and the industrial wasteland next to the opposite bridge approach was being razed by bulldozers. Engine noises from both banks rose into the air and met in a swirl of sound overhead.

Close to where he stood, link fencing was going up in place of the crowd barriers and police cordon tape, and he asked one of the men at work on it where he would find the office. He was directed to a mobile unit parked on the far side of the approach road. A man stood smoking at the entrance, and another man waiting inside turned and stared as Ron stepped in. The place was airless and muddy and smelled of sweat and warmed-up plastic. Two men in shirtsleeves sat behind a cluster of desks, one young and slight in a way that marked him out as the junior. Both had wads of paper in front of them, and the older one was arched back and swivelling in his chair, speaking on the telephone. On the wall by his desk was a board with a year planner and a postcard that read "A Man without a Woman Is Like a Neck without a Pain". Ron stood at a respectful distance.

The man in front of him was talking in halting English to the younger man behind the desk; after a while he called in the second man from outside, wrote down some figures for him, and after protracted translation, both signed some papers and left. The young man now had his head down writing; the older one was gazing upwards with the telephone at his ear, listening with obvious exasperation.

Ron stepped forwards. "Excuse me, I'm looking—"

The young man looked up. "Skills?"

"Construction. General building, labouring. Transport, mainly."

"Transport? HGV? Excavators? Got rough-terrain experience?"

"LGV. And PCV. Just… driving. I'll do anything. Don't mind heavy work." Ron paused. "I just want to help."

The man handed him an application form.

"Pens over there," he said, and motioned him towards a narrow ledge at one side of the unit. "Answer all the questions, mind."

Ron took his time, turning his back as he took the card of the Glendarroch Bed and Breakfast from his pocket and copied the details down under "Address", and in brackets wrote "temporary". He covered his prison years with a lie about working for a contractor in Spain, with names and places he'd long ago memorized for precisely that purpose. He handed the form back just as the older man finished his call and turned to his colleague, running his hands through his hair and groaning.

"Nae fucking use, Davey. There's naebody else to try till Monday. They'll have tae fucking swim."

"It's a difficult situation, Mr Sturrock."

Mr Sturrock glanced over at Ron's application, lying on the desk. "Transport? Can he drive a fucking boat?" he asked his colleague, sourly. He looked at Ron. "Eh? I'm a couple of guys short. I've eighteen men from Inverness starting this side eight o'clock tomorrow and I've naebody to get them over. Don't suppose you can handle a thirty-foot boat with an outboard, son?"

The young man shook his head over Ron's application. "Doesnae say so here, Mr Sturrock," he said.

"I can, I've worked boats," Ron said recklessly. "Never thought to put it down, it was a while ago. Fishing, harbour boats. A thirty-footer's no problem."

Mr Sturrock stared at him. "You kidding me?" He paused. "I'm no' talking fucking barge holidays on the Norfolk Broads, mind. Have you got your ICC?"

"Doesn't need an ICC," the first man said. "He's UK. Have you got your NPC?" He scanned the form. "No, well, you won't, you're fifty. Have you got NPC equivalent?"

"Not on me. But I could send for it," Ron said. He could prevaricate over it for a while, if need be.

The two men looked at each other. "He has to be qualified, Mr Sturrock. NPC, or equivalent," the first man said.

"Aye, Davey, but we're desperate here. If we give him a wee try-out now and he's OK," said Mr Sturrock, "that'll get us by for tomorrow at least. Alan's down at the boat now, he can give him a go and see how he handles it. See what I'm saying?"

"Mr Sturrock, he has to be qualified."

"Come on, Davey, you want to spend the rest of the day trying to get somebody else frae fuck knows where?"

"I'm just trying to be thorough."

"I've worked boats on and off since I was fifteen," Ron said.

"But there's the local knowledge," the young man said, pulling a thick sheaf of papers from the desk and turning up the right page. "You'd need to familiarize yourself with 'local seamarks, local traffic practices, mudbanks, shoal waters'," he read. "You'd have to 'demonstrate knowledge of heights of tides, neap and spring tides and tidal streams, and local safe landing places according to differing weather conditions'."

Ron nodded. At least not every term he'd just heard was unfamiliar. "It would be a matter of learning the local conditions. And being always safety-aware," he said. "I learn fast."

"Aye, and nobody else we could get at this fucking notice is going to have local knowledge either, are they?" Mr Sturrock said. "And he's qualified. Aren't you, son? Mind you, I'll take experience over a fucking certificate any day o' the week," he said, looking hard at Ron. "Paperwork to follow, eh? We just need a copy for the file here. You'll get your paperwork in to Davey here right enough, won't you?" He turned to his colleague. "I'm not paying eighteen men to stay idle for the sake of a wee bit of paper when I've got an experienced guy standing in front of me. Send him on down, and if Alan says he's OK, put him on the day rate. Put 'paperwork to follow' and we're covered."

The younger man shrugged and Mr Sturrock smiled, and Ron signed.

I slept and slept, and I fell into dreams like long perilous ruts, channels of movement that swept me along helter-skelter, not in pursuit or escape from anything I could name, but with some formless, looming jeopardy present all around and above me. I slept all that night and for spells the following day, and if when I woke I saw or heard Silva nearby, stepping into the trailer or fetching something outside, I felt as though she was permitting me these collapsed hours as kindly as if she had put me to bed herself and told me to close my eyes and rest. I would come to, and lie there, slowly calculating the passing of seconds against the beating of my heart (would my baby have a beating heart yet?), while my waking thoughts began to tick once more to the rhythm of the day – of which, thank God, a little less would remain. The shaking that had been going on inside me since I walked out of the Invermuir Lodge Hotel abated. As I began to feel steadier, my sickness eased somewhat.

But my mind was empty, as if it were choosing to turn away and live outside of what was happening to me. I slept through another night, and the next day I got up. But between sleeps, all I could do was sit outside wrapped in blankets, looking at the river. Silva watched me closely. I told her I had a nervous stomach, and she said she sometimes had one, too. The next time I felt sick she wouldn't let me lie down or drink water. She tore a ragged triangle off the corner of a slice of bread, spread it with jam and made me eat it. I felt better at once.

136

She was taking me in hand in some way, and I was grateful, but she didn't know I was pregnant, of course.

She was restless. In the middle of the afternoon she took two empty containers and walked up to the service station. She was gone nearly three hours. Her absence filled me with terror. Having had her company for just a day and a half left me in such agitation at the thought of being alone again that when she came back I asked her sharply why she had been away so long.

"I needed to fill up with drinking water. I wanted to see what was happening. I was finding things out," she replied, dumping the full canisters on the kitchen counter. She told me the place was crowded with sightseers and journalists and drivers with trucks of supplies for the salvage work. There were also a lot of rough sleepers, turned off the wasteland behind the car park, and quite a few police. Not all the vehicles had been pulled out of the river yet, she said.

"There were thirteen survivors, and they found nine bodies in the river. There's four cars still in there. They can't get them out yet because of the weather, it's the big spring tides or it's too deep or it's the winds or something. They know who they are, all the people still down there. There's seven."

"How can they know, if they can't get to them?"

She looked surprised. "Because they're missing. Seven are missing. They've got their names. Their photos are in the papers, everywhere. They've told the families."

Why did this shock me? Of course the victims would be counted and named; that anyone should die randomly and also remain anonymous would be an unbearably compounded sadness, and people are inquisitive about the deaths of others, even strangers on a list of lost and missing. The papers would keep a tally and reveal names and faces and describe good lives cut short and families bereft, it being one of the obligations of tragedy to ponder urgent reversals in the

137

lives of those left behind, to bow gently in the direction of other people's grief.

"So who are they?" I said. "Did you get a paper?"

"I saw them on the news in the cafeteria. There was a van with a father and his son and another man, they cleaned carpets. A woman tourist in a rental car, and a man and his secretary on business. Oh, yes, and a retired man coming back from golf. That's the seven. So there you are." Silva's voice was newly fresh and relaxed, and her eyes shone. "You see? Nobody else."

"You actually saw them? These people's faces?"

She nodded. "They're clearing that dump down near the river. I saw trucks going in, same thing on the other side. There were people there just watching. I saw a man I know," she said. "He was in the shop that day, I was talking to him the moment it happened. He asked if I was all right. I said it's those poor people and their families I'm sorry for."

I didn't speak. I was picturing Col and trying the word *families* up against him, and it didn't suit him. I couldn't think of just the two of us as a family, and that was a relief. He would not suffer long or deeply for loss of me. He might remember things about me: my face, some words stored somewhere in his mind. I might even for a while warm his heart with an idea of love, now forever abstracted and beyond test, kept perfect by my absence. Then he would forget me, probably. I hoped he would.

"This man I was talking to, he said they might never get them out."

"What does he know about it?"

"Oh, he knows. He's something to do with boats. He's working for the contractors, running crews across. He took some divers out to the middle, where the cars were sunk, and they said they might not ever get to them," Silva said. "They might get washed out to sea and break up and the bodies would just disappear."

For a few hours after that she moved lightly about the place preparing for Stefan and Anna, setting little circles of order around herself, folding clothes, lining up shoes, separating cutlery and mugs. She began to ask me about myself.

I told her I used to live in England and I had lost my job and I had no house any more because it belonged to the mortgage company after my father died. That wasn't so far from the truth. But what also seemed quite true to me was that I was not and never had been the woman tourist probably trapped in a rental car in the middle of the river. Nor did I feel I was really tricking either of us to imagine that this had happened to some *other* woman tourist; watching Silva dart around cleaning and tidying for them, I told myself that her certainty of Stefan's and Anna's safety was more to be relied upon than an assumption that they had been in the car. Suppose just after I left them Stefan had taken Anna to the service station for lunch? Then the car might have been stolen from the roadside. Or the man who had changed the plates that afternoon might have been driving it. Silva knew her husband best. Sharing her faith in him to stay alive was the only way I could spare myself the distress of believing them lost. It was also the only way I could help her.

And she was helping me. She asked me more and more, and I began to talk more easily, building my new history bit by bit as from her questions came my answers, like little blocks appearing in my hands that I could turn and consider to see where they fit, and set in place, one by one. After I lost my house I had spent three months in a hostel trying to get a job, until I had to leave. Then I had taken the coach all the way up to Inverness because I had two spinster cousins there. We hadn't been in close touch, but I'd met them a few times when I was younger. They would be elderly by now, maybe frail and glad of my help in the house; I'd been thinking I could even move in with them. At least they wouldn't turn me away while I got settled. As I told it, the story gained credibility for me; even though before I said all this the idea had never existed, it did now. I wanted Silva to think it brave and commendable of me, making a fresh start in the north of Scotland, closer to family. I did not want her to think me desperate or degraded. But then, I told her, despising the rise in my voice, it turned out I'd been sending the cousins Christmas cards for years and all for nothing (though I had to admit I hadn't had one from them for some time). When I got to their address, they had long ago moved away. Nobody had even heard of them. The young couple living in the house now were very nice to me and had agreed to keep my luggage in their garage until I got myself organized. I'd been looking around Netherloch for shop or bar work and a roof over my head when the bridge went down. I'd got stranded without enough money on me for a hotel, and then I had got sick.

Silva looked at me with cool, curious eyes. It was possible she didn't believe a word of it, but as long as she didn't say so and as long as she let me stay, maybe I didn't need her to. Whatever was true or not true, known or unknown – cars plunging off a collapsing bridge, Colin, the baby, Stefan and Anna, *other* people trapped and drowned – the fact was I could not bear to think of any of these things for more than a few minutes at a time.

In return, Silva told me about Vi's shabby little general store and how Vi was drunk a lot of the time and how she put up with it because it meant cash, no questions about work permits. Vi hadn't even asked exactly where she was from; she didn't care.

"She sometimes says 'your lot', but she doesn't even know who she means." Silva shrugged. "To her I'm just foreign. Just as well."

I remembered Stefan's demand that I ask no questions and how, when I did, his cold, pinchy face had softened.

"I don't know where you're from, either," I said.

She shook her head. "It doesn't matter. We went first to Greece and then Italy. Anna was born in Italy. We got to London, then we had to go to Glasgow. There were bad things. Things went wrong. So we came here." She looked at me seriously. "We are better than this, we are not people who choose to be like this, Stefan and I. We used to have a place, a proper life. We are getting things better, soon we will be away from here. We will have our life again."

She sighed and got up. A while later she made tea and we ate some bread and jam, and I had another nap.

So the day passed. Whenever she grew restless, she went off alone along the riverbank towards the bridge, or up to the top of the track, where she told me she just watched the traffic going by. When she wandered away, I stayed awake, watching over the place and keeping the fire going. We went our separate ways, both waiting for Stefan, each believing she was looking after the other. Later I heated a pot of water and cooked some rice, and when she came back we made a kind of stew with tomatoes and beans. As the afternoon began to fade, she set off again for the service station. Stefan and Anna might be there, she said, or most probably she would meet them on the road.

On Monday I got up early, before six. It was cold inside the trailer, and the air was pale and empty. I dressed quickly and brushed my hair. When I put away the brush, I banged the cupboard shut on the wall above Annabel's head, which woke her up.

"I have to get going," I told her. "I need extra time. Maybe there's a bus up to Netherloch and over the little bridge and I can get to work that way." I hesitated. "Stefan knows I won't be here. He'll come and find me at work. So—"

"Do you mean – do you want me to—"

"Stay. You can guard the trailer. Go back to sleep."

I got to the Highland Bounty at twenty to ten, more than two hours late. It was raining and the shop was locked up, but the outside lights were on. Probably they'd been on all night after Vi went across to her place at the back. It was a horrible cottage, water-stained walls behind a scraggy hedge and the garden nothing more than dead grass. I banged on the door and waited. There was brown moss sprouting at the base of the water pipe. The rain was cold on my head.

I had to stand back when the door opened and the smell spilled out, the thick, salty smell of the stuff Vi ate, those pots of flakes she just poured boiling water into, and the smell of dirt, as if she kept sweating dogs in there with the windows shut. But she didn't have any pets, she just never cleaned.

142

"Vi, I'm sorry I'm late, I had to get a bus to Netherloch and then I walked."

Half of her face appeared round the door. Under the orange-shaded ceiling light in the hall, she hardly looked human. She couldn't get her mouth to work.

"I'm not dressed," she managed to say. There was some scrabbling behind the door, and then one hand and her dry arm covered in yellow nylon appeared. She shook the bunch of keys and a bag of coins at me.

"Here, don't keep me out on the doorstep! Go and open up."

I took them and went back across the tarmac, unlocked the shop and turned on the lights. I opened the till and counted in the coins, switched on the radio and wiped down the counter with the spray and a paper cloth. I wiped the old words off the sandwich sign and wrote on both sides, OPEN MILK SOUVENIRS GROSERIES ICECREAM, and I carried it outside. Then I swept off the steps and emptied the litter bin. I mopped the floor near the door and then I lit the paraffin stove in case Vi came in later. She couldn't stand the cold. By this afternoon she'd be at the vodka just to keep the cold out, or so she said, earlier if she couldn't sit in the hot fug around the stove.

The shelves were full of gaps. I restocked them and put on the kettle, then I wrote a list of things Vi needed to get from the Cash & Carry when she was sober enough to go. I poured a mug of tea and took it across. I rapped on the door, opened it, and called out that I was leaving it on the hall mat for her. I heard the toilet flushing upstairs.

Then I walked back slowly in the rain. I didn't mind being at work, but today, with you still away, I didn't know where to find the energy. The day had only just begun, and already my strength for any more of it was leaking away. Whatever I did it felt like dragging about a heavy load on my back, and for what? If all it came to was this, trying to get through as a person alone – how could I face that? I asked you. I felt sick with loneliness, sick to my heart of simple, ordinary things that only I was there to notice: water drops landing in the puddles in the tarmac, the greenness of the wet verges in the rain, the aroma that would meet me when I stepped inside the shop, of wrapped bread and firelighters and tea dust. I had never needed you more.

But you were coming back. Somehow I would have to wait out the day in the wobbly heat haze from the stove, listening to the grating of the freezers and the tinking of the turned-down radio, and watching the weather outside strike rainy shadows off the pegboard walls and racks of empty shelving. And go on waiting, if I had to, for as long as it took.

When I came around the corner to the front there was a Land Rover parked outside. Two men in work gear were in the shop. One of them was Ron.

"Hello, Blondie," he said, smiling, dumping tea, instant coffee and sugar on the counter. "How are you? Had a nice lie-in?"

The other man called over. "Yeah, I was down here at half-past eight, wasn't I? Eight till eight you're supposed to be open, aren't you, love? Where's the milk?"

We were out of fresh milk. "There's only long-life," I said. Then I tried to say there might be fresh later on, if Vi got an order in, but my eyes were stinging with tears. I picked up the box of tea bags to ring it up, but I couldn't read the label. I fell into Vi's chair and covered my face and burst into tears.

"Hey, hey, Blondie!" Ron said. "Hey, never mind him."

The second man said, "Whoa, no offence, love, OK?" and then came Ron's voice telling him to go and wait in the Land Rover and he'd only be five minutes, then I heard the *ting* of the shop bell. I looked up. The radio was squealing, distant and yappy like a tune tapped out with a fork on a wire.

Ron stepped around the counter and switched it off. "Having a rough time," he said. It wasn't a question.

I shook my head. "A bad start. I was late. Coming the Netherloch way now, it takes much longer. Then the walk from there."

"You live on the other side? Where?"

"I used to get the bus over the bridge. Twenty-five minutes to here. Now it's longer."

"That's tough. Going to be tough for a while."

"I will have to get up more early. I'm sorry, it was silly to cry."

"How're you getting back tonight?"

I didn't like that he was so nosy. "Same way," I said in a sharp voice. "No problem. Like on the day the bridge fell. Walk to Netherloch, get a bus. Maybe get a lift. People are kind."

He was staring at me. "There's nobody to help you? Nobody with a car? Where's your husband?"

I was proud he had noticed my wedding ring. "He's away. Just for a while. He has to be away, for work, he is looking for work," I said. "But I am not alone. I have a friend. She stays with me."

"But the friend hasn't got a car."

"No."

'When do you finish?"

"At six. It's not a problem."

"OK, well, here's what we do. You finish at six. I come back here at six and take you over."

"No! No, I can't do that. I can't. I don't know you."

"You really think I'd do you harm?"

I hesitated, and then I had to smile. "No."

He nudged the things on the counter towards me. "Good. Now I need to get going. What's this lot come to?"

I totalled it up and he paid. "I'll see you later," he said at the door. "Stop worrying. I'll take you safe over the river."

145

I got up and put away the bedding, and tidied up the trailer just as I had seen Silva do. But she was gone, and it was so quiet, and after a while I couldn't bear the memory of the sounds of yesterday – our feet up and down the steps, a pan scraping on the fire stones, most of all, our voices – against the silence I would have to endure before I would hear them again. The gap of solitude that opened up between the memory and the expectation of her company was too great, so wide and dark I was afraid I would fall into it and never get out. Nothing but lonely sounds welled up from the river, the geese landing and feeding, the calls of gulls following the tide. In the salty, white stillness of the air I thought I heard the faraway wash of sea waves. I couldn't stay. I cleaned my face and did what I could with my clothes. Then I closed the trailer and set off up the track towards the road.

Not far along was the place I had stopped the car to look at the map. Had that been only five days before? Now the jagged bridge ends stuck out from the far bank on the last bridge piers left standing, and the twisted lanes of the roadway, torn and still, dipped down to the river. The reflections of a line of emergency lights along the remaining edge of the carriageway splashed in broken bars of blue and orange off the grey water and detonated behind my eyes in tiny explosive after-images. The helicopters still roamed above, hovering low enough for gusts of air to blow flecked and juddering waves in circles around the wreckage sticking up from the surface. In the middle of the river, where three spans of the bridge had collapsed and vanished, the water was flat and empty. From here, the people struggling to save themselves would have looked like flies spinning in a puddle.

When I got to the service station, I didn't go in. Instead, I cut across to the start of the track that led to the waste ground. All the cars had been cleared from that part of the car park, and the space was now the arrival point for trucks on their way down to the southern bridge end. There were policemen on duty, some with dogs, keeping spectators behind lines of tape on either side. I joined the back of the group and watched. The track entrance had been widened and a mobile office set up, its interior garish with strip lighting. Inside, boxes and computers and telephones were crowded on tabletops. Office chairs and filing cabinets, still wrapped in plastic, stood against the windows. Men in yellow hard hats went back and forth with flapping sheets of paper and two-way radios, checking trucks and sending them on, past two bulldozers and a digger that were levelling and pushing heaps of rubble into a low, loose wall at the site's edge. Some of the trucks were covered, and most of the others carried machinery I couldn't guess the use of, but I also saw two carrying more portable cabins, and on another a cluster of massive lights and chains and metal bars. The air was loud with droning generators and grinding wheels.

Across the river, upstream from the slanting northern end of the broken bridge, a muddy access road had been cut between newly felled trees down to the water's edge. There, a long area had been levelled and a crane was at work, directed by salvage men stationed on the last slope of bridge road and in boats around the wreckage. A row of huge sheds was going up, and there was now an iron jetty with dinghies moored to it, lifting and falling in the slight swell of the ebb tide.

My attention was drawn back to my side of the river. Upstream and some way over to the left was a stretch of scrubby land where a few sheep grazed. Beyond the sheep, I could see some of the people from the wasteland coming and going around a fire they had just managed to light. Smoke swayed low and horizontal over the fields. Paused in a landscape in which only fire smoke and a few sheep moved, the human figures looked stranded out of their time, gazing across into another age. But their displacement was timeless, just another of the world's arrhythmic visitations of calamity upon dispensable, unrecorded lives.

I turned away. I was hungry in a way I hadn't been for days. I went first to the service-station shop, bought soap, a toothbrush and toothpaste, and washed at a basin in the Ladies. In the café I ordered shepherd's pie and a pot of tea and took them to a window table from where I could watch the trucks and workmen. As I unloaded my tray I realized I was almost enjoying myself. I sat down, poured out my tea and began to eat. These transactions with strangers, no more than a few words and a polite glance over the paying for things and the taking of change, were so easy. Nobody I encountered had bothered to look at me. In a matter of a few days everyone would have forgotten the face in the papers of the woman tourist drowned in a rental car. Until then, invisibility, it was turning out, could be pleasurable.

I started to make plans. Now that I was getting my nerve back, renting a room somewhere as Annabel Jones wouldn't be any more difficult than ordering a pot of tea and the lunch special. When Silva came back this evening, Stefan and Anna might be with her. In the morning we'd explain everything, Stefan and I. We'd divide the money and I'd be on my way, arranging my new life properly. I'd get a place to stay and a few clothes and look for a job like Silva's, one that paid in cash. I could work for months before the baby was born, and by then I would be used to my new name. For the first time in days I was managing to look ahead. That was when, through the window, I caught sight of Col.

I did not know until that moment how well I had come to read his feelings from the hunch of his shoulders, the bowing of his thick head. He stood motionless and alone, close to where I had stood only minutes ago. I was surprised that he was there at all; my disappearance would have delayed his return home on Friday, our departure date, but once he learned that my car was in the water with my body inside it, what could he achieve by staying? There was nothing to wait for, nothing he could do here. What was to be gained by staring at the bridge with puzzled, blinking eyes, tipping his head back and scanning the sky in a gesture of endurance, looking so bruised and forsaken? I felt a flare of anger. How dare he appear in this way, as if some truly dreadful blow had been dealt him, when all he had lost was *me*? There could be no possibility he was truly suffering; he had made it perfectly clear he could take or leave me. I could hardly bear to look at him.

Yet I stayed at the window. He had only to turn his head and some invisible wire connecting us would have fizzed to life and directed our eyes straight towards each other's, and my deception would have been over. For a moment I was so curious I almost wanted it to happen. Or, if he didn't turn his head, I could just get up from here and go to him. But it was too late for any such move. *If you want to make a go of it with me, fine, I'll make a go of it with you. But not with a kid.* I remained where I was. Then he took out his mobile phone, snapped some pictures, and trod heavily away.

Soon he was out of sight. I waited another half an hour until I could be sure he had gone, and then I returned, walking fast all the way, to the trailer.

By the time I got there it was pouring, and I sat inside and stared as raindrops pitted the water. When it stopped I went outside. The river lay like a swathe of thick, dull cloth under the pall of the clouds and seemed barely to flow. I could not stay here. The sight of Col had shown me that I had to act urgently to put distance between my old life and the new one. It was distasteful to linger in this way, like a mourner at my own funeral. The trailer was damp and falling apart; what had been asylum was now a rotting prison. If I did not get out at once and rejoin the living, my defiant vanishing act would amount to nothing but a self-imposed shackling to a dead end where I was alive to nobody on earth except Silva.

Besides, I could do nothing for her by staying. How would it help for me to stay and witness any more of her faith that Stefan and Anna were coming back, when I was too cowardly either to encourage her hopes or to destroy them? The best thing I could do for her would be to leave some money and be gone by the time she returned. I would write her a note explaining – only in part – why I had left. I could not be sure that she would be able to read much English, and she might ask someone she knew – her employer, probably – to read it for her. I could not tell her anything that mentioned the car and gave me away. But the truth was I could not tell her everything anyway. I did not have the courage.

The only paper I could find was a colouring book of Anna's, and I carefully removed a page she had already scrawled over and wrote on the back of it.

Dear Silva,
Thank you for the food and accommodation and for looking after me when I was unwell. Your hospitality was very welcome at a time when I needed it, and I valued your company very much.

I apologize for telling you I didn't have enough money on me for a hotel when I first arrived. It wasn't true, but for complicated reasons I had to say it. It is a long story how I came to turn up at your place. I enclose herewith a sum to reimburse you for expenses incurred during my stay and also as a token of my gratitude. I hope it will be useful to you in the future, whatever it may bring.

I regret I was unable to let you know in advance that I was leaving today. I hope your husband and daughter are now back safe and sound.

    Yours,

      Annabel

I knew my letter was formal in a way that was odd in the circumstances, but I didn't know how else to do it. It took me much longer to compose than I thought it would. I had deliberately let my mobile phone run out of charge, so I could not know the time exactly, but I had reckoned it was the middle of the afternoon when I began the letter. By the time I had finished and folded fifteen hundred pounds into the single sheet of paper, I could hardly see to write. Daylight was fading and the sky was lowering with waiting ice. Maybe it was later than I had thought, after all, and I remember thinking that this was a good thing. It shortened the interval until Silva's return, when the trailer would be unattended with the money inside, lying on the table. But when I closed the door and went down the steps onto the shore, I saw at once that I couldn't leave.

Downstream, between where I stood and the wrecked bridge end, two small fires at the river's edge were burning through the blurry dusk. It was not difficult to gauge their distance from me; the nearer of the two had been set on a jutting-out part of the bank where three or four felled tree trunks lay on the ground. I had wandered down there several times in the past few days; it was a tricky walk over slippery rocks and around ponds of mud, and possible only at low tide, but it took no more than ten minutes. If the tramps displaced from the waste ground had encroached as far as that already, they could easily come farther. The trailer was set well back and under trees, and could not be seen from their bonfire, but if any of them wandered along and found the trailer empty, of course they could easily steal the money and take the trailer over for the night. And for all nights to come. I might trust to the coming darkness to keep them from exploring any further today, but I would have to stay outside on the lookout in case they did. And I was going to be very cold. I couldn't risk drawing their attention by lighting a fire for myself.

Vi was sitting at the stove with a shawl round her shoulders and a tumbler of red wine in her hand when Ron returned to the shop. She looked up from a magazine spread over the counter. Her eyes were sour and watery, and her mouth was puckered and stained dark with wine, like a patch of decay starting on a small, bruised piece of fruit.

"Cold out there," Ron said.

"You'll have to be quick, I'm closing early."

"Where's Silva?"

Vi pushed herself up a little in her chair. "Silva!" she yelled, then slumped back. "You come from the river?" she asked, swinging her glass towards the darkness on the other side of the window.

"You could say that."

"Terrible thing."

Ron wandered farther into the shop, looking at the shelves, sniffing gently as if he found the air, laden with paraffin and wine, too heavy to breathe.

"It's self-service," Vi said. "Take a basket. Aye, terrible thing, that bridge."

She gulped some of her drink and returned to her magazine. Ron brought a packet of biscuits back to the counter.

"Drowning your sorrows, then," he said, placing a five-pound note on the counter.

153

"Keeps the cold out," Vi said, but she stood up and placed her glass out of sight under the counter. She put the note in the till and started pulling coins out for the change, counting aloud, but her voice slowed. She stared at the money in her hand, dumped it all back and started again.

"Can't add up the day," she said, trying to smile. She made another mistake, turned the coins from hand to hand, counted them into her open palm, and dropped them. They fell rattling over the counter and cascaded onto the floor. Swearing, she ducked to pick them up and almost knocked over the stove as they rolled away. As she resurfaced, she swayed forwards and gripped the back of her chair, but it screeched away from her and she nearly fell.

Ron looked over his shoulder. Silva was walking down from the back store with her bag on her shoulder, wrapping her scarf round her neck, smiling.

"That'll be four pounds, twenty-five pence I'm owed," he said, turning back to Vi.

"Well, it's on the bloody floor. You'll need to come back for it."

"I'd like my change, please."

Vi slammed the till shut. "You'll have to come back the morn. We're closed."

"Come on, Vi, I'll do it," Silva said, moving behind the counter to open the till. Vi shoved her away. "Don't you touch my bloody money! We're closed!"

Silva looked at her for a moment, then pulled her purse from her bag and counted out four pounds, twenty-five pence.

"Here, take it," she said to Ron. "It's better not to argue with her. It's all right, I got paid today. I'll get it back tomorrow."

"Sure? Well, thanks." Ron took the coins and picked up his packet of biscuits. Vi was now back in her chair with her glass in her hand.

"Are you locking up, Vi? Want me to do it?"

"I'll do it myself. In my own good time," Vi said. She lifted her glass and swigged. "Go on, fuck off home."

"Bye, Vi. Don't fall asleep there, now."

Vi didn't hear. She was bending into the shelf under the counter, looking for her bottle.

Outside, Ron lit a cigarette while Silva picked up the sandwich-board sign and took it inside. When she came back, he nodded towards the Land Rover and Silva clambered up into the passenger seat. As they drove off, Vi was staring out at them across the window display of faded boxes and dusty bars of fudge with her drink in one hand, waving with the slow, clawed fingers of the other. Ron pulled onto the road and turned left towards the bridge.

"Stop, what are you doing? This is the wrong way!" Silva said. "We can't go over the bridge, we have to go to Netherloch. To the little bridge."

Ron shook his head. "There's a bottleneck at Netherloch. If we go that way it'll be over two hours. This way you'll be across in less than twenty minutes. You won't even get your feet wet." He smiled. "Don't worry, I won't make you row. Trust me."

"Row? We are going in a boat? I can't! I can't go in a boat!"

"Why not? You want to swim?"

"I can't swim!"

"Well, you'll be better off in the boat then, won't you?" Ron laughed, rolled down the window and threw out his cigarette end.

"I can't go in a boat!"

The sudden rush of air from the window felt white and clear, a beam of cold light. Silva was aware he had half-turned and was looking at her and at the same time was somehow, almost magically, keeping his attention on the road. He had careful, strange eyes, and he put them to work like a camera; they travelled out and over her as she sat there, dissolving the shadows around her so that she might be unconcealed to him, fixed and memorized. She felt she was being recorded as a specimen, categorized; she was an example of something or other, but she had no idea what.

"You can go in a boat." He spoke matter-of-factly, winding the window up. "You'll be fine."

For a while Silva stared ahead at the road until she felt safe enough, in the dark of the cab, to look at Ron again. She could see that his face was grainy with white stubble, and his square, shaved head sat on his shoulders like a boulder on a ridge. Why had she agreed to this? She had no reason to trust him. The back of the Land Rover was dark but obviously not empty: every bump and curve in the road brought dull clunking noises from the uneven mass of vague, heavy shapes behind. There could be guns in there. Knives. Chains. Rope. Even with just a pickaxe and spade he could kill her and nobody would ever know. Or out there on the river, in the pitch dark, he could push her overboard. She turned back and gazed through the window. Her body might be buried among the trees or under the dark hills or lost at the bottom of the river, and Stefan would never know where she was. Would Anna, growing up, explain her mother's absence to other people with three words: *she went missing*? It came to her suddenly that disappearance was worse even than death. *Where were they?*

"You're not from round here," Ron said.

"No."

"But you're not a tourist. Are you a student?"

"No."

"Your husband. What sort of work was it you said he was looking for, again?"

"I didn't say."

He gave a short laugh and lifted his hands from the wheel for a moment, in mock fear. His eyes rested on her again.

"OK. None of my business. Here we are, anyway," he said, tapping on the steering wheel with straight, thick fingers, and turning off the road on to a gouged-out patch of land lit by a single orange light and bordered by a chain-link fence. He parked beside a security shed and got out, took a hard hat and a torch from the back of the Land Rover and spoke a few words to the man at the shed window. The man snorted and shrugged, then handed another hard hat out through the window, which Ron told Silva to put on. The man came out and unlocked the gate in the fence.

"'Night, then, Ron. 'Night, madam," he said, assessing Silva as she walked through. "Mind how you go."

"She's just going across the river," Ron said.

The man laughed. "Hard hats must be worn at all times!" he called after them.

Ron led the way down a track of deep tyre ruts, past giant machinery and stacked stone blocks and mounds of sand, still under a misty glow from the moon. Bright electric light and music and men's voices from other sheds at the far edge of the site spilled over the darkness. When they reached the jetty, Ron handed Silva the torch and swung himself down a metal ladder into a motor launch bobbing in the inky water. Silva handed over her bag and the torch, and he helped her down and onto a long seat that ran around the side of the boat. He started the motor, and at once from somewhere among the sheds and piles of machinery the barking and howling of several dogs rose into the air. The engine stalled. The barking grew louder and more vicious; a man's voice shouted. Silva turned to Ron.

"Security. They're locked in. Don't worry."

At that moment the boat surged away from the jetty with a force that pushed her hard against the stern. Her hands found a rope, and she clung on. Icy spray flew up and soaked her face as the boat cut a way through the water into darkness and into a night wind that carried the scent of oil and seawater.

Out on the river it was impossible to speak above the noise of the engine and the wind. Ron took off his hard hat and motioned to Silva that she could do the same. Immediately her hair flew up in a tangle, and as she pulled at it and tried to gather it into a roll under the collar of her jacket, she heard him laugh. The pitch of the motor rose, and the boat rocked and raced on. In another two minutes they were more than halfway across, and Ron slowed down. The wind eased and the black water turned satiny under the light of the mooring they were heading for, the pontoon at the construction site near the bridge's south end. But Silva could see that the bank was dotted here and there by tiny bonfires, glowing on the shingle between the river and the heavy dark shadow of the scrub that grew almost to the water's edge. She strived to get her bearings in the dark. Beyond the last of the bonfires, the bank curved inwards, and set deep and hidden in that curve some way farther up was the trailer. The last fire couldn't be all that far from it. Or were there more fires around the bend in the river, presently out of her sight line – or could there be one *at* the trailer? Could it be Stefan? Ron cut the engine, brought the boat to, jumped out and attached the rope. He helped Silva onto the jetty.

"That wasn't so difficult, was it?" he said. "You made it safe and sound."

Silva was peering anxiously upstream. "What are those fires?"

"Tramps, turned off their patch. Where they camped out, it's the salvage site now," Ron said. "They won't be bothering you. Don't worry."

She fixed her attention on the lights of the service station up ahead, across the cleared waste ground, then glanced again at the bonfires receding into the dark of the riverbank. "Well. Well, thank you. I should go."

But she stood where she was. How could she move from here, not knowing what the fires meant? She didn't know whether to run towards or away from them.

"Where to?"

"I don't know. I mean—"

"Where do you live?"

"I – up there." She nodded in the direction of the service station and the road. "Not far from there."

"Come on, then. I'll go with you."

"Aren't you going back across?"

"Don't need to rush back. Come on."

He steered her up from the jetty and across the ground that, just as on the opposite side, was now a site for the bridge salvage and rebuilding.

When they got to the service-station entrance he said, "You hungry? I am. Want some coffee?"

Silva shook her head. "I need to go."

"You always look frightened. Are you in trouble? Where are you going?"

She waved a hand vaguely down the road. "Not far."

"How far? You can't just head off into the dark on your own on a busy road."

"It's really not far. I'll be fine. My friend will be waiting for me."

"Well, I'll just make sure of that. I'll walk you home."

"It's all right. I don't need you to come."

But she did, and Ron was already walking ahead. "Come on," he said, turning back to her. "Damn, I forgot the biscuits," he said, searching his pockets. "Never mind. Come on. It's too bloody cold to hang about."

Some time after it was properly dark, one of the bonfires went out. Soon after that the other grew bigger, burning fiercely enough to send smoke high into the night air, where in the moonlight it drifted like a grey veil over the river. As the flames flew up I thought I caught the sound of faint voices raised in satisfaction, or triumph. Maybe some form of cooperation was at work and two groups had joined around one big fire, or maybe one group had overwhelmed the other. I couldn't tell. I stayed outside wrapped in wads of bedding, listening for anyone who might be approaching in the dark along the shore. From time to time I dozed.

My first thought when I heard footsteps from the track and then Silva's voice, followed by a man's, was that she had found Stefan. But in an instant I knew it wasn't him. The voice was older and deeper, and she was speaking as if to a stranger.

"I am here now, thank you." The man said something I didn't hear. I got to my feet and called out.

They came around the side of the trailer, and we all stood for a moment, trying to see one another in the dull moonlight. The man was solidly built, that was all I could make out. Then Silva gave a cry and rushed forwards to hug me. I felt my breath catch in my throat, and my eyes filled with tears, but over her shoulder I saw the man watching us steadily, as if trying to find something out. Would not a normal person have looked away at such a moment?

160

"They haven't come up here, have they?" Silva asked, withdrawing from me and looking downstream. "Are you all right? They haven't come this way?"

The man was gazing towards the fires.

"Thank God you're back," I managed to say.

"You're so cold," she said.

"I had to stay out to watch. I couldn't light a fire. If I'd lit a fire they'd have come."

"They might have done," the man agreed.

"This is Ron," Silva said. Her voice lifted when she spoke his name. "He brought me across the river. This is Annabel, my friend."

He nodded at me. "You all right?" He spoke without smiling, though his words came through the dark as if he required an answer.

Silva said, "You're so cold. Come on, get inside."

We went in and lit candles. Silva used the gas ring to boil water and make tea. Ron and I watched her, and in between we watched each other. The trailer was cramped, and we settled onto seats and moved as little as possible, like tired roosting birds. We hardly spoke. It was too late – and our being all together too unexpected – for polite conversation among strangers. Besides, all the questions that came to mind (*Why did you come here? Where do you live? Who are you?*) would, out loud, have sounded not curious but distrustful. And the remarkable thing was that although I knew I should be wary, because everything about his sudden appearance here with Silva begged such questions, I felt I could trust him.

Stefan, I wonder if you would have liked her. Over the three or four days we were together I had got used to her, but when I saw Ron staring at her by the candlelight in the trailer, I could see what he saw. It was not that she looked strange or remarkable, though she kept the shape of her body disguised in her clothes and had a lumbering, secretive walk that suggested neither woman nor man, adult nor child. There was nothing about her, apart from her clothes, that stayed the same long enough for me to be sure she looked a particular way and not another, that she was a person like this, not like that. Her face changed with every turn of her head, her eyes large and seeing, then hooded and looking away, her lips drawn in tightly, then spilling with words. Her skin would be white and soft and new-looking, then dry and unhealthy. Her hands were as heavy as clay in her lap until her fingers fluttered like pages falling from a book as she pushed her hair back off her face. And the tangled reddish hair on the top of her head reminded me of kemp on the back of some aged mountain animal, and then she pulled it around, and behind her ear it dropped on her neck in silky, baby-like coils the colour of charcoal. She looked neither happy nor sad, rich nor poor, old nor young. She had not an appearance at all so much as an atmosphere about her, of doubt and restlessness. It was as if, although present, she could, in her mind at least, leave and rejoin our company at will. In the close, glowing space we three shared that night in the trailer, she came and went like the ghosts of many people.

I watched Ron study her, wishing that he would not find her worthier of his scrutiny than I was, yet what I felt was not jealousy. It wasn't that. It was a need for him to know about me, and about you and Anna. I didn't want him puzzled by her instead. There was a satisfaction in knowing there was more I could have told him about her than he would be able to tell from looking. Dressed, she was almost sexless. I had seen her naked. I could have described the line of her back, the tilt of her breasts, the curve of her flank. I could have mimicked the sheltering, modest gesture of her hands across her stomach as she stood in the bathtub under the flow of steaming water over her shoulders. I liked keeping all this to myself. My knowledge of her body, that there was a baby growing inside it, had a power only for as long as I did not share it.

"Yes, they might have come here tonight," Ron said again, "if they'd seen a fire burning. But I don't think they'll bother us now. It's late."

When he said "us" I knew he intended to stay. He got to his feet.

"But I'll sit out another couple of hours, just in case. You two should get to sleep." He nodded at the long window seat. "If it's all right with you, I'll bed down there in a while." He opened the door.

Annabel said, frightened, "But they'll come when it's light. If not tomorrow, then in a day or two."

"Sure enough, they'll be along," Ron said. "We'll look at it all in the morning."

Annabel and I got ready for bed, shyly, saying little. Ron's presence was an excitement that neither of us chose to find words for, nor were we able to admit that he made us feel safer. When we were lying down and the candles were blown out, I think we were both grateful for the dark, for not having to see each other's faces. But then came the tears that I had been holding back since the morning.

"Don't cry," Annabel said.

How could I not cry? You were gone. I hid my face in the bedclothes and cried until I was exhausted. She lay in the dark and said over and over that you were surely safe somewhere and would return soon. Maybe both of us knew that this was a prayer and not a belief, but I let it comfort me anyway, and I fell asleep.

In the morning, Annabel was up first. She had hauled a tub of cold water round the back of the trailer and was splashing in it and singing, very badly, probably to let Ron know to keep his distance. I went outside, leaving him on the long seat stretched out under his blankets and his hands folded on his chest, like a dead saint. Down-river, the bonfire remains were dark smudges on the shore; nothing moved. The geese bobbed on the water, and I heard the sad, wavering cries of the gulls scavenging on the incoming tide. Annabel's voice rose from behind the trailer, and I laughed and called out to her to stop frightening the birds. The geese flew up from the water with a great flapping of wings. Across the river, my deserted cabin stood unchanged.

The cabin. It was the answer. It always had been the answer. You were wrong about it and always had been. We should have been there long ago. But surely even you could see that it was necessary and ur-gent for us to go now. There was no danger there, nobody had been near the place for a year and more. We would go across and live on the other side, and the tramps would stay on this bank of the river, near the service station and Inverness. They wouldn't want to come across, even supposing they could. There was nothing for them in the forest. They could take the trailer if they wanted, I didn't care. The leaks were getting worse, and it wouldn't last another winter. We would have a proper little house, not large but much bigger than the trailer. We would make it comfortable. Besides, I had to live on the other side now to get to work, and from the cabin there would be a way up through the trees to the road, and from there it would be only a mile or so to the Highland Bounty. And Annabel had nowhere else to go and nobody to care for her. She needed someone. She could stay as long as she liked, and I would look after her while I was waiting for you and Anna.

And you'd know to come and find me there. That was the best part of it – knowing that when you came back and found the trailer taken over by tramps, or empty, you'd guess where I was. That's if you even had to guess! Standing where I was now and looking across, you'd be able to see me sitting on the jetty, waiting, the cabin door open. Oh, Anna, I can see you watching me. I would hear you the moment you called out for me.

I went back inside and shook Ron.

"Ron! Ron, wake up! Will you help us? Can you get us back over the river? To our new place? Come, come and see. I need to take everything, it will be many times across and back. Please, will you help?"

It was Silva's idea entirely. I let her excitement enter me; even so, it floated only on the surface of my feelings. Underneath, dread at what I was doing and where it was leading me, like an undertow, pulled and ebbed. I had to get away, and yet I did not go. I did not go. In small, unguarded moments my fear swamped me, physically, leaving me nauseated and struggling for breath. I fought it down; I ascribed it to pregnancy, to shock, to the pure panic of displacement, to anything but my guilt and the need to outdistance it. I denied and resisted it. I was determined to erase the picture in my mind of Col's face as he stared at the wrecked bridge. I would not test my reasons for disappearing from my life with him, for fear that the ingenuity of my excuses might fail. Yet I did not go.

I had to inhabit the here and now, I told myself, live in the present and pay no heed to the past. So, wanting to believe that the future would take care of itself and that, meanwhile, constancy to Silva would make me a little less reproachable for what I had done, I went along with her excitement about the new place. Maybe I could be on my way once I'd seen that she was settled and safe. It did not feel like a trick of avoidance, quite, to dwell on her pleasure in her plans for the cabin, and to share in it. It was simply that, for the sake of Silva, the baby, and me, I could not leave her now.

Ron set off early along the road to get back to the boat and work his shift, promising to return later. Silva did not go with him, and was surprised when I asked if it was all right for her not to turn up for work.

"Sometimes I have other things I have to do," she told me. "Vi doesn't care. I'll go tomorrow."

"But shouldn't you call Vi and let her know?"

"Sure, I'll call."

I don't believe she did. Soon we saw again, downstream, bonfire smoke in the air and slow, dark figures moving at the river's edge, and we began loading Silva's belongings into bags. With our arms full, we made our trips singly to the old jetty upriver, so that the trailer would not be unattended for even a few minutes. It did not take us long to strip the place; although the jetty was a few hundred yards away over difficult ground and we made several trips each, the bags and implements and tools did not amount to much as a whole family's belongings. When we had finished, there was nothing to do but wait in the trailer, not just for Ron to finish work but, as he'd warned us, for the tide, which would not be high at the jetty until about six in the evening.

The light was fading when we heard the boat and watched it chug past us and up to the jetty. When it was moored, Ron came down to the trailer and helped us with the heaviest things. He disconnected the gas burner and brought it along with the gas cylinder, and went back for the water containers and mattresses and seating. There was nothing we might not need, he said. The cabin might be completely empty. Silva shrugged. Ron and I exchanged a glance, but neither of us added that it might not even be weather-tight, it might not be habitable at all.

I waited while Ron and Silva took the first load over. Ron returned alone and made four more crossings, bringing me over on the fifth with the last load. The jetty on the cabin side creaked and swayed, and the white rowing boat moored there was a useless wreck, half-submerged and filled with rotting river flotsam. I could not see how it even stayed afloat.

Silva had been all around the place, trying to peer in through the curtained windows. Up close, the cabin, set on a plain concrete platform, was unromantic. What had looked like silvery, weathered timber from the other side of the river was a scaly wash of grey paint over blistering, prefabricated hardboard. The flat sloping roof of cracked bitumen sheeting was covered with a ragged blanket of dropped branches and cones and dead pine needles, and bright-green streaks ran down the back and side walls as if the embrace of the forest were an encroaching stain. Moss and tree debris clogged the gutters that were supposed to channel rainwater into a covered water butt at one corner. The door was cheap, with a plastic handle, and was padlocked. Ron had a toolbox in the boat. He took a lump hammer, split the thin panelling around the hasp and dug into the frame with a chisel until the door hung open.

It struck me later, not at the time, that Ron stepped across the threshold and held the door open as if it were his own place, and that as we followed him in, all his attention was directed to us and not to the room we were all seeing for the first time. The disturbance of stagnant air as we entered raised dust and the warm, peppery smell of wood and linseed, and I sneezed, catching also the sharpness of old fire ash and cigarette smoke. The patchy linoleum floor was grainy with dirt and dead insects and soot blown down from the stove. Ron pulled back the curtains on their sagging wires, watching us like an eager host, scanning our faces for signs of disappointment.

In silence but for the scrape of our feet and the hollow creaking of the floor, we roamed and inspected the place as if each of us were there alone, privately assessing it against the unspoken measure of our own hopes for it, and our own needs. Within the small space, the distances between us expanded and grew vast.

The cabin must once have been a restroom or shelter for forestry workers. A black stove stood in a brick alcove, and a pile of magazines, a bucket of logs and a poker sat alongside. The magazines, all dedicated, unsurprisingly, to naked girls, were dated between 1999 and 2002. In one corner a plywood tabletop and its two trestles were stacked against the wall next to a shelf holding a beer glass and three pub ashtrays. Two wall boards were marked with fuzzy, darker rectangles where notices and pin-ups must have been displayed. The gingham curtains bore shadow stripes of pale grey where light had fallen on the original dark blue, and they were oddly homey, perhaps made by a wife or a girlfriend; perhaps there had been times when the workers had stayed here overnight. Behind the main room was a windowless kitchen with a sink and plastic-fronted cupboards. A small fridge stood open under the counter, the handle encrusted with dirt and rust. A door at one side led to a tiny vestibule, from where a back door, sagging from its frame, led outside. We could have squeezed through it instead of busting the lock on the other door; now both would have to be mended. Off the vestibule there was one other door, behind which was a chemical toilet and a shower of the kind people use in caravans.

There were two much smaller rooms next to the main one, completely empty. In the one at the back, the window glass was cracked and had been sealed over with tape, now a dry, flapping shred. The floor was dark with mould and sloped downwards, and when I trod near the centre of the room, it tipped a little and a gap opened under the bottom edges of the walls that met in the far corner, and a draught of cold air blew in around my feet. Roots had lodged themselves there and were pushing in like damp fists. I went outside and saw that some tree roots had split the concrete platform and were taking hold in the join between the side and back walls and along the line of the cabin's base. I thought of calling out to Ron to ask if it could be mended, and then I wondered why I was so ready to consult him. He was a stranger, and my inclination to depend on him was foolish. I would not ask.

I wandered down onto the jetty, and very deliberately I turned and gazed back; for Silva's sake (I believed) I needed to see the cabin from a little distance, to judge the idea of living in it as plausible or not. As I looked, Ron came out and pulled a couple of bags from the doorway over the threshold. I saw him move across the window, while Silva rose and carried a bundle of something inside, out of sight. They passed to and fro for a while in this quiet little duet of housekeeping, and I felt a pang of exclusion. I was glad when Ron came to the door and beckoned me back.

"Place looks OK for now," he said, to both of us. "The logs are dry and the flue's all right." He looked at his watch, then nodded towards the boat. "I have to go." I glanced at Silva. Did she feel, as I did, a sudden unreasonable resentment, as sharp as fear, that he was going? Silva and I, even between us, might not get things right. I didn't want to be left, and I was annoyed with myself that I didn't want to be left.

"I'll have a proper look round tomorrow," he said, addressing me as if he knew. "See what needs doing."

"Why are you helping us?" I asked.

"I thought you could do with it." He motioned across the river. The trailer looked deserted and hopelessly vulnerable. The bonfires still burned.

"Maybe, but that's not the point. Why are you—"

"I'll be back tomorrow. So don't be frightened if you hear the boat."

"I'm sure it's very kind of you. But why?"

"I want to," he said, awkwardly. "I do what I can."

"But why?" I knew nothing about him. "Do you live here? Where are you from?"

"Be quiet, Annabel. Of course, we'll pay you," Silva said, quickly. "And we are grateful."

Ron shook his head. "I do what I can," he said again, "and you don't pay me anything."

"Come tomorrow and there will be food," she said. She sounded shy. "Not grand food, but you will be very welcome."

He smiled and nodded and left. As he turned the boat into the river tide I called out to thank him, but he didn't hear above the noise of the motor and the cries of the geese as they rose. Silva and I stood for a while on the jetty, watching the frill of the boat's wake disappear and the geese glide back in pairs onto the silver-smooth water around the black rock.

I was angry. I suppose she didn't know what it is to live in a country where you have no right to be, where you are grateful for an empty shack. She didn't understand that you're always afraid. She didn't understand that going unnoticed and surviving without begging counts as success. People don't mean to be cruel, not always, but they only help their own. You never hope – never mind expect – that anyone is going to help *you,* so you don't start asking questions and looking suspicious because someone shows you kindness. If you have the luck to find it, you take kindness. You take it while you can and put it down to the way this world works, and if something good can come along, then something good can also be taken away. You take the good while you can.

But after Ron left I didn't say any of that, because I thought maybe she was that way because of her baby. It makes you cautious, being pregnant. And she wasn't suspicious about everything. She wouldn't have been here at all if she hadn't put her trust in me, another stranger – and I did want her here.

I turned and walked off the jetty. I was angry, and there was all the stuff still lying outside, the place dirty, so much to do. I hadn't thought much about furniture yet, but there was the matter of cleaning, and a water supply. And what about power? There were light switches in the place as well as the fridge and the shower, so they must have had some electricity. Ron looked as if he would know about water tanks and generators and that kind of thing. You didn't, not really, but you always managed to work things out well enough to get us by. You were always so proud of getting us by. You must be on your way home now, with Anna asleep on your back, I was thinking, and meanwhile I had the whole of our new house to fix up. Already I thought of it as our house.

She watched me take the gas burner and cylinder inside, and she watched while I filled a water container from the river. All the time I think she was wondering if she believed in it, if it was worth all the work to get the place ready to stay in. A little while later she followed me in and stood watching me in the kitchen. I had set up the gas and was heating the water to scrub the cupboards before I put plates and dishes away.

"Silva, you don't need to," she said. "I mean, we don't need to do all this. We don't have to live here if we don't want to."

"What do you mean? It's a good place."

"We could rent somewhere."

"Don't be stupid. I don't make enough to pay rent."

"I've got some money." She pulled out an envelope and showed me a bundle of money. She looked ashamed of it.

"Where did you get that? You said you had nothing. You said you didn't have enough money for one night in a hotel. Did you steal it?"

"No! I didn't steal it. It's mine. I mean, I want… It's for both of us. The point is we've got it. So we could pay rent."

"How much?"

"Three thousand."

It sounded plenty. It was a lot, the amount we had saved and you had on you, minus whatever you needed to get by until you came back. But then I thought about it. Around here we would have to pay expensive holiday rents, even if there wouldn't be so many tourists this year because of the bridge. The money would be fine for a while, but it wouldn't last long. The summer would come and go. Soon there would be a time when she couldn't work, and then what? I couldn't go and live in a place I wouldn't be able to keep. While I was thinking all this, looking at the money she was holding out, the notes began to shake in her hands. The sickness was coming over her again, and she was looking at me, scared, her eyes begging me to save her while her face and her lips were turning white and grey. She shoved the money into her jacket and stumbled outside. I waited for a few moments while she retched, and then I followed with a cup of water and a biscuit. She was leaning against the cabin wall sucking in huge, deep breaths. I pulled her over to the heap of mattresses on the ground and made her sit down. It kept surprising me how little she knew about taking care of herself.

"It's a waste of money to pay rent," I said. "This place is free."

She drank down the cup of water. "It's a wilderness." She looked towards the steep bank of pines around the cabin. Beyond the trees that stood like guards three or four deep at its edge, the forest rose up into darkness in the shadow of the hill.

"How do we get out of here except by boat?" she said. "How far is it to the road? I can't even see a path."

"There must be a path. People got down here once, didn't they? We'll find a way up through the trees. It's peaceful here. It's safe."

"But suppose I... what if one of us got ill? Suppose one of us needed something and we were stuck down here?"

"There would be two of us. And that's only till Stefan comes. Everything will be all right when Stefan and..." My voice gave out. The single word of my daughter's name was too much to say.

She turned away from me. "Yes, soon you'll have your husband and your little girl," she said. Was she scared I wouldn't let her stay after that? But she sounded more sad than scared. Maybe she was jealous, but she would have her own baby soon.

"Yes. I'll have Anna back," I said, and tears rushed into my eyes. "Anyway, you won't be ill much longer. It passes."

She decided to ignore what I was really saying, and lay back on the mattress.

"This place makes me feel lazy," she said. "I like the sound of the river. You can hear it now there's no traffic on the bridge." She sighed. "I'm so tired. I could fall asleep."

I wasn't tired at all. "So we should stay here. We shouldn't waste that money on rent. If we went somewhere else and I lost my job, Stefan wouldn't know where to find me. If I'm not at the Highland Bounty, he'll think of here at once. He knows I'd come here. He knows I love it."

She didn't trust what I was saying, but she wouldn't say so. I could tell she believed you'd left me and taken my baby away. She didn't know you, and what it was like, the three of us together.

"Anyway, soon you'll need your money for other things."

"Well, but I'll get a job, at some point."

"You'll need money for your baby."

She sat upright. "Why do you say that? Could you tell? How could you tell?"

"Do you think I'm stupid? Of course I can tell. Where's the father?"

She shook her head. "He's got nothing to do with it. I'm not with him. I'm going to manage on my own."

"It's hard. You don't know what it's like."

"I'll manage. Plenty of single mothers manage."

"You don't know anything. You're lucky you've got me."

She didn't argue with that.

"Listen," I told her. "Tomorrow I have to get back to Vi's. You can come with me as far as the road. We'll find a way up, then you'll see. Then you can come back and unpack some of our things. Sleep. You can have the little room at the front. Get us some firewood. There's lots of firewood. You'll be fine. I'm going to look after you."

Part Two

He rose at five o'clock in the morning, was always first up and clattering to the shower before anyone else, trying to make as little noise as possible because the men he shared with worked until late at night. Because of his hours he'd got a place in a mobile sleeper unit on the site, which he shared with other men who couldn't get home between shifts. It was spartan – three narrow beds in cubicles, a small recreation area and a shower room – but it was an improvement on sleeping in the Land Rover. Another identical unit was stacked above his, and alongside stood a third. He saw little of the other men; they pitied him his early start, but he relished it, the quiet and space to himself before he would be caught up in the flow of another day filled with people. Much as he liked being no longer alone, he found it exhausting.

On the first day he'd been instructed to take the boat across and bring back the catering staff, but after he'd done that and made several more crossings for other work crews, they hadn't known quite what to do with him. He'd driven up to the Highland Bounty Mini-Mart to buy stuff the guys in the sleeper unit wanted: tea, coffee, cereal. Then he'd done a few more boat runs and waited out the day until it was time to collect Silva. On the second day he'd been busier. By the third day, his work was acquiring a pattern.

By half-past five he would start the launch and set off to pick up the catering crew. Within half an hour they would be back, unloaded and preparing breakfast in the canteen unit, while he crossed the river again to bring over the first of the day's relays of workers. In the course of the first week, the emergency teams faded away and were replaced by people recruited for salvage and urgent repair work. The boat held only twelve people; Ron would be busy for the next three hours or so, and then he would moor the boat and get a late breakfast at the canteen. At first he made do with tea and toast; by the fourth or fifth day Jackson, the massive, tattooed cook in charge, knew Ron's schedule and kept some hot food for him. Ron tried to thank him.

"Plate's hot, mind," was all Jackson said, passing it over in huge hands etched with blue-black thorns and wine-red roses that entwined all the way up his forearms.

Around nine o'clock each day Ron presented himself at the site office, and now either the younger man or Mr Sturrock, neither of whom had mentioned Ron's paperwork again, would assign him here or there to fill in for absentees or where an extra man was needed for unskilled labour. They would also give him a list of river crossings scheduled for that day; as well as contingents of workers there were police officers and accident investigators, engineers, contractors and dozens of officials whose role it was not Ron's place to know.

Mid-afternoon, when the crew would be finishing with clearing after the lunch service and getting ready to return to the jetty for the trip back to the Inverness side, he would return to the canteen. That was how he found himself included in the distribution of the day's leftovers to the staff; Jackson counted him in, he supposed, because he knew that the men who stayed on-site overnight had to microwave their own evening meals.

Small kindnesses such as these and the routine of work and sleep and waking up in the same place each day put Ron in a more even mood than he had known for years. He was friendly but remained a little reserved. He didn't join in the daily, mainly obscene banter of the men; he never topped a dirty joke with one of his own. Nor did he care for the taunting that went on among the work teams, for almost every man was singled out for something – having red hair, no hair, being good at darts, unable to whistle – and given a nickname and a greater or lesser amount of teasing about it. Though the banter was not at heart malicious and Ron himself escaped it, probably because he was the boatman and not part of any one team, it sapped his energy to withstand the relentless camaraderie, even as a witness. He dreaded being made conspicuous for any reason at all.

That must be why, he decided, he looked forward all day to the peaceful company of the two women. He carried pictures of them in his head, and he thought about them carefully. The older one, Annabel, was the softer-natured of the two and at times even seemed the younger. Silva didn't order them about, exactly, but she was always first to be clear about domestic matters, and there was an edge in her way of asserting that things had to be done thus and not otherwise: how long to boil potatoes, how to get their towels dry, which wood burned best on the fires she lit to heat water for washing and where in the forest to find it (about which she was often wrong). Annabel never tried to assert control, and so neither did he. Annabel appeared, actually, to welcome Silva's bossiness, meeting it always gently, and over the course of an evening Silva's abruptness would subside a little and slowly she would become less brittle.

All around him at the bridge site there was pilfering going on, not on a big scale but in so matter-of-fact a manner it was clearly, up to a point, tolerated. So on his tasks around the place he was always on the lookout for things Annabel and Silva might need. Being discreet, and keeping his acquisitions modest, he took the small things: pallets for kindling sticks, canisters sloshing with the dregs of something useful – a good spoonful of lubricating oil, or bleach, or detergent – a handful of screws and nails, small amounts of sand and cement.

What tools he needed for work on the cabin he borrowed, returning them always to the same places. With one thing and another, there was never an evening when he turned up empty-handed.

Every time he went, there was daylight a little longer into the evening by which he could work on the repairs. He brought offcuts of timber and bitumen sheeting and sealant, and after he'd sawn back the tree roots that were forcing their way into the cabin's back room, he replaced the split and rotten wood and secured the join between walls and floor. There was no glazing work going on at the bridge, so he took the window measurements and got one of the Inverness men he ferried across each day to have the glass cut there. If the man was curious about why the boatman needed a pane of glass, he didn't say so.

As soon as the window was mended and the back room dried out after being leaky for so long, Silva, who had been sleeping in the main room while Annabel took the front room, moved her things in. She set out a mattress from the trailer on the floor and kept her own clothes in a couple of deep plastic tubs at the foot of it. Along one wall she arranged a bank of Anna's and Stefan's neatly folded clothes and shoes. Anna's dolls and teddy bears perched atop the pile, staring into space.

On the first evening after she was installed there, while Annabel cooked, Silva wandered with Ron upriver. They were supposed to be collecting firewood, but she began to pick the sparse little wild flowers, really just flowering weeds, that grew in the narrow strip of soil and light between the forest and the bank of stones on the shore. Back at the cabin, she put them in a mug of water on the floor in one corner of her new room and surrounded it with photographs of her husband and daughter, propped up against the wall. Ron was surprised at the satisfaction this appeared to give her, arranging the mug on a clean white handkerchief like a votary at her altar.

"And look!" she said, when she brought him and Annabel in to admire, "See, there's this as well."

It was a drawing in crayon on a scrap of paper, childish but not done by a child. It showed a wobbly little house surrounded by trees. A mummy, a daddy and a little girl stood smiling in front of it. Water flowed past their feet in snaking horizontal blue lines.

"Oh! That was on the wall in the trailer," Annabel said. "I'm glad you brought it. You see?" she said to Ron. "It's the cabin. It's where we are now."

"Stefan drew it for me," Silva told them. "From across on the other side. It was a joke, then. Now it's important. It doesn't matter what guides him here. As long as something does, like this. This will bring them here."

She propped the drawing up at the back of her shrine. The paper was flimsy and it curled over and slid down the wall. The others watched while Silva fiddled with it until she just about managed to make it stay. Ron could see that with the least draught across the floor it would fold in upon itself again and float away.

"I could you make a frame for it, if you like," he said.

Silva turned and thanked him, her eyes shining with such piteous gratitude he could think of nothing more to say except that it was nice for a picture to have a frame.

Most nights after supper they sat outside for a time, since Silva kept up her old habit of lighting a campfire. They watched the river and listened to the creaks and rustles of the wind in the trees and the furtive scrabbling of animals, most likely squirrels and badgers, Ron said, or deer. The noises from the bridge had lessened, or perhaps they had got used to them. For the first few days they saw on the far bank the trailer doors open and a fire lit nearby, and then one night there was no sign of life at all. Annabel told them she'd watched that morning from inside the cabin as the tramps had been escorted off the riverbank by policemen with dogs.

"Dumped back in Inverness, probably," Ron said. He'd heard the men talk about it, too.

None of them said a word about returning to the trailer.

Each day Ron and Silva had bits of overheard news and gossip about the bridge, to which Annabel listened with patient interest, but she never craved information. They would sit at times in silence, and even when talk ranged more widely, they asked one another very few questions. Silva said nothing about Annabel's luggage, supposedly still being kept for her by kind people in a house in Inverness. Nobody asked Silva about the country she was from, not even idle enquiries about language or food or customs. Ron once referred vaguely to losing touch with his family, and neither Annabel nor Silva followed it up. They all avoided speculation about when Stefan and Anna would return.

It was courtesy, not indifference, that kept each of them from probing into the others' lives, a delicacy that prohibited the seeking of answers that might make it necessary for them to lie to one another. Even sincere answers would surely be imperfect and unreliable, anyway. Perhaps they could assume that for all of them it had been a long haul to get from the past all the way to here, and their friendship (if it was that – friendship was another word they didn't use) was not rooted in curiosity about what that past had been. Soon conversation would return to practical concerns: how to fix the rattle on the door, how deep the water was around the jetty. Would the matches stay dry longer in tin or in plastic, would it rain again before morning.

Ron liked to watch the two women together across the failing light and the smoke from the fire, saving up the images for when he was alone again. Later, as they walked him down to the jetty, he would always manage to mention what tasks he could do next, what he

would load into the boat that night: borrowed tools, water containers for refilling, rubbish for disposal, to be sure they were expecting
him back. And as he turned to wave to them standing there, he liked
not knowing which of them he found more touching and beautiful,
nor whose approval gave him more pleasure, nor of which of them
he was growing fonder.

Within a few weeks of being at the cabin, my sickness vanished and I noticed a firming and swelling of my stomach. The weight of my fear began to drop away, like a stone somehow melting, and a different, pleasing heaviness gradually took its place. My breasts acquired a high, proud outline. I wondered every day about Col, testing over and over in my mind the possibility of going back and trying to explain what I had done and asking him to forgive me, leaving aside any thought that he might need to be forgiven for anything himself. Any affront I might have suffered for the apparent misdemeanour of carrying his child did not enter the equation; I assumed that even a notional reconciliation would be on his terms only. In my head, I heard myself plead with him to understand that I could not give up my baby; I begged him to let us become a family. And that was where I always stalled, for no reply came. I could not conjure up his voice speaking any words of acceptance.

I realized I had to allow Col his silence. I resolved to let him become a distant regret, to turn my concern for him into a conviction that he was better off without me. It was not that difficult. I needed only to recall what he had said that day at breakfast to be convinced again that by staying away I was saving him from the sight of a child he didn't want growing in the body of a wife he didn't love.

His loss, I told myself, although it was some time before I really believed it. Several times a day I would run my hand over my body, slipping it under my clothes to touch my naked skin. I was touching myself and also my child. Col didn't love either of us, and so I would have to, and I did. I loved us both.

With that love came elation, and amazement, too, for I had never associated love, certainly not self-love or love of the unborn, with happiness. Yet it took me only a short while to trust in it. And as must be common enough in pregnant women, I grew reflective of my own mother, and myself as a child. I had been a teary, clingy little girl, always scared by my mother's brisk, dutiful care of me. The patting-on of talcum powder after my bath, the tying of hair ribbons, the cutting of birthday cakes – all were guiltily rushed along and done with before there was time for me to experience pleasure small or great or, indeed, to cling. (And as must also be common, I made whispered little vows to my baby that we would do all these things differently.)

But if love is blind, happiness is kind. I felt no longer bitter, but merely sad and generous towards both of us, my mother and me. I saw now that the reason for her roughness and hurry must have been that she had not wanted to give herself time to dwell upon the anxious, ashamed frugality of her affection. I saw that she must have regarded my being born to her at all as a bewildering miscarriage of justice. For her, it must have been beyond comprehension that she of all people should be granted a live baby girl, let alone one who survived babyhood. But what could she do about a moral error that could be only God's? Since I was alive and remained so, she discharged her obligations as a mother with ruthless attention (being nothing if not conscientious), but she refused herself any joy in my upbringing.

On the Friday five days after the photograph in the garden was taken, on an identical, shrivelling-hot afternoon after everybody had stopped saying the weather was lovely, my mother went next door to mind baby Annabel while Marjorie popped out to pick up the developed film from the chemist's. Annabel had been fractious all day – too much sun, probably – but she had gone down to sleep in her cot at last, and Marjorie didn't want to risk setting her off again by putting her in the pram and lugging her on and off the bus in the heat. But she was desperate to get into town that afternoon for the pictures, because the chemist was closed on Saturdays. There were lots of new ones of Annabel, as well as last Sunday's tea party in the garden.

None of these details was mentioned while my mother was alive. I heard them from my father afterwards, over the years, in faint, unintentional allusions and references and little wisps of fact, never the whole story at once. And in retrospect, the thirteen years of my childhood before my mother died, before I knew a single thing about Annabel Porter, seem to have been a strange kind of waiting time, when I was learning, without understanding what it was, to live half-drowned in the backwash of an old disaster. It was always there, never spoken of but still the reason why certain words and phrases could bring conversation to a halt: *Heatwave. Died in infancy.* It hung around like a kind of eerie damp rising up from a long-ago flood that was now a stagnant pool in the cellar of a house where the words *flood* and *cellar* were unmentionable.

On that Friday afternoon Marjorie wouldn't, she told my mother, take so much as a peek at the snaps before she got them home, she'd wait and they'd look at them together. I thought of all the pictures I would take of my own baby, and I could imagine Marjorie, glowing with the kindness of her gesture, sitting on the bus with the packet warm in her hands, the crackly waxed paper around the photographs still sealed. Brave, barren Irene, she was thinking, so disappointed and deserving and sweetly interested in Annabel, a perfectly sensible woman when she wasn't going overboard on the religion. A book of illustrated Bible stories when the baby was a week old, honestly! She could be given at least this, a little share in the immaculate newness of the newest baby photographs.

Had Marjorie really thought all that, sitting on the bus? I didn't know, and my father had no patience with that kind of conjecture, but in those early days at the cabin, I was certain that she had.

And now here she comes, open-hearted Marjorie, through her own back door, calling out to Irene to get the kettle on and they'll have a dekko at the snaps over a cup of tea. She drops the packet of photographs and her handbag on the kitchen table, kicks off the shoes that have made her feet swell and peels away the chiffon headscarf from her soft tower of hair. Irene, looking frowsty and blue about the gills, walks to the sink with the kettle. She's been feeling off since the heatwave, everything turns her stomach, it must be her age, once upon a time she would have been in the sun all day and loving every minute. Over the running of the tap she says she looked in on Annabel twice and she's flat out and there hasn't been a squeak; the mite must have worn herself out this morning with her fractiousness. Marjorie lights the gas, takes the kettle from Irene and sets it over the flame. She puts a saucepan of water onto a gentle simmer and lowers in the sterilized bottle of baby formula. She pulls at two or three escaping strands of hair and tucks them back into the nest of her hairdo, then heads up the stairs in her damp stockinged feet to bring Annabel down for her feed.

It begins as a high keening, a wail that strangely comes and goes as if Marjorie's whole body is spilling away into a place that's bottomless and echoing, as if she is drowning in her own agony and also trying to struggle up out of it, screaming with terror. It rides over other sounds: the whistle of the kettle on the gas, the last bubble of water boiling dry in the unwatched pan, and the snap of glass as the feeding bottle bursts, the hiss of milk curds roasting on searing-hot tin.

And Irene is rooted in the kitchen doorway and has no words to meet anything as fearsome as this, Marjorie with that look on her face, clutching her dead baby against her and screaming, Marjorie bursting her way out of the front door and making off down the road still screaming, holding out her child to people who are now coming from their houses to see what the noise is about. Irene cannot follow. She is trying to stop her bones from shaking themselves loose inside their thin wrappings of muscle, she has set her jaw against letting her own screams escape; she holds on to the doorposts, but sudden pains are shooting inside her and she can't control the noxious rocking in the cavity of her stomach, which now is slopping with vomit and disgorging it, without warning, all over the floor.

Though she survived another thirteen years, I am certain my mother was never free of the noise of that afternoon in her head, its heat on her skin, the taste of it in her mouth. It made no difference to her that the inquest concluded three weeks later it was a cot death. She had never heard of cot death. Babies sometimes just stopped breathing for no known medical reason, it was mercifully rare but becoming more common? That was no explanation at all. The doctor and coroner were merely giving a name to some newly invented peril for healthy babies. Cot death? The child had died in Irene's care. She should not have touched her. She should have picked her up. She should have covered her, uncovered her, turned her on her side, not turned her, opened the window, closed the window. She should have kept her alive. In taking the blame on herself she was not discouraged by the Porters nor, it seemed, the whole town. Nobody else had heard of cot death either.

My mother came to believe, once she could no longer deny that the disturbance in her own body was a pregnancy, so late and unlooked-for it felt unnatural, that she had taken Annabel's life as surely as if she had stopped her throat or driven a blade through her chest.

Because there must have been a moment when she had sucked the life out of the baby's unconscious body and drawn it up, somehow, into hers; that must be why she had left the darkened nursery forgetting to whisper *God bless you*, and feeling even more nauseous and drowsy and faint.

And it wasn't enough that she believed she'd done it, my father told me, she still had to know how God could have let her. She spoke to her priest, not that it helped. He couldn't convince her that some force within her had not stolen the child's life. It must be, she reasoned, that in smoothing Annabel's hair with too much yearning, she had tapped a well in herself that was not love at all but something distorting of love, something visceral and needy and covetous. She had craved her own baby too much, and there had been nothing to protect Annabel from such aching, unguarded cupidity. The child had been christened, and had that done a thing to keep her sanctified soul moored within her body? I imagined a flummoxed young minister reaching for the orthodox comforts about baptism and the life everlasting. But my mother would have shaken her head. No, God had declined to lift a finger to save Annabel, and so where did that leave it, the soul? Unprotected. Anywhere. Nowhere. There was nothing eternal, or still, or unique about it. It did not – it could not – belong to God. It was not merely unsanctified, but unsanctifiable. She knew.

She left the church. Henceforth her soul, unsafe like every other, would have to look after itself just as Annabel's soul, taking its chances, had proved itself restlessly and promiscuously fluid, capable of passing from person to person, its tenure always provisional upon the beckoning of its next nascent host. So it was that my mother, slaking some ancient thirst for her own child, had drawn Annabel's supple, migrant soul out of her sleeping body and into her own, where it was to alight, and embed, and animate the simmering, multiplying cells that were even then readying themselves to be expelled exactly thirty-seven weeks later as me, the deplorable little thief whose veins raced with lifeblood stolen from Annabel Porter.

Cot death or not, new phenomenon or not, it was a calamity so woeful and mythic that it had, in fact, brought a chorus of women wailing onto the streets to prise the corpse of an infant from the arms of its deranged, barefoot mother. I think it might have saved my mother's sanity had her part in the affair been condemned outright as diabolical; an explanation, however anachronistic, that blackened her reputation with the name of witch might have been preferable, in the months that followed, to her neighbours' askance looks and hasty crossings of the street. The Porters moved away. I was born, and for the next thirteen years my mother did not leave the house to go any farther than the back garden visible behind the fence in the photograph.

When Ron began to help us, I thought it was because he is kind, now I think it is because he likes us. We are doing very well. Annabel is eating like a pig. He has noticed it, and that must be why he brings us so much food as well as all the other things. But I do not think he has noticed why she is so hungry. Her stomach is beginning to show, but he doesn't look at her body, or at mine. He watches our faces. When he finds out Annabel is having a baby, I think he will help even more. He is a good man. When you come back, he will be like a grandfather to Anna.

Sometimes, when Annabel is thinking about something far away, or is asleep, the look on her face is so smooth I could cry, for envy. Sometimes my stomach and throat shut themselves tight when I think of her body getting ready, the way mine did with Anna. I feel a prickling in my breasts the way I did when our baby was suckling. When you come back, I want us to have another baby.

Of course I have wondered if you are dead, but you aren't. It isn't possible. I need you too much for you to be gone for ever. You can't be dead, because if you are Anna must be, too, and that isn't possible, either. I need her too much for her no longer to exist. There is no other need or purpose or reason in this world stronger than my need to hold you both in my arms. You are coming back.

Until then, I'll watch Annabel grow heavy and lazy, and I'll take care of her as if the child inside her was mine. We can stay here for a long time, as long as we like, as long as we need. Until you come back and we have our own new baby, there will be Annabel's to look after.

I didn't know until now how beautiful the forest is. The trees stand all around us like tall, guarding giants, and they have a smell that is strong and clean, and the sound the branches make at night is a safe sound, like me saying *shoosh-shoosh* to Anna when she cries.

The Porters left; why didn't we leave, too? There was nothing about the house or my father's job at the council that could not have been replicated elsewhere. Was it courage that made my father choose to stay and stand by his wife in front of the whole town, or was it simple obstinacy? Or was it a lack of imagination – at a time when every family in England that wasn't doing it themselves knew of some other family, someone at the office or down the street, that was packing its life into ocean-going containers and emigrating to Australia or Canada – that he could not envisage the three of us embarking on a journey even as far as the next county? I think it most likely that by the time he thought of moving us anywhere it was already too late. Our lives were too ingrained in the causes and effects of my mother's entrapment to withstand any such uprooting.

He cycled everywhere; his bicycle clips were as redolent of his presence in the house as the sound of his voice. They would be on the draining board, or hanging out of the top pocket of his jacket over a kitchen chair, or (to my mother's consternation) balanced on the Wedgwood clock on the side table in the hall. He went to work and shopped and ran the errands on his bicycle; he fitted a seat to the back of it, and until I was old enough to ride my own bicycle he fetched and carried me to and from all the excursions of my small life: school, the dentist, the cinema now and then, a birthday party. He would take back to my mother an account of films we saw, he brought her news of happenings in the town: businesses opening or closing, roundabouts and supermarkets springing up, the switching-on of the shopping-centre Christmas lights, new benches along the riverbank. Over the years we all grew used to this rhythm of forays and reports, but he never gave up suggesting gently she might care to see these things for herself, and she always said when she felt a bit more like it she might just do that. But she preferred to stay at home *for the time being*.

I found myself wishing, those first weeks in the cabin, that I had known then what I was discovering now: that it is possible – not easy, but possible – to draw a life to a close in one place and start another, not only somewhere else but *as* someone else. It would have helped my parents to believe in just the possibility; to dream of it, even if it had remained always a dream, might have saved them. And I still wanted them to know, as if somehow they had time remaining to them to change anything, that with the right moves it could be done, and so I went about the cabin as if they were watching. I wanted all the tasks of cleaning and clearing and getting the place fit to live in to look transparently sensible and natural to them. I wanted to convince them, by taking the strangeness out of it, that I was making a success of this odd turn of events. You see, I was trying to say, it's all about taking a risk, getting out while you can, finding somewhere to fix up and call home. You can just *go*. They were present to me every bit as much as my baby was, and I was sure they were pleased to see me perform this act of reinvention for the sake of their grandchild.

The weather improved, and this, too, I could not see as anything other than approval, a kindly warmth cast on my enterprise. During the first two weeks I scrubbed the cabin from top to bottom: walls, floors, ceilings. I carried out bucket after bucket of filthy black water floating with dead insects and cobwebs and dumped it all in the pit we had dug at the back, a little way into the trees. I unstuck the windows and kept them as well as the doors open all day, and the sun dried out the place and left behind a smell of soap and resin and sawdust. I washed the curtains and hung them back up (they still looked shabby but would have to do for now). I pulled out the linoleum flooring completely, and Ron took it away in the boat to dispose of. At the end of each day, Silva came back down through the trees with pine needles stuck to her shoes and in her hair, and I would make a point of spending the first hour or so showing her all I had done. She needed distracting when she got home at the end of another day without word or sight of Stefan and Anna.

Ron would come later, after his work on the river, either with something we had asked him to get for us or more often with something he had seen we needed: oil for the creaking doors, a pane of glass and some putty, paraffin lamps, a plastic picnic table. I gave him money for the things I asked him to get, but usually he shrugged and refused it, as if the notion of paying for things just didn't interest him for the moment. He had access to all kinds of tools and materials; he secured both doors and cleared the roof and gutterings and got the water collection tank off the roof, cleaned out, and working again, with new piping. He was looking for a small generator, he told us, so we could run the fridge, and use the shower instead of heating up water in a tin bath outside. He brought containers of drinking water every day, saving Silva the trouble of getting it at Vi's and carrying it down through the forest. Often he brought leftover food: big slabs of lasagne or bags of meatballs, half a cheesecake, for which I was grateful because I was always hungry. He was staying in a kind of bunkhouse for the workmen who lived on-site during the week, and the catering was crude and generous.

By the middle of April the bridge was secured, the salvage work scaled back, and the investigation into the cause of the collapse, as far as Ron could tell, all but wound up. For the time being the diving teams had been stood down and the five vehicles still in the water left wherever they might be lying; strong spring currents were pushing what was left of them to and fro among hunks of submerged rubble and steel, making further recovery dives impossible. Ron heard people say they would never be brought out. They and the bodies in them would probably be washed all the way down the estuary by underwater currents and devoured by the sea.

On the site there was a lull while what Mr Sturrock called "the fuckin' powers that be" considered tenders ("twiddled their fuckin' thumbs") for the rebuilding of the bridge. But Ron was if anything busier; almost every day he took Mr Sturrock and groups of surveyors and engineers out to examine the bridge piers that were still standing, and every day he overheard them discuss the latest analyses of the wreckage.

Mr Sturrock also had a new task. The trouser-suited young woman called Rhona whom Ron had seen from time to time in the site office (there were few women on the site, and no others as memorably glamorous) turned out to be in charge of public relations for the project. However preposterous he thought the very idea of public relations, every other Saturday Mr Sturrock had to "keep the community updated" by meeting groups of people who signed up for guided walks of the reconstruction site. Ron would take him over by boat, and all the way across Mr Sturrock would complain his job wasn't "being a fucking tour guide". On the other side, Rhona brought the people who had assembled at the service station down to the bridge end, from where, wearing an assortment of hard hats and clutching information packs, they would walk along a section of the old roadway, listening to Mr Sturrock.

Ron listened, too, and he learned that the bridge had been old for its type, opened in 1956 and due for replacement in 2012 anyway. This was fortunate, because work that was already in hand on a provisional new design could be brought forward for almost immediate adoption, with a great saving of time. Not that the bridge's collapse could be directly related to its age, nor had anything been discovered that pointed to faulty structural design or construction. The maintenance records were up to date, and the routine repairs, neither critical nor urgent, that had been completed three months before the bridge collapsed were not considered to have been in any way connected with the accident. Metal fatigue due to heavy traffic had been ruled out.

The bridge was of a deck-truss design (here Mr Sturrock produced from his pockets a handful of metal rods and sticks and laid them one against the other, explaining tension, compression and load transfer), and in the collapse six of its spans had been destroyed. The final tests on the concrete and steel were still underway, but one theory was that salt used on the roads in winter might over several years have seeped into the concrete and corroded the reinforcing steel rods inside it, causing one or more piers to fail.

But why then, Mr Sturrock's listeners sometimes asked, were steel and concrete to be the main materials used in the new bridge? Why was the new bridge also to be of deck-truss design, a pre-cast, post-tensioned concrete box-girder bridge (as the information pack had it), to be exact?

"Your concrete technology nowadays," Mr Sturrock told them, as patiently as he could, "is a far cry from what it was sixty years ago. Your concrete nowadays contains chemical additives that retard the corrosion of the steel rods. Plus," he went on, "in this region, grit is now favoured over salt for treating icy roads, so salt residues are a thing of the past. Plus, modern span-bridge design nowadays incorporates what are known as redundancies, which means if there is a failure, the entire bridge doesn't go down, and single spans can be repaired."

Invariably Rhona led the groups away, reassured, to the service station for their complimentary refreshments, and invariably Mr Sturrock complained all the way back over the river.

To Ron it was quite marvellous, this collaborative amassing and expending of expertise and ingenuity, and all for the future sake of perfect strangers crossing a bridge that was still to be built. He took it as evidence of something miraculous, this practical goodwill from one set of human beings – the surveyors, designers, engineers, builders – towards countless other, unknown human beings, many of them yet unborn. It was more than professional responsibility; it was more even than an assumption of good intent between people. Even while Mr Sturrock was ranting about fucking busybodies and amateur know-alls, Ron felt there was no word for it but love. Then he would give himself a shake for getting soft, because whether these guys were filled with tenderness towards others or were just doing their jobs, bridges got built, and they got built to stay up. Filtering out his feelings, Ron presented an information pack and all the technical bridge-building facts he could remember as unsentimentally as possible to Silva and Annabel, who weren't in the least interested. They wanted to know about the cars still in the river.

"The poor people inside. I am so sorry for them," said Silva, while Annabel nodded but said nothing.

But Ron had nothing to report about that, though he, too, was sorry. He was also sorry for some of the people who showed up for the bridge walks. He didn't tell Silva and Annabel that many of them came and left white-faced in wretched silence, and that every time at least one person broke down and wept. Some were so stricken they had to be physically supported, and once a woman had fainted. He didn't mention the regulars, either: those who turned up time and again, tense for new explanations, and those already weighed down by what they knew but who could not keep away. There was the ghoulish evangelical who, until Rhona barred him from coming any more, enjoined the others in prayers of contrition because the disaster was the act of a displeased God. There was the big, solitary, tongue-tied man who drove up from Huddersfield every other weekend because, he said, he'd been in the area when it happened and, for reasons he wouldn't bother the others with, couldn't get it out of his mind.

After we had been here for about three months there came, in late May, a week of rain. The river ran high for two days and a night, and when it subsided it left a tide of stinking, sticky mud along the bank. Right in front of the cabin a swarm of flies spewed out of a dead fish stranded in a mesh of washed-up reeds and sticks. I had to take a shovel and push it back into the water. Inside, the cabin walls swelled and mould bloomed on the ceilings. On the third night of rain I found silvery slime trails and a snail on my bedding, and couldn't sleep. I lay wide awake, deciding I had to talk to Silva about buying camp beds and some other bits of furniture. There was no need to sleep on the floor and keep everything in boxes, as if we lived in a tent. Even after spending over five hundred pounds on the generator we could surely afford it, and Ron could pick up whatever we bought from Inverness in his Land Rover and bring it up to the cabin by boat.

We had electric light now, a fluorescent strip in the kitchen and single bulbs hanging from the ceilings. The friendly buzz of the little fridge and fresh milk were still novelties. There were also two or three sockets, so for just a bit more outlay we could have a lamp or two, maybe even music, and with the rainwater fast collecting in the roof tank we might soon be able to use the shower – although, like Silva, I had grown to enjoy the ritual of our outdoor baths in heated-up river water. The prospect of such luxuries was thrilling. There would be no harm in spending a little money on a few more comforts. I began to think about a cot for the baby, a small chest of drawers, pretty curtains.

Then on the following day, for the first time, I was bored. The weather was depressing, and there was little I could do around the place. I was desperate for company and had too much time on my hands. I began to have doubts. Why, if I really wanted to get away and start my life again, was I holed up in a water-soaked shack within sight of the scene of my "death"? What was wrong with me that I couldn't tear myself away from the ruined bridge or from Silva, the only connections I had between my old life and this one? Why was I willing to use money to establish an invisible existence at the cabin, when I could just as easily use that money to travel away from it?

I tried to tell myself it didn't matter how far from that old life I had managed to go, as long as I had gone. I told myself it was not merely natural but necessary to stay. I had to stand by Silva, and besides, it would be wiser for the baby's sake to remain here for the time being rather than find a place elsewhere, and alone. It was a period of rehearsal; I needed practice at living in Annabel's skin. But was I nursing the same delusion – that she preferred to stay at home *for the time being*, until she felt a bit more like going out – that had kept my mother captive for thirteen years? The fact was I had chosen confinement and concealment. I remained in a hideaway rather than risk venturing into the open. I had struck out for the freedom to go anywhere in the whole world and was afraid of freedom.

So that evening I was agitated and upset with myself long before Silva came back from work. As usual her spirits dipped on finding there had been neither sight nor word from Stefan, but this time she didn't recover her optimism. She didn't sigh patiently and wonder if a sign of him might come tomorrow. Ron's quiet saintliness I found for once a little irksome. Although I had longed all day for their company, I discovered I didn't have much to say to them after all.

A wet haze of mist lay over the surface of the river and blotted out the far bank. It was too humid to eat outside, so we had brought in picnic chairs and set them around the trestle table, and we sat with the door and windows open to catch the slightest breeze. But the air was chill and heavy with water; nothing stirred except an unpleasant cloud of midges in the doorway and the rainwater that had collected in the chimney and was dripping down the flue, hissing on the logs in the stove. Ron had managed to light it, but the flames were sallow and weak, and curls of bitter smoke leaked through the glass.

He had brought a tinfoil parcel of leftover baked potatoes. After hours wrapped in their own heat their skins were wrinkled and soft like warm glove leather, and they smelled like moist leather, too, salty and dank. I had fried some onions and heated up a tin of beans, and those smells mingled with the wood smoke and wet rust smell of the stove and the wormy aroma of rain. I was irritated by the glances Ron and Silva cast me as we ate.

"I'm starving," I said, not caring much. I did not mean it apologetically.

"She's always starving," Silva said. She was eating less and less. Ron watched me scrape the remains from her plate onto my own. I couldn't help it if he thought I was greedy and fat. I started on my third potato.

"Really, I feel like eating meat," I said. "I would even eat rabbit. I think there are rabbits in the woods."

"I don't think I could shoot a rabbit," Ron said, "even if I had a gun."

"Trapping is better," Silva said firmly.

"But tomorrow's Thursday," Ron said brightly. "Carvery day. The meat tends to go, but there'll be Yorkshire puddings over, and gravy."

"Can you bring back burgers from the shop or something?" I asked Silva.

"I might get a bit of beef," Ron said. "Or pork."

"Sausages. I could eat sausages," I said.

"You need proper meat," Silva told me. "There's a butcher in Netherloch. Maybe I could get there, somehow." She looked at Ron. "Ron, you know why she wants meat? I will tell you. Your wife, did you have a wife? Did your wife have babies?"

"Silva!" I protested, with my mouth full.

"It's all right," Ron said. "She… no. We didn't have children." He pressed a finger and thumb against his closed eyes. After a moment he looked at us and said, "My wife, ex-wife… Kathy. She was cleverer than me, younger, career-minded. Made it to regional manager, never wanted children. And proud of it."

"Proud she didn't want babies?" Silva said. "Didn't she love you?"

"Oh, I think she did," he said. "For a while."

"But *proud* she didn't want babies?" she said again, shaking her head. She didn't understand it.

"Some people are," I said. "They just are."

"I thought there'd be time if she changed her mind. Later on… when we got divorced, I thought probably it's just as well. No kids involved, getting hurt." There were tears standing in Ron's eyes now.

"You see, Ron, Annabel is soon having a baby. Annabel is going to be mama."

"Silva! What are you telling him that for?" I said. "Anyway, it's not soon! Not that soon."

"Yes, soon! So why he shouldn't know? A baby, it's good news." Silva shrugged. "Anyway, it shows already. Soon you will be very big, then he'll know."

Ron was staring at me, and then at Silva, not sure if he was allowed to be pleased.

"A baby?" he said. "A baby, well. Well, then. Does that mean—" He hesitated and turned to me. "Does that mean, as long as... I mean, you might... I mean, will you be staying here?"

"Yes," I said. "I'll be staying here."

I did not know if at that moment I was making the decision or just announcing it.

"And the... the baby's..."

"The father?" What could I say? "The father. He never ... he's like your ex-wife. Never wanted kids and proud of it. It's over, and he won't be bothering us. Ever."

At last Ron's face showed relief. "Right," he said, standing up. He was smiling carefully, softly. "Right, so, that's the case then. Well, there's plenty I should be getting on with."

He went outside, and soon I heard the regular chop of the axe on a fallen log he'd dragged down from the woods. Silva and I sat on for a little while until she said she was going off along the shore. She did that more and more, disappearing downriver for long spells, needing privacy. When I asked her once where she went, she said cagily there was a place she liked to sit. I finished everything that was left on the table and then I washed up.

An hour later, the weather broke. Gusts of wind, suddenly cold, banged the door shut and pushed and pulled through the trees. Then I heard distant groans of thunder, and the sky that had been oppressively still for days began to move, first with a crazy, pinkish-yellow shimmering in one high eastern corner and then with clouds, darkening and roiling together low and close to the land. Slow, huge drops of rain hit the river. The thunder advanced, shaking the ground and crumpling the air, and after the second or third shot of lightning, rain began to stream from the sky. It spiked the ground around the cabin, obliterating the river and the far bank. A sheet of water cascaded from the edge of the roof and poured past the windows. From the door I could hear nothing but the drumming of rain over my head and the gurgle of the overflowing gutterings. Ron dashed up from the jetty carrying the axe and some tools he'd rescued from the boat. He dropped them just inside the door, grabbed his jacket and ran out again, heading downriver. I waited, watching the sky throb with lightning, and after about twenty minutes he came back with Silva drenched and clutching his arm, shivering under the jacket.

I heaped more sticks into the stove to try to get a blaze going, and fetched towels. Silva changed into dry clothes and Ron stripped down in the kitchen and wrapped himself in a blanket. I arranged his sodden things over chair backs. Then, because lightning was fizzing all around the cabin, I thought it best to turn off the electricity, so I made tea on the gas ring and then we sat by the stove in candlelight, and the storm went on and on. There was some whisky that Ron had brought ages ago, and he and Silva both took some to warm them up.

Silva had retreated into herself. I said she looked tired out, and she sighed and said she did need some sleep, and went to bed. Ron and I stayed by the stove. There was nothing to talk about, this late; we had made every remark it was possible to make about the weather. The thunder was distant now, and the rain had lessened but went on falling. Our candles burned down and went out one by one, until I looked up and saw by the light of the last one that Ron's cheeks were wet.

"Is it the smoke?" I said. "It's got very smoky."

He wiped his eyes but didn't answer.

"It's late now," I said. "There might be more lightning on the river. You can't go back tonight."

He didn't. Picking up the candle, he followed me into the room where I slept, and I rearranged the cushions and mattresses so we could both lie down. Without a word he took me in his arms in an

207

embrace that was natural and warmth-seeking, nothing else. The smell of his skin was male, pleasantly sharp, like clean metal.

The rain pattered on the roof over our heads, and after the candle had burned down and died, he said quietly, in the dark, "A baby."

He reached out and just once, over the covers, stroked his hand gently across my stomach, and then we slept.

This is what I learned after you went missing. I learned I would not die of my distress, not even when I wanted to. I would not altogether lose my mind, not even when I was afraid I must.

To begin with, the passing of time with no news sharpened the pain to the point that I couldn't bear any more. Then there came a day when the passing of more time with no news blunted the pain a little. No news was better than bad news, it meant hope, and it brought a little calm. This was the beginning of fooling myself, the beginning of knowing that fooling myself was what I must do. A way must be found to survive, and it was in my nature, then, to find that way.

And after another little while, the pain, which I didn't expect would go away, burrowed deeper into my life. It found its place and made its home there, and I let it. It took up room that everything else in my life moved over and made for it. It was just with me, like the sound of my own breathing, while I did all the other things that happen every day. I brushed my hair, counted change, put on my shoes, took off my shoes, and it was there alongside me: pain, and no longer shocking. It became ordinary, as familiar as the mug I drank tea from in the morning. By the time it was like that, that was how I wanted to keep it. I was grateful to be at least used to it.

I discovered also that I could not lie awake weeping for ever. Sleep came, if only in short, fretful waves, and when it did, it brought dreams that were sometimes merciful. I dreamed once of walking into a small, bright field, sunny and sweet-smelling, and all at once I forgot the way I had come to arrive there and did not want ever to leave it. And that was how it was also sometimes when I was awake. I could be busy in the shop, or talking with Ron, listening to some story of Annabel's, or just sitting on the riverbank watching the birds on the rock, and suddenly I would notice that for the past little while I had been carefree, as if I'd been standing in my small bright field. I had let go of everything in my mind that lay behind or ahead of the little pleasure of that moment. Then I would be ashamed, for what sort of mother and wife enjoys herself when her child and husband have disappeared? By being careless of you even for a minute, maybe I had made it harder for you to come back. As soon as I could, I would hurry to my room and place fresh flowers for you, light a candle and pray for your return, but also for your forgiveness. I would swear never to let you out of my thoughts again, I vowed to walk a thousand miles barefoot to find you. And when, as it always did, my despair returned, I gave in to it quietly, knowing I deserved it.

Yet the world goes on, and I went on. I rose every day and managed to dress myself in the wrong clothes, clothes that were happy and summery, soft old cotton skirts, trainers for getting up through the forest in the morning – I even tied up my hair with that plastic flower you bought me last year at the service station. The tourists had come, so the shop was busy and I was working more hours. Vi was having one of her good spells. The warmer weather helped her. She stayed sober, mostly, and sometimes even took half-days off and disappeared in her rusty red van, coming back with her hair done, and once a birdbath from the garden centre. But she was also harder to please. One day she told me if I didn't learn to smile at the customers, I could make myself scarce, and I did try, by thinking of the cabin and imagining you back there with Anna, counting the geese on the water. I told myself the world goes on, and the river and the sun go on, and if I also could go on, and even smile, then you could, too. You were still in the world, and you would come back. It could not be otherwise. Now, after all these weeks, the way that I walked each day up through the forest to the road had become a path, well worn and easy to tread.

Watching Annabel grow big made all this both better and worse. Everything she was becoming was a mirror of my own childbearing and of my aching. Her belly began to swell as mine had, sooner than she thought it would, and I also watched her become happy in a way she wasn't expecting. But I was. I know what it does to you to carry a child you love before it is born. When you love that way, the baby knows it, and grows. I remembered a woman from our village, they talked about how she married a brute, a real rough brute, because of his land and businesses, and her misery to be carrying his child. She couldn't bear the bulk of it, its weight in her like his weight upon her, they said. She couldn't forget her disgust over how it got there, that boulder of a child filling and stretching her. Blameless thing, that baby withered and died inside her, and they said it was hatred of its father that killed it.

Never mind. That was a long time ago and far away. There was much to do here, and Annabel was not as good at thinking ahead as she thought she was. She had nothing to do all day but take care of things at the cabin, and she did, in her way. Not in the way I would, but I didn't complain. It was important not to upset her, so I did not let her see that her standards were not my standards. I was glad to have Ron there in the evenings. He kept the peace without knowing it. He was so sweet and quiet and grateful, and he did so much for us.

I wasn't surprised when I got up the day after the storm to find him in the kitchen making three cups of tea. Too dangerous last night to go back in the boat, he said, so he'd slept in front of the stove. I was sorry he hadn't had a mattress, but I liked it that he stayed. With the storm going on outside, I had lain awake for a while thinking that if our cabin had been put here for just this purpose, to be filled with people who needed a haven, there would surely be another place like it somewhere that was sheltering you. I prayed for your arms to be around her, wherever you were, and I fell into a deep sleep. I was sure a part of me knew Ron was there all night, and that was why I slept.

The weather had cleared, and Annabel got up and went to wave him off from the jetty. When she came back I said to her that Ron was a blessing, it was good he had stayed. She nodded.

"It would be good if he could stay more," I said. "We should get something for him so he doesn't have to lie on the hard floor."

For once Annabel had been thinking ahead, because she agreed with that as if she had already planned for it in her mind.

To keep her happy, I let her go off shopping the next Sunday with Ron. I wanted to be by myself, and with her gone I could attend to some of the cleaning she hadn't done very well. There was nothing I wanted to buy anyway, but she needed some bigger clothes, and there were places in Inverness where they could get folding beds, some pillows and other things. She was excited about going out, and I tidied her up, I brushed her hair myself. But I couldn't do anything about the sleepy, foolish look that had come into her eyes. She hadn't been away from the cabin for many weeks and she looked strange and distant, drugged on solitude. Ron had the Land Rover waiting on the road, and she set off up through the forest in her unironed man's clothes with her belly large and her hair thick and springy, panting with every step. Soon she wouldn't be able to make it up the steepest part. As I watched her go, I was anxious. I hoped she wouldn't attract too much attention. But I was also afraid to be letting her disappear out of my sight and into a world that could swallow up the people I loved.

As Ron drove towards Netherloch, my excitement disappeared and I felt only fear. The people at the Invermuir Lodge Hotel would certainly know that one of those lost on the bridge had been a guest there; quite probably the press had turned up to interview the staff about the tragic couple. What if one of them, the nice waitress, say, saw me and remembered me? And don't people always notice pregnant women anyway? I would have to spend the entire day with my collar up, staring at pavements, my heart thumping and sweat pouring down my body. I gazed out of the window and wondered if my mother, noticeably pregnant with me, had once ventured out like this and also found her courage melting away the moment she left the shelter of the house.

Ron said, "Some year for foxgloves, this. Just look at them all."

There were lots of them, growing tall in the banks among the bracken and at the forest edges under the shade of the pine trees. I agreed, pretending I had noticed them, too.

"Sure sign of a good summer, foxgloves," he said. "A hot, dry summer."

"Lovely," I said, not meaning it, imagining the hot, dry summer my mother was carrying me and Annabel Porter died. Maybe someone raised an eyebrow at her rounded stomach and crossed the street, maybe a neighbour, bitter on the Porters' behalf, hissed "*child-slayer*" as she walked past. Or did the people she met assess her with remote,

213

grieving eyes and say nothing? Perhaps things like that happened, perhaps none did. It's possible that every single bit of evidence of my mother's defamation she conjured up herself, out of nothing but her sense of sin.

"A hot, dry summer. We don't get many of those," I said.

"Not like we used to. Not like the summers you look back on, when you were a kid."

I wanted to tell Ron that I never did look back on them, at least I tried not to. I wanted to tell him about the later summer, when I was thirteen, the one my father said sent my mother over the edge, though in truth the weather had little to do with it. We both knew it had been coming for years, but we needed an additional factor, one beyond our control, to blame for an occurrence that we failed to prevent.

It was the summer holidays, and nearly all the girls I knew from school had gone to the seaside or to visit relatives. We, of course, were staying at home.

"Here," my mother said one afternoon, "take this on down to your dad at work. It's just a list. A few things we need to get." She handed me a small envelope. "Tell him I'm not up to much," she added, as if her not doing the shopping was unusual and required explanation. Her voice sounded careful and hurting, as if there were too many bones in her throat.

She was lying on the sofa with a handkerchief balled in her hand; tears had been spouting from her eyes all day. I didn't ask why she had put a simple shopping list in an envelope. I asked if it was her hay fever, one of several euphemisms we used to cover her various states of collapse. She said it was.

"I'm just not up to much. Stay while he reads it, you hear?" she said, with her eyes closed. "Don't skip off. He'll need you." More tears trickled from under her eyelids.

"You mean I'm to stay and help carry things back? I'll take a basket then."

She took my hand and looked at me.

"Go now and you'll be down there before five. You'll find him all right, he's doing holiday relief in the outer office."

I nodded. "I'll push the bike home. He can carry the basket."

She closed her eyes again before she let go of my hand. "I'm sorry," she sighed. "I need some peace and quiet now. Be a good girl. Mind the road." I put the shopping list in my pocket and left her alone.

But before I set off I went into the bathroom, and that was when I discovered the blood between my legs. I went quietly up to my room. I knew what was happening, in theory; some of the girls in my class had already started, and one or two actually talked about it. But I felt disorientated and shy, and there was the practical problem of what to do about it. Before I could go out I needed help from my mother and I couldn't go to her; she was vacant and inaccessible, crying on the sofa and wanting peace and quiet. The afternoon was muffled and hot, and I realized then that warm sunshine no longer meant, and never would mean again, perfect play weather, hours and hours for swings and sandpits and running across the grass. I would never be carefree again. The day had turned wearyingly complicated and the heat treacherous; it would make me sweat, and itch, and smell. I lay on my bed unbearably dismayed, with my hands folded over a wad of paper tissues pushed up between my thighs, and I fell asleep.

I woke less than an hour later, in a panic. It was after four o'clock, and I couldn't delay it any longer. I went in search of my mother. The house was empty. I found her hanging from a flex attached to a metal spar in the garage roof, her face black and her neck broken.

The note in the envelope in my pocket said,

Dear Gerald

Please forgive me there is nothing else I can do to keep going. It is taking me over and getting worse and worse. Thank you for everything Gerald I know it hasn't been easy. You are a good man, you will both do better without me. She doesn't need me any more she is not a baby any more. I can go at last. I know I am a coward but I have to let go of it all. Please try and understand it's for the best.

Love to you both

Irene

If she ever has a baby you need to warn her, make sure she knows it can happen just out of the blue.

Just then I must have shuddered, because Ron asked if I was all right and suggested stopping for a cup of coffee. I refused and said I'd gone off coffee, so I was surprised when he turned into the car park by Netherloch bridge.

"Why are we stopping?" I asked.

He was already halfway out of the Land Rover. "You can have tea instead," he said simply. He walked round to my side, opened the door and held out his hand. "Come on."

We paused on the bridge to watch the river flow underneath and widen into the loch. Three or four men moved around with buckets and bags far away down on the stones of the loch's north shore, dark hunched shapes under the floating veil of morning mist, but we couldn't make out what they were doing. We walked on into the town. Set in the shade of mountains, it was a place of water and stone. Even in June there was a mineral, chilly scent from the river and loch, and the echoes of traffic and voices rang off the hard grey buildings. The main street was unspectacular, but there was an enigmatic undercurrent about it, as if it operated according to a closed, parochial logic unintelligible to all but its inhabitants. I kept noticing oddities: three strands of tinsel tied around a lamp post, an ironmonger's shop with a basket of eggs in the window, a handwritten card on the door of the chemist's saying "Shona left Bermuda on the 17th". If I had been alone I would have been slightly unnerved, but then I heard Ron laugh, and I laughed, too, and wondered why I was taking it all so seriously.

We went into a gift shop that also had a few tables and a microwave and a sputtering coffee machine. Ron ate a massive wedge of lemon cake, but for once I wasn't hungry. I was entranced, to begin with, by the modern hardness of the place; after the damp pine woods and river shore and our shabby, mouldering cabin, the chrome fittings of the coffee machine, the bleached counter and plate-glass window looked to me impossibly new and sharp-angled. I looked around at the girl behind the counter, and two women at another table, and none of them paid me any attention at all.

Ron looked at me. "People seeing us, they might think I'm the father," he said.

"Does that bother you?" I asked, feeling suddenly the force of the insult to me that was implicit in how much it had bothered Col.

I didn't mean it cunningly, but the question seemed to present Ron with layer upon layer for measurement and consideration. The answer might be strewn with implications, his silence seemed to say; whatever he replied might be a blunder. Maybe, I thought, I'd asked it mainly because all my conversations about my baby and its father had been with myself. I didn't really need an answer for any other reason than to satisfy a thirst for words on the subject from another person, the way I might ask for a glass of water. To avoid a long fall into silence, I stood up and said we should get going, and as we walked back over the bridge and set off in the Land Rover down the opposite side of the river towards the city, we began to talk again of this and that, the weather, the way people drove, the cost of things.

I pointed out a brash-looking house with a Spanish balcony and pampas grass in the garden, and Ron laughed and said he bet it was called the Hacienda.

So the miles to Inverness, our voices saying nothing in particular, the day itself: all passed along. I bought my clothes while Ron went to a DIY shop, and then we had lunch in a shopping centre, looking not so different from every other couple there. Ron had been given a cap in the DIY shop to promote something or other, and I put it on and he burst out laughing and said I looked like a boy of seventeen. I kept it on, partly because it amused him but also because it felt so good to be light-hearted about the matter of staying unrecognized. Together we shopped in a department store for the things on the list we'd made with Silva, and Ron insisted on paying half. We arranged to drive round to the customer collection point at the back, and we even picked up leaflets about applying for the store's charge card. By then I felt soothed by the ordinariness of our day; it made me absurdly happy to be out and behaving like everyone else.

It was as if the strange fracture between my past and future had been imaginary, and my real life could now once again stretch before me flat and horizontal, within the taut, functioning predictability of the world. Before we left the city, we bought delicious things to cook for dinner and lots of wine, thinking that Silva must be given a treat for having missed the outing, and on the drive back we talked about recipes and our favourite foods. Our unfinished exchange of words in the gift-shop café that morning had got lost in the gentle curve of the day.

In the middle of July, the tide dislodged the silver Vauxhall and nudged it along the riverbed in a gentle veering curve seaward and closer to the north bank of the river, until it came to rest in about twenty feet of water some twelve yards from the shore. Though the car was still submerged, people came to see the salvage barge and crane barge that were towed out and moored nearby. Barriers went up again on both sides of the river to keep spectators back. The television crews returned.

Rhona put out a press release. The car was believed to be the rental car caught on camera on 19th February as it passed onto the bridge only moments before the collapse, the car believed to be driven by the woman holidaymaker missing since the day of the accident. Her next of kin had been advised to prepare themselves for the worst. The vehicle would be lifted by crane the next day, in a delicate operation calling for skill, ingenuity and teamwork. Members of the public were urged to stay away so as not to hamper proceedings.

Ron, Silva and Annabel heard the news over supper in the cabin (they had a radio now, tuned to the local station), and Ron had also been keeping them up to date with the reconnaissance dives and crane movements earlier in the week.

"What next of kin?" Annabel asked abruptly.

"There's just her husband, I think," Ron said.

219

"How can they say that – prepare for the worst? He knows the worst already, he's known it for months. He won't come to see, will he?"

"I think they'd advise against it, even if he wanted to. Poor guy."

"Will he have to identify the body?"

Ron shook his head. "They may not find one. Even if they do, the guys were saying there won't be much left by now. Jewellery, maybe clothing, that'll be about all. Poor guy."

"Maybe if he'd been with her it wouldn't have happened," Annabel said.

"You can't blame him for the bridge going down," Ron said mildly.

"I don't mean that. I just mean if he'd been with her, things might have turned out different. If they were spending the day together, they might have been somewhere else at the time."

"Well, but that's still not his fault."

"I'm sorry for him and for her," Silva said. "But at least he can put her in a grave now."

It was a warm evening, but Silva had had enough of river and forest walks, she said, and she went to bed tired and sad. Ron and Annabel strolled up the shore, chucking little stones in the water. Ron kept her supplied with pebbles, because bending down was now an effort for her.

"So, the car. They're bringing it up tomorrow?" she asked. "What time?"

"Midday. They've got the press coming. I'm supposed to take a load of photographers out in the boat so they can get their pictures."

"Horrible," Annabel said. "Who wants to see pictures like that?"

Often now, Ron slept in the main room on a pull-out bed that they used as a sofa in the daytime. That night when they got back to the cabin, Annabel, turning to say goodnight, suddenly took hold of his hand.

"Would you stay with me tonight? Like last time?" she said, her head bowed. "Just tonight? I keep thinking about that car."

He led her to her room. As he closed the door behind her, she gasped. Then she smiled and said, "Oh! The baby's kicking."

He said, "I want to see," and he undressed her, and then himself. When they were lying in her bed, he said, "I want to touch." She drew his hand over the mound so he could feel the baby inside, bumping against the soft wall of her body. Then he said, "I want to touch you," and he began to explore her without her guiding him at all, and they made love quietly and saying nothing more, mindful of Silva in the next room who, they knew, would be staring wide awake into the dark.

He left the next morning without waking them up.

Later, after Silva had set off for work, Annabel waited an hour. Then she dressed in what she considered her least noticeable clothes, pushed her hair under the cap, and left the cabin.

I followed Silva's pathway up through the forest. It rose steeply all the way, and often disappeared completely. In places the hillside had collapsed into soft, lumpy terraces and banks that bulged with the roots of fallen trees, and the broken spars of trunks lay criss-crossed and horizontal. I struggled to keep going, using them like climbing bars to haul myself up; under my weight several of them split, each time with a crack that echoed damply through the trees and sent pigeons and rooks flapping into the sky. I would pause, panting hard, until the quiet returned and I could be sure there had been nobody nearby, only the birds to hear me, and then I fought on, huge and heavy among the spindly, brittle boughs and branches that shivered and shook and swung back against my face as I climbed.

It took me nearly an hour to get near the road where the forest levelled out, and I had to rest for several minutes leaning behind a tree to catch my breath. When I felt better, I brushed from my clothes as best I could the black and green streaks and scrapes from the wet bark, and got rid of the mulch and pine needles from my hair and shoes. Then I set off towards the bridge.

After only ten minutes I came across one, then another, then more and more little groups of people on the road, most of them in walking gear, heading in the same direction. I was relieved to be no longer conspicuously solitary, but I didn't want to be spoken to, so I slowed my pace to an unobtrusive stroll and went on alone, trying to look neither lost nor in need of company, just one of the straggle approaching the bridge. I had to trust that everyone's interest would be focused on the spectacle to come and not on a dishevelled, pregnant woman trudging along by herself. But my heart was beating hard.

I had my jacket pulled around my belly and my hands jammed in the pockets, and I secretly stroked the baby as I walked, and I fancied she wriggled and kicked to let me know she could feel my touch upon her. And I thought of Ron and how his hands had roamed over her, I remembered what followed – his directness, so unexpected, yet thoughtful, and so pleasing. And afterwards, sleep: peace inspired by and in each other, somehow. His awkward tenderness was already playing in my memory like a little grace note, and I didn't care if I was being idiotic or sentimental. Whatever might happen after this, I felt that I had been favoured, and that thought made me surprisingly happy.

I couldn't get near the river, nobody could. I walked the road as far as the old bridge approach and went beyond that, farther up the bank towards the sea, and stopped on high ground some way from where the gathering of people was densest. Anchored together on the river, as Ron had told me, were the crane barge and the salvage barge. Around them, a dozen small boats swayed on the water. Speeding among them were three or four police launches that threw out white, frothy trails. The helicopters were back, one of them with the logo of a media group slashed in red across it. For half an hour or more, nothing much seemed to happen; I watched as men walked about on the barges, though I could not determine what exactly their purpose was, and I began to wonder if the operation was going ahead at all. Then quite suddenly two small dinghies moored to the back of the salvage barge moved out onto the water and the men left on deck took up positions at the far end. The crane swung out over the river. The winch chains, black against the pearly white water, unwound and dipped below the surface. The men in the dinghies went to and fro, guiding the chains down to the divers underwater. After another long wait, the chains tautened. The dinghies returned to the back of the barge. The crane head juddered and cranked and began to wind in its load, and a few moments later a dome of water began to rise and bubble and then the surface of the river darkened and swelled and broke, and up came the car like a drowned, hanging corpse, crushed and sodden and bleeding dark mud. It hung, swinging, as river water streamed off it. The helicopters came lower and hovered. All around me people were lifting mobile phones into the air and taking pictures, or scanning their screens for live news. One man fiddled importantly with his iPhone and relayed details in a loud voice to his wife and two teenage sons who stood beside him, gaping and pointing. Others gathered to stand within earshot.

He said, "There are six divers down there… weather conditions almost ideal… very little wind… but operation may be hampered by strong currents and low visibility underwater."

Then out on the river we heard a faint metallic cranking, and the crane jerked and shook and pulled the sagging pendulum of the car a few feet across. Then it stopped. The car hung in the air above the salvage barge until the arc of its swings diminished, and then it was lowered slowly onto the deck. As soon as the winch chains came off and were swung clear, tarpaulin screens went up all around it. A few minutes later three police vessels came alongside the barge, and several men were brought on board.

There was nothing more to see. The small vessels around the barges began to move, some towards the jetty on the far shore, some over to our side. Ron's boat would be among them, I supposed, but I was too far away to make out which was his. Around me the knots of spectators loosened, shifted, dispersed, but I stood where I was, and so did the man with the iPhone and his little audience.

I knew what I should expect. Why then did I not expect it?

"First images of the vehicle taken from vessels adjacent to the rescue suggest there are human remains inside," he announced. "Police are not confirming anything at this stage and will make a statement later today."

The man's two sons gasped and stared. One of them said, "Human remains, wow!" and grabbed at his brother and they sniggered in mock revulsion, caught up in the thrill and horror of it. They weren't being cruel. Laughter was the only route they knew away from what dead bodies in a car might actually mean.

I turned to leave. I had to find Ron. How could I tell Silva? What could I tell her?

The police announced that night that post-mortem examinations were being carried out on two bodies found in the car, neither of which was believed to be that of the missing woman. They would not comment on the speculation in some news reports that one of the dead was a child.

At the bridge site, the discovery of the bodies – the wrong bodies – unhinged the operation for several hours. Ron was busy into the evening with unscheduled relays of police, salvage crews and journalists, and could not go to the cabin that night. He knew that Annabel's mobile phone sat unused and uncharged on a shelf, and he could not bring himself to call Silva's. They would have heard the news reports themselves on the radio. But the real reason was cowardice. Late that night he had a missed call from Silva but did not reply. He could not have borne to hear his own voice tell her there was a chance that the people who had died in the car were Stefan and Anna.

The following day he took Mr Sturrock across the river for the Saturday bridge tour. They were surprised to see more than thirty people waiting at the jetty; over the weeks the numbers had been dwindling. Rhona said she'd been swamped with bookings since yesterday, and this was, at last, evidence of the "penetration" she had been working for. The news of the found bodies was providing an essential "enhanced human-interest factor" for the journalists, while being at the same time, of course, a tragic twist.

Mr Sturrock led them to the end of the bridge approach, gave his stern welcome and fished out his notes (he never spoke without them). Ron knew the speech by heart now, and as he half-listened he watched the audience. They were younger than usual, and many had camcorders and cameras. There was something else different about them, too. They were warmed up for something. This was a gathering of ghouls. Gone were the quiet attention of the regular audience of locals and the earnest types interested in bridge design, the sad concentration of people hoping for answers, paying respects to the dead.

Mr Sturrock was telling them about concrete. "We're well ahead of schedule," he read from his notes, "partly because we are fortunate in having suitable sites downriver for the casting sheds, thus minimizing the cost and transportation time for the replacement concrete components. Needless to say, we inspect every casting and reject it unless it meets our strict criteria."

As he spoke, three or four people detached themselves from the group, wandered away and began taking pictures. Mr Sturrock counted on his fingers. "One, concrete has to cure properly, in temperatures above zero degrees centigrade. Two, on top of the temperature, you have to think about what we call air entrainment, which is—"

"Excuse me, are there any more bodies still down there?" somebody asked. Others murmured with interest.

"What about that woman? Have they found her yet?"

"Are the divers down there now? Have they called off the search?"

"That's a police matter," Mr Sturrock said. "Three, your basic concrete recipe has to suit your actual conditions. There are various chemical—"

A few more people drifted away; two or three began a conversation.

"How long would it take a human body to decompose down there?"

"The fish eat everything, that's what I heard. Everything. Hey, mister, is it true after five months there'd just be bones?"

227

Mr Sturrock paused and looked past the crowd. Two of the first defectors had strolled to the barrier at the end of the bridge road and were scanning the river with camcorders, homing in on the crane barge that had lifted the car. Their safety helmets sat on the ground at their feet.

"Hoy!" Mr Sturrock yelled. "Hoy, you! Stop right there! You're in breach of regulations!" He pocketed his notes and strode towards them. "You fucking jokers, get your hats on! Get your fucking hats on and get your arses off the fucking bridge!" One man stopped at once and reached for his helmet. But the other swung his camcorder round and began filming Mr Sturrock.

Ron wasn't in time to stop it. Mr Sturrock let out a roar, broke into a run, lunged at the man and wrenched the camcorder away. Holding the man off with his free hand and ignoring his shouts, he strode to the barrier and flung it into the water. Then he swung round to the rest of the group. "Aye, and that goes for the lot of youse! This tour is cancelled! Fuck off! You are no longer authorized on these premises! So fuck off, the lot o' youse!"

Rhona came forwards, protesting, but he held up a hand. "Rhona, hen, just get them out of here, OK? I'm no' having it. Hear me? Get them fucking out of here."

He strode off towards the jetty, stepped into the launch and took a seat in the bow, as far as possible from where Ron operated the boat, and stared out at the opposite bank. Ron followed, started the ignition, and when they were mid-river he slowed the boat right down so they could feel the soft tilting of the tide against the sides. The quieting of the engine or their distance from the shore, maybe the rhythm of the waves, calmed Mr Sturrock. He turned and shuffled down until he sat close to the stern.

"Lost my rag for a wee minute there," he said. "Maybe I went a bit far, eh?"

He had never before talked to Ron in a tone of voice that invited a reply.

"No, served them right," Ron said. He smiled. "Shouldn't have taken their hats off, should they?"

Mr Sturrock laughed. "Aye, right enough, they shouldnae." He shook his head. "See how they were carrying on, like it's entertainment? Nae respect." He paused. "It's on my mind, I suppose. Him that wasnae there the day, the English fella."

"What English fella?"

"Fuck's sake, yon English fella, he's here every time. Big quiet fella, comes up from Huddersfield."

"I know who you mean. He wasn't here today. First one he's missed," Ron said.

"That's what I'm *telling* you," Mr Sturrock said. "You ken why? Rhona told me. See, she had him on his own for a wee minute, one time, over the coffee kinda thing. She makes an effort, Rhona. Turns out it's his wife. The lady that hired that car, it's his wife, for fuck's sake. That's why he keeps coming. And see thay bastards the day, going on like it's a photo opportunity..." He glanced back at the jetty. "Enter-fucking-tainment. Imagine being him when that fucking car came out the water."

"Will they ever find her body?" Ron asked. "So at least he'd know what happened to her?"

"I've nae fucking idea," Mr Sturrock said. "Poor bastard. Put a bit of speed on, will you? I havnae got all fucking day."

Ron's phone rang again, and he didn't answer. After he'd delivered Mr Sturrock to the jetty he checked for messages. The call was from Silva's number, but it was Annabel's voice.

"She's heard about the car," she said. "I've been trying to get you. Can you come today? Please come."

When he arrived he found Silva sitting on the floor in her room with photographs of Stefan and Anna in her lap. She'd been that way, Annabel told him, since the news came.

She had taken Stefan's drawing of the cabin down from the wall and lit candles around it. She was rocking to and fro with her hands clenched against her mouth as the candles burned, gazing at the drawing and whispering to the smiling stick figures he'd made of the three of them in fierce, spitting bursts of language of which Annabel and Ron understood not a word.

All through Saturday and Sunday they tried to care for her, but she would scarcely be deflected by entreaties to eat or rest. When Annabel spoke to tell her there was food ready or to suggest she lie down and sleep, her voice seemed to reach her, if at all, from too far away to be understood. When Ron helped her gently to her feet and brought her to the table or to her bed, she walked carefully on her numbed legs and did not look at him. She ate and slept only to regain enough strength to return to her place on the floor.

But she did not weep, and on Monday morning she was up and ready early to go to Vi's. The radio was now repeating that the police had confirmed the bodies were those of a man and a child and that the car was the one hired by a woman tourist, who was still missing. And so, Silva announced to the others, these were the bodies of two other people. Stefan never hitched lifts when he had Anna with him, because he always said if he ran into trouble he could defend himself all right alone, but he couldn't be sure of defending her as well. Besides, she said, the police didn't even say the child was a girl.

She spoke in a firm but faded voice, as if she were under a kind of hypnosis of both hope and dread; an entranced, defiant look had entered her eyes. She got through the next few days at Vi's, returning exhausted to her candles and photographs and incantations. On the fifth day she did not go to work because she woke after a vivid dream of Stefan who had borne a message that the answer to her prayers was nigh. This would be the day they came back. She waited all day, and the next, and the next.

For the whole week Ron's workmates at the bridge traded rumours about the occupants of the car. People sat on in the canteen past their break times, talking and arguing. Ron just listened; nobody asked for his opinion, and he gave none, and least of all would he have said anything about Silva and her vigil for Stefan and Anna, or about the husband of the missing woman and his presence at every bridge walk. Even if he could have strung the words together, Ron believed he had no right to offer up for their scrutiny any stories, and such desperate ones, that belonged to other people.

One rumour was that the child was strapped in the back and nesting in a tangle of blankets as if asleep, and the man's body was floating free and twisting, arms outstretched, towards her. Another had it the other way round, the child reaching for him; another, that the child was cradled in his arms. And who were they, the workmen speculated, and where was the woman who had been or should have been driving? Were they hitch-hikers? No sane woman alone picked up hitch-hikers. But had she stopped for these two (had it been raining that day?), either for the child's sake, or because the very presence of the child had made her feel safe? But suppose the man was just a car thief, albeit one who operated with a child in his care, and he had stolen the car. Where then was the woman? Was he also a murderer? Had he killed her in front of the child? So where was her body?

The word went round that when the car was hauled from the river, the driver's door had not been closed. Ron sat quietly and heard the theories: the door lock must have burst on impact with the water; it had been broken in a collision with other wreckage; it had been corroded and prised open by the tides. But the favoured version was that a third occupant, the woman driver, had managed to open the door and get out, but had not made it to the surface. She must have been drowned and her body dragged out to sea. The bridge workers had it all worked out, they reckoned, on the balance of probabilities; meanwhile the police investigation continued with what they considered perverse slowness.

Ron was grateful that the patterns of his physical life – work on the boat, food, jobs at the cabin, sleep – kept him immersed in practical tasks and with little time to think. Whatever had happened to the woman, and whoever the man and child had been, all three were lost. And while the deaths of people he had never known were losses abstracted and at a remove, loss recalled all losses. He was sad for their deaths and felt they should be contemplated in silence, in the unshared privacy of his own mind; the thought of their suffering hurt and frightened him. He returned at the end of each day to the cabin, where such matters could not be discussed.

After two weeks, no next of kin had come forward. On its front page, under the headline "Police Appeal to Family of Mystery Victims", the *Inverness Herald* printed a photograph of the man's neck chain and the half-perished remains of a toy giraffe. It also reported that DNA tests showed that the bodies were overwhelmingly likely to be a father and child. Ron brought the paper with him that evening as well as a can of diesel for the generator, a tub of leftover coleslaw and a bottle of whisky. Silva was once again at her devotions. He showed the front page to Annabel, who was peeling potatoes at the table. These days she sat down to do such tasks.

"Oh, God, no," she said. "Don't let her see it. Oh, God, what are we to do?"

"She has to see it," Ron said. "She's bound to see it sometime. It's better if we're the ones to show her."

"Why?" Annabel said. "What good will it do?"

Ron was taken aback. "If it's not Stefan and Anna, think how relieved she'll be," he said simply.

"But it is them... I'm sure it is. She won't be able to bear it."

"If it is, she has to know. She'll have to know sooner or later."

Annabel gazed at the door to Silva's room, her face suddenly white. "She'll have to know sooner or later," she repeated stupidly. She turned to Ron. "Don't leave tonight. Stay. Don't leave me alone with her."

Silva's door opened, and she wandered in, casting a severe little smile at Ron. Her eyes were over-bright and her hair, as it always was these days, was pulled back under an exuberant purple plastic chrysanthemum that looked doubly absurd above her pinched face. She glanced at the pan of potatoes and slumped into a chair at the table.

"Not hungry," she said. Then she caught sight of the paper lying under Annabel's hand, and snatched it up.

"Silva, wait. Don't. Silva!" Annabel said, getting to her feet.

Silva cried out, once, and in the next moment she was at the door. She flung the paper down and was off and running, sobbing, stumbling over the rocks to the jetty, her screams sounding back across the wet stones of the shore.

She was simply trying to get to them. I do not believe a thought of her own death was in her head. I still think it was blind need that drove her to the water, to be where they were, where they had died, and that was all. It was not an actual intent to kill herself.

Ron dashed after her, ahead of me, but he wasn't quick enough. I came out of the cabin just in time to see her throw herself forwards off the jetty. The strange thing was that from the moment she surfaced, everything was very quiet. She had stopped screaming. There was no kicking and flailing of arms, no splashing or wailing. Perhaps it was the shock of the cold water that stilled her. Then her head sank. The purple flower in her hair bobbed for a second and disappeared, and the back of her pink cardigan floated up behind her and for a moment billowed across the surface of the river before its own waterlogged weight pulled it under and around her submerged shoulders. By then Ron was in the water, and I ran down to the jetty as he dived under and seized her by the jaw and struggled to drag her face up to the air. If she'd fought him harder and got a few feet farther out and into the current, she would have been swept away, but the strength went out of her. She surrendered. He brought her to the side of the jetty and dragged her out of the water. She collapsed against him as if all her limbs were broken.

I got her out of her wet clothes and dressed her in a thick dry shirt and pyjama trousers. Ron heated whisky with sugar in it and made her drink a lot of it. She sat for a while by the stove until her shivering and sobbing subsided, and then I put her to bed, leaving her candles burning and her door open. She fell asleep, and Ron and I sat up for a long time, wondering how she would be when she woke and what we might do for her. I stopped him wondering aloud about Stefan and Anna and how they had come to be in the car. For shame, I could not tell him my part in it. "Don't go on about it," I told him. "It makes no difference. It won't bring them back. We'll probably never know."

My back had begun to ache, and Ron said I looked tired and should go to bed. He kissed me on the forehead and once, gently, on the lips, and he settled himself on the sofa bed in the main room so as to be nearby if Silva needed us in the night.

She slept until daybreak. It must have been the *click* of the door that woke me as she left the cabin; as soon as I discovered her bed empty I hurried to follow her, leaving Ron asleep. But this time she hadn't gone to the jetty. She was standing on the shore some yards from the water, mirror-smooth under the early light. She'd picked up some pebbles and was studying them or counting them in her hand. I started to go to her and nearly called out, but stopped myself and drew back to the doorway. She didn't move. Her head in cameo stillness against the silver-and-lemon sheen of the sun on the water was bowed and sorrowing. I was helpless – worse than that, culpable.

All of a sudden she looked up and flung the pebbles from her hand, and they landed scattershot, wrinkling the water with hundreds of colliding circles. She watched until the water was smooth again, and then, her lips working and her arms wrapped tight around herself, she turned and wandered down the riverbank. Now and then she lifted her head and paused, looking at the river and all the time talking to herself. Or maybe she was talking to Stefan, to Anna, to a God who let such things happen. Who could tell?

I couldn't go back to sleep. I went inside and wrapped myself up warmly and found some shoes, and then I left the cabin, intending to follow her at a distance to make sure she was safe. But by the time I came out of the cabin again and had got down to the river edge, she had already turned and was walking slowly back. She looked up and must have seen me, but she walked past me as if I weren't there, still mouthing words nobody could hear. When she reached the cabin she went straight to her room. I heard her lie down, and then, at last, she let out a low, desperate moan and her weeping began.

Ron was awake and had to leave; it was one of the Saturdays for the bridge walk. I went down with him to the jetty and made him promise to come back as soon as he could and to tell no one about Stefan and Anna. He looked puzzled for a moment, I think because the idea of doing otherwise had never crossed his mind. I didn't want him to leave, but I couldn't say if that was from a desire to be with him or because I was afraid of coping with Silva alone. Two weeks ago we had made love, he and I, but not since, nor had we talked about what happened. So we were not lovers, exactly, but what were we? The question was tangential now; Silva was our only concern. Maybe it didn't matter at all. He promised to return in the afternoon.

In the boat going over, Mr Sturrock, huddled in his waterproof jacket, said, "Did you see that, the wean's giraffe? In the paper?" He wiped a fleck of rain from his cheek. "Wee soul."

Ron nodded. He wanted to tell Mr Sturrock about Silva, bereft and weeping. He wanted to tell anyone who would listen how she was suffering. It grieved him that Stefan and Anna were to be unclaimed and dispossessed in death as they had been in life, the small history of the family as erasable, finally, as a drawing in an exercise book.

"The poor mother," he said.

"Aye, whoever she is," Mr Sturrock replied.

Rhona was waiting under a lime-green umbrella. She had pacified the irate customers from the last tour with lunch vouchers for the service station and had also cut the bookings back down. The small gathering now with her stood with the sombre decorum of the previous groups; despite their garish wet-weather clothes, they looked like people at a funeral. The big, reticent widower from Huddersfield was there again, aloof in his sadness.

Summer was already in decline. The early morning sun had vanished, and there was a spit of rain in the chill wind that blew up the estuary, raising short white combs of spray off the water. The tree shadows cast on the river margins had grown longer, and in the forest a single stand of larch trees was turning from green to bronze.

Mr Sturrock introduced himself and began his talk, counting the same points off on his fingers, inserting the same statistics, breathing in the same places. Ron stood at the back with Rhona, who was absorbed in sending text messages. The audience stood lulled, reassured, a little bored. Following Mr Sturrock, they tramped with a scraping of feet between lines of hazard cones along the bridge approach to the farthest point of the old, ripped-up roadbed. At the barrier a few dozen feet from where the jagged edge of the tarmac dipped down towards the river, they halted and gathered in a semicircle. Collars and hoods went up; out here, squalls from the river blew hard around their heads and down their necks. Calling above the wind, Mr Sturrock launched into his lecture on the nature of estuaries and the design options for the estuary bridge designer.

"...here you can see that each tendon contains twenty-seven strands of steel and each strand has seven wires. The post-tensioning counteracts sagging and adds strength to the spans."

This was the point at which he invited people forward to see the new concrete and steel segments, and warned them about slippery surfaces and going too close to the edge. One by one people broke from the group and went to look. But the big man hung back, staring at the ground, and paid no attention when Rhona touched his arm.

"You OK, Colin?" she asked.

Colin looked up, pulled his arm away and walked to the barrier. When he reached the edge, he turned to the others and raised a hand.

"Ladies and gentlemen, just for today, if I may have a minute of your time." He opened and closed his fists as he spoke, and his voice and big body were full of confused, flashing energy. "I have something I want to say."

Rhona froze. Mr Sturrock took a few steps towards him.

"You're all right, son," he said. "Remember where you are, now."

Colin threw out an arm to hold him at bay. "There's something I need to say!" He paused, expecting to be stopped. "I want to... well, anyway... here..." He reached in his inside pocket and brought out a small toy dog with floppy ears and huge, mawkish eyes. A red felt tongue lolled out of its mouth. From the other pocket he fished out a posy of artificial flowers set within a ruff of plastic lace and tied with a ribbon.

"My name's Colin. I wanted... It's just a gesture," he said, reddening and unfolding a piece of paper. Aloud he read, "For the two victims."

Ron strained to hear the words above the sighing of the wind. Colin threw the posy and toy dog into the water, and took from his pocket a red rose, a rigid, dry-looking thing on a long stem.

"My wife... This is for my wife. She also died here. And I just want to say to her, not that she can hear me now... you don't know what you've got till you lose it. It's no good wishing for a second chance, but if I could make it up to you, I would." He sucked in a huge breath to steady himself. "I didn't give you flowers when you were alive, and I should've. I'm sorry. I'm really sorry."

He let go of the rose and a current of air caught it and blew it high into the sharp wind. It all but disappeared against the grimy rain and river spray and lowering clouds, until it finally came to land on the water too far away to look at all like a rose any more. It floated there diminished and misplaced, a dark, untidy twig. Rhona stood openmouthed. Gradually people fanned out past Colin to the barrier to watch his offerings bob on the waves and begin to sink.

One man turned back. "Well said, there, sir," he said.

Someone else said, "So say all of us," and began to applaud, and the others joined in. Colin broke away and walked off fast, back up the ruined road. Rhona hurried over to Ron.

"Christ, what next? I can't take this! I *so* can't take another drama. Could you go after him for me? Get him a coffee or something, see he's all right? I have to stay with the group."

Ron followed the man up across the site and into the service-station café. At the counter he caught up with him.

"I'll get this, mate," he said. "Go and find us a seat, OK?"

He bought coffee for himself and hot chocolate for Colin, remembering something vague about sugar and stress. When he brought it to the table, Colin was sitting with his hands over his face.

"Here you go, Colin."

Colin lowered his hands and nodded thanks. His eyes were red-rimmed. "Was it OK? Me coming out with all that?" he asked in a shaky voice.

Before Ron could speak, Colin waved his answer away. "I had to say it. Needed saying. Even if nobody was interested."

"I'm very sorry about your wife. It's a terrible way to lose somebody."

"Yeah." Colin's eyes filled with tears. He wiped them away, lowered his head almost to the table and took a slurp of his hot chocolate. "Well, there you go."

"People say the worst part is the waiting, don't they?" ventured Ron. "The not knowing. I can believe that."

"Five months I was waiting. Then when they brought that car up and she wasn't in it, the police were straight round. I thought they'd come to tell me she could still be alive. Still hoping, see? Stupid, but I was. Only they acted like I'd killed her. Took the place apart, went through the whole thing over and over again."

"Bloody hell. Must've made it even worse."

"Had to rule out foul play, they said."

"Were you married a long time?"

Colin screwed up his face and shook his head. "You married?"

"Was once," Ron said. "Long time ago, now."

"Got kids?"

"No."

Colin shrugged as if he'd lost interest. He picked up his mug and stirred his drink hard and began feeding it into his mouth with his teaspoon. Ron watched him, wondering if he was too upset to talk any more or if he was a person who didn't mind long silences. He thought it likely to be the second, and a few months ago would have accommodated it easily, being then that kind of person himself. He could leave now and tell Rhona that Colin was all right. But he said, "So you come up from England, is that right? I've seen you at every walk. Where are you from?"

He didn't in the least care where Colin was from, but it was necessary to pull words, on neat and neutral subjects, into the empty space between them.

"Huddersfield," Colin said dully. "Know it?"

"Passed through a couple of times. Nice place to live, is it?"

The silence returned. Just as Ron was about to give up – he couldn't keep this going all on his own – Colin said, "My wife didn't like it. People don't unless they're from there."

"Where was she from?"

"Way down south. Near Portsmouth."

There was another silence.

Colin said, "She would've got used to it. She was only there a few months."

"Is her family in Portsmouth still?"

"No. There was just her dad, and he died last year. Nobody left now." Colin squeezed his eyes tight. "There's nobody to talk to about her. I went down there, found her old address, saw where she grew up. Spent two days just walking about. How stupid is that? Same again?"

He was already on his feet and on his way to the counter, and Ron could not find the heart to say no. When he came back he tried harder, since Colin had mentioned not being able to talk about his dead wife and seemed to want to, insofar as he wanted to talk about anything.

241

How had they met? What did she do? What were her hobbies? Colin answered with a handful of words or skirted the questions altogether. It struck Ron that the more he said, the more distraught he became. Colin wanted to tell someone things about her, but not these things; Ron was asking the wrong questions and had no idea what the right ones might be. He sneaked a look at his watch.

"Sorry, mate, you don't want to hear me going on. A total stranger," Colin said.

Ron felt terrible, because it was true. "No, no, it's just I need to watch the time. I have to get Sturrock back across the river. Talk all you want. If it helps."

"Nah, I'm no good at talking. That was part of the problem, maybe. But thanks, mate. Maybe it helps a bit."

"Any time. Anything else I can do for you, feel free."

Colin stood up and shifted on his feet. Shyly, he held out his hand. "Thanks. Appreciate it."

Ron got up and accepted the handshake. "Well, I'd better be getting back to the boat," he said. "Take care, now."

"Actually there is something," Colin said abruptly. "But maybe... No, you probably can't help."

"What is it?"

Colin looked at him directly for the first time. Behind the thick socket bones and pouches of his fleshy face, his eyes were small, bewildered dots.

"Over the other side, is that where you're going?" he asked.

"That's right. The forest side."

"Well, it's just... I've never been there. Never thought of it. Then when I did I couldn't face it, but I could now, I kind of want to. I mean, that's where she was trying to get to, across the bridge." He raised his arms and let them drop against his sides. "Never made it, did she? And they're doing a memorial garden over there, aren't they? For all the victims. Putting up a proper memorial. If I went over in the boat with you, I could, well, you know, have a look round."

Ron had heard something about the garden. "It's not planted yet. They've only just decided where it's going. Don't think there's much to see."

Colin shrugged. "Never mind, doesn't matter." He turned away. "Just thought I'd ask. See you around."

"No, no, wait," Ron said. "It's just, it's not up to me. Depends on Sturrock. We can ask."

Mr Sturrock turned out to have a view of his own. Colin's gesture at the barrier was a lovely wee tribute, he said. As if the wean's giraffe in the paper wasn't enough.

"Och, go on, then, we'll take you over the once," he told Colin. "Only the once, mind. Compassionate reasons, OK? And you'll need to get yourself back by Netherloch."

They chugged over through the blustery wind saying nothing, the tang of diesel mixing with the smell of cold rain. When they reached the other shore, Sturrock hurried away to the site office to pick up his car keys. Colin stepped off the jetty and followed Ron's directions to a new walkway. The garden, Ron said, was going to be on the bank on the far side of the bridge, a short way downriver. He watched Colin go, trudging through the mud, his eyes on the ground and his big shoulders stooped under the rain. Then Ron cast off again to go upriver to the cabin. He really couldn't do any more.

If Silva slept at all, she would often wake distraught and wander about the cabin with rage in her eyes, pulling at her hair and clothes. She would not be held or comforted. Other times she would lie helpless and weep for hours until the skin on her cheeks was raw from her tears. Sometimes I found her, as I had the first morning, staring at the water and unable to move. Every couple of days, I think to get away from me, she would wander off farther downriver and come back hours later, exhausted. She hadn't the strength to go far. I tried to judge when to leave her be and when to talk. I kept her warm, covering her when she fell asleep, and I cooked her tiny meals of eggs or pasta and coaxed her to eat, not that I managed to get her to take much, often she'd only accept tea. Her grief terrified me, and all the time I looked after her I hardly spoke. When I did, something about her made me whisper.

I cared for her on my own, until Ron came in the evenings. I looked forward all day to seeing him, and by the time he arrived was desperate for his company. With Silva he was circumspect and solemn, hardly less reticent than I, and I was pleased if she went to bed after supper and I could have him to myself. I was delighted when he noticed how much bigger I was getting and fussed over me a little. Now each night he would lie with me for a while, sometimes shyly stroking my belly and sometimes not, but always peacefully, without intensity. I was grateful. When I was nearly asleep, he would go back out to the main room and bed down next to the stove.

Silva began to sleep longer and more deeply, and slowly she began to eat a little more. After several more days she was almost alert again and more talkative, but she was also restless and weepy, and she tired so easily. She hadn't been to work for weeks. We had sent Vi a text message when Silva first missed work saying she was ill and would be back when she was better. There had been no reply. One evening Ron suggested she might try going back.

"Routine," he said. "Good thing, routine."

I didn't think it was such a good idea. I was afraid Silva wouldn't be able to stand up to Vi in one of her difficult moods. And there was still some money left; we didn't need to worry yet.

"It's a bit soon," I said. "Why not wait a little longer?"

Silva listened as if none of it had anything to do with her, and I took her calm as a sign she was getting better.

You are not gone. I am full of pictures of you that spill through my head in an unending stream, and I have your voices all around me. You are not gone, because what I see and hear are not memories. I am not remembering the sight of you both, your sounds and your words, I am not bringing you to mind as you once were. It is *you* I see and hear. But there is no comfort in it, because I know you are dead. I have not gone mad. You are dead, and how can there ever be any comfort from that? I no longer have you, though I see and hear you. It just means that nothing in this world is as real as you are. You will never be gone, but no more will you ever come back to me. You are both dead.

I remember the first few days only as a time when I thought my throat was blocked with stones and I wanted my heart to stop. Every beat of it hurt me. I tried to stop breathing. I wanted my lungs to choke, I wanted to sink to the bottom of the river and be with you, not that that made sense, even to me. Of course I knew you were no longer there, for they had lifted you, poor drowned souls, out of the water.

Yet the river is, for me, where you were and will now always be, down under the water, your faces calm and your skin as clean and white as shell. You do not perish. Slowly, patiently, you blink your eyes, and your dark, curling hair still grows, and all day long the river current plays with it, spinning it in wafts around your shoulders. You

246

let the water turn you this way and that, and your hands rise and fall, your fingers open and close. You are waiting for me now, just as I, since the day you disappeared, waited for you. This is why I will not go far from the river.

Other people are waiting, too, official people. They are waiting for someone to come and tell them who you are, and to bury you. And I can't, because the official people have got rules. They are holding behind their backs all the rules they have for people like us, and as soon as they knew I didn't belong here, they wouldn't let me near you. There are laws, they will say. They wouldn't let me bury you, and they'd send me back, and then I would be farther away from you than ever.

So, soon they will have to bury you without your names, and I won't know where. But at least you – no, not you, only the discarded shells of you they brought to the shore – will lie together, and not far away. I will stay nearby and go on talking to you every day, and every day I will watch the river for a runnel in the tide, a flicker of light, a wave feathering the surface that will tell me you are waiting.

I have heard them since I was a child, but I never felt before now the truth of them, those fairy tales of mortal people who step off dry land leaving not a single footprint, drawn to the sea or a lake or river for love of a lost one who has been taken and transformed into an underwater spirit. But the oldest stories turn out to be true, at least in this: the vanishing from sight, the yearning of the one left waiting for the beloved who is never coming back. An old story, my love, is what we are now, and all we have.

Annabel and Ron try to take my mind off all this. They think it is not good for me to spend my time wandering between my bed and the river. They think I talk to myself. Ron thinks I should go back and work for Vi again, Annabel doesn't, but she doesn't know what I should do instead. I don't want them to worry so much, especially not Annabel. I want her to think I am beginning to recover.

Meanwhile she is very kind, and Ron would do anything in his power to make me comfortable, and it is calming to know I am not wholly alone. I am grateful for them. If they were not here, there would be no reason not to go mad. Annabel herself is growing heavier and slower by the day, and there is a certain calm in that for me, too. She is stupidly content. She does not know I am waiting for her baby just as much as she is. She does not know her baby is my reason to stay alive a little longer.

I wasn't so out of touch with reality as to want to give birth in the cabin, without help. I knew I would have to see a doctor eventually. I wanted to be the one to choose when, that was all. I would go when I felt ready. For months I'd imagined it as if I were watching myself in a film, enacting the scene where I present myself to a jovial doctor with some story about being new in the area, and my bump would be routinely examined and we'd make arrangements about the delivery. *Well done, mum, you're doing fine, we'll expect you at the hospital when baby decides to put in an appearance!*

Now I could see it might be more difficult than that. I needed time to prepare myself, but there was no hurry. By the middle of August the northern summer had begun to give way to autumn, but still I had no proper sense of time passing. Across the river on dry days now the combines were at work in the fields, raising clouds of pale dust in long straight rows. I went for walks under rainy skies, grateful for a new sharpness in the wind off the water, utterly content. I don't know where my complacency came from unless from pregnancy itself – some merciful, hormonal muffling of the very idea of risk – but I was sure everything was fine. The baby was growing and kicking, and didn't thousands of women gave birth every day? There was nothing to worry about. There were times when I was tempted to give up on the idea of the doctor and just let nature take its course. I had ages to go.

It was worth putting up with Silva nagging me about it, and about everything else, to hear her talking again, or so I thought. At least she had come far enough out of her torpor to care about something. Besides, nothing upset me much. I felt safer than I had ever felt in my life, attuned to my body's growing weight, its rhythms, even to its small lapses and betrayals; I swelled and sweated, I gasped with heartburn, the veins on my legs bulged like coiled worms. I had to pee a dozen times a day, and I could no longer lie flat on my back. But I accepted everything that was happening to me. I marvelled at the willing, aching vessel my body had become for the child, whose size was now quite terrific, and I gave myself up easily to its night-long pummelling under my ribs. I was happy.

But unlike me, and although there was no reason for it, Silva was edgy all the time. At the cabin she watched me constantly, and although she cared about the baby, she wasn't kind to me. Her attention was scrupulous but disapproving, as if the baby needed her guardianship because it was being born to a mother too hapless to deserve it. And she was full of opinions, all of them superstitious and most of them closer to witchcraft than to midwifery: I mustn't stand for more than half an hour (as if I wanted to), because I'd draw blood from the baby's brain; I shouldn't cut my hair because the baby would then be born with weak hair. I suppose I was touched, but nonetheless her scrutiny was wearing, and if I objected mildly to any of it or took a shade too lightly some silly piece of advice, she got angry. I learned to overcome the urge to laugh her concerns away. There was some respite when she went off on her wanderings along the river, but when she returned she would be more dogmatic still, with plans for more unpleasant, punitive little rituals that I would have to undergo. I lay with my feet pointing to the ceiling, I inhaled bitter, steaming concoctions of boiled leaves for lung strength. All, of course, for the baby's good. Often the cabin seemed unbearably small, yet when Ron came there would always somehow be more room, not less.

The worst days were the ones when I got ridiculously hungry. I could eat half a loaf of bread in minutes, impatient with the time it took me to spread the butter and jam, folding each oozing slice over and shoving it in my mouth, chewing as I spread the next. This put Silva in such a rage I would have to wait and gorge in secret when she was busy getting firewood or washing her hair outside in the tub, or had gone walking along the river. I could not explain to her the need to fill myself up in this way, the strength and pleasure it gave me, the floppy collapse in my mouth of bread slick with butter, the tingle of strawberry syrup on the tongue. Afterwards I would lie still and feel my stomach gurgling and squirting its juices and doing its work like the wondrous factory I now trusted it to be, transforming the heaps of food I had eaten into the bones, flesh, hair, fingernails of my baby. I thought of its face in the dark of my womb, blinking its wet eyes and smiling a sated, gummy smile.

Other times, I craved sugar. It would hit me suddenly, the need to crunch and suck on glassy grains of it, squeezing them through my teeth; some days I stole so much sugar I made my tongue sore with abrasions from working its sweet, scratchy crystals against the roof of my mouth. Then there were days when I needed sugar to slide around inside my mouth all smooth and golden and chewy, and I walked around salivating with a desire for soft lumps of toffee. Once I was so desperate I set about making some without a recipe, just melting and boiling up sugar with butter, and Silva lost her temper. She lifted the whole seething pan of it from the gas burner, carried it outside and tipped it all out on the ground, shouting at me that it was bad for me, bad for the baby, a waste of gas, a waste of sugar, I had ruined the pan. Not even then did I do more than protest I hadn't meant any harm. Actually I had already made up my mind to get Ron to bring me as much toffee as I could ever want. Silva need never know.

After that she wrote down her rules for my diet. She made a time-table with my hours all set out, for domestic tasks, periods of rest, gentle exercise. I wanted to laugh. She was rationing my knitting to an hour a day because, she said, pregnant women who knitted too much could produce confused babies. I went along with it, more or less. My days were all now so much the same, so uneventful and poised for this last period of waiting, that I didn't care what I did. It hardly mattered that Silva wanted to shift me along from one activity to the next according to her notion of what was good for the baby.

In fact, it suited me to let her do the thinking. While time was of course stretching forwards, I was basking in a dream that it stood still. Insofar as I bothered to grasp that everything was about to change, I was enjoying not knowing quite what to expect. I never once thought of pain, for instance. I had the dreamiest notions about breastfeeding. I trusted myself to deal with these things naturally, when the time came. It was as much as I could do, day by day, to heft around this massive body of mine and make sense of the idea that all it was, for the time being, was a vault for the round bulk of baby pushing harder and harder against its walls.

Still, eventually I said I should find a doctor and make arrange-ments. Silva was reluctant at first. I don't think she wanted me to hear any advice that might compete with hers, or get the idea that anyone but she was managing my pregnancy. So, more for vigilance than support, she came with me.

I stood no chance of making it up the slope through the pine trees, so very early one morning Ron took us in the boat to the other side of the river where he picked up the catering crew. Silva and I walked to the service station and waited there for a bus. We were in the centre of Inverness before half-past six. It was a blowy, colourless morning, and the pavement at the bus station where we stepped off was dark and cold in the long, early shadow cast by high buildings; seagulls squabbled over discarded food wrappers blowing along the gutter. The air was brackish with the exhaust fumes of arriving and departing buses, and already the city was noisy with traffic. We hung around until the bus station coffee stall opened at seven o'clock, and we bought muffins and tea. There wasn't a proper seat in the place, just a ledge, and the ground was littered with cigarette ends and was dark with the stains of drink and dropped food and urine. My back ached and I kept yawning. The tea was both weak and bitter, and I said I felt sick and wished I was still in bed.

Silva told me to shut up. It wasn't unusual for her to say that kind of thing, but away from the cabin it sounded harsh and different, a way of being spoken to that I should not have had to get used to. Still, I didn't let it bother me. I remember gazing at her profile as she swallowed her tea and thinking how thin her cheeks were, how much more in need of a doctor she looked than I did. I took her hand and whispered my thanks to her for bringing me. And then, although it hadn't crossed my mind before, I told her that she would be the first to hold the baby. She turned with a gasp. Then she squeezed my hand and smiled, a shining smile full of delight that I had never seen on her face before and that revealed, perhaps, her delight in having me confirm something she had already decided.

We waited until nearly eight o'clock and then caught a bus to the surgery, which opened at half-past. Of course, we had had no idea how to find a doctor in Inverness, so Ron had done an Internet search for us and printed out details of the largest surgery in the city. It wasn't in the centre, but it had ten doctors as well as nurses and mid-wives and other staff, and I hoped it would be busy and impersonal, too system-bound to probe into my circumstances. I didn't want to be treated as a person, just as a container that might need technical help to empty it of its load of baby.

I was glad to see that the building was modern and low, an austere, small institution, its entrance doors plastered with notices. Inside, we joined the queue at the receptionist's window. When my turn came, there were several people behind me and within earshot. Silva kept turning and glaring at them.

"Yes?"

I opened my mouth and stalled. The receptionist had begun writing and I didn't like to speak to the top of her head.

"Hello, *yes*?" She looked up with a micro-smile, no more than a twitch of the mouth.

"Sorry, yes, hello… I've just moved here," I said. "I wonder if I—"

"You want to register," she said, rolling herself a few feet back on her office chair and reaching into a filing cabinet. "Both of you?"

"No! Not me," Silva said. "Only her."

"Do you want the forms in English? We've got them in other languages," she said, rolling back.

"I'm just having a baby," I blurted. "I don't need a doctor for anything else. I'm just having a baby."

The receptionist sat up higher in her chair and looked at my belly, nodded, then swung herself over to another filing cabinet.

"You want Maternity Services. Here's the antenatal questionnaire as well. We'll need details of your previous GP. Once you've registered, we book you in for an assessment with the community midwife. Antenatal clinic's Tuesday morning, you need to attend weekly from thirty-five weeks. Postcode?"

"Postcode? Oh, I don't know," I said. "Sorry."

"What's your address? You have to be resident within the practice area."

"Oh, yes. I mean, we're just moving in. I don't have it on me."

I had thought up an address, but suddenly I didn't dare give it. I felt certain this woman had an encyclopedic memory of Inverness and knew the sound of every doorbell in every street.

Silva pushed forwards and pulled at my arm. "Come on, we don't need this!" she said fiercely. "Let's go, come on!"

"Silva, wait. Just a minute," I said. I smiled at the receptionist. "Sorry."

Silva pushed her face to the window. "She'll come back another day. She has many weeks still, maybe eight, nine. It's not urgent."

The receptionist ignored her and handed me several sheets of paper through the window. "If you want to see a doctor today you'll need to wait till the end of surgery. First you need to fill in the new patient registration form, the patient questionnaire, and also the antenatal questionnaire. We'll also need your medical card, passport or other photo ID, proof of address, and contact details of your previous medical practitioner."

She looked past me to the next person in the queue. "Yes?"

Silva steered me out and strode off. She kept walking until we were several streets away and slowed only as we reached a park with paths and litter bins and a tatty children's playground. She marched through the gates and sat down on a bench, and I followed, exhausted and sweating. She pulled the papers from my hands and sifted through them.

"Questions, so many! For one baby! Why?"

I pulled the papers back and began to read them. I could give a false name and address. I could make up a name for my previous doctor. I could say I had lost my medical card and leave my National Insurance number blank. They might not follow those up straight away.

But the questions became more nosy, more dangerous. How would I rate my feelings about my pregnancy from one to five,

255

extremely negative to highly positive? Did I live with a partner? How many adults, smokers and non-smokers, were living at my address, and were any unemployed? Were there domestic pets or other animals at the premises? I could give false answers to all of them, too, but if I turned up every Tuesday at an antenatal clinic, there would be more and more questions. Soon I would make a mistake or give something away. If I registered, but didn't go to the clinic, they would make enquiries and find out I had lied. And once they knew I wasn't Annabel, what else would they uncover? The newspapers had said nothing about the missing woman tourist being pregnant, but that didn't mean Col hadn't told the police that I was.

Col. I had a sudden recollection of him as I had last seen him, his stricken face as he turned away from the wrecked bridge. But I could not undo what I had done.

"They want to know everything," I said. "If I don't tell them they'll find out anyway."

Silva's face was white. "You shouldn't go back there," she said. "If you do, when the baby's born they'll take it away. It was a stupid idea to come."

"What am I supposed to do when I go into labour? I can't have the baby all on my own. What if something goes wrong?"

Silva stood up and started walking. "You just have to go to hospital. Ron will take us. It will be fine."

I was surprised at how relaxed she was about it.

"You mean just turn up?" I said. "They'll think that's very odd, they'll ask me all sorts of questions. They'll interfere."

"So? Have you done a crime, to have a baby? No. They will look after you. Then afterwards we'll leave with the baby, they can't stop us."

"And you'll come with me?"

"Sure, of course! Ron will take us in the boat, then the Land Rover. Then after, he comes again to pick us up in the Land Rover. Four of us!"

She looked almost happy.

"Then everything can get back to normal," I said. "Then we'll decide what to do next."

On the way back she was silent. Just before we got off the bus, she turned to me and said, "I'm going to look after you."

There's that rock in the river you used to watch, the one you only see at the ebb tide, a long, low, shining lump of black. The geese and gulls land and feed around it, but no bird nests there, because once a day the water swirls over and covers it again and the birds fly off. Between it and the forest bank of the river, there are other, smaller rocks in the water, some flat and some jagged, set in a loose tumble as if they landed there from a prehistoric avalanche. For all I know, they did. The water collects and turns all around them, and maybe it's also because of the rocks that the river flows in strongly just there and has worn a curve in the bank. Or maybe it's because the ground in that particular place is so soft to begin with, formed of nothing but disintegrating acid shreds of forest soil that are easily licked out from the pine roots by the tongue of the tide. Either way, the water has washed the soil away and borne it down to the riverbed, and it has hollowed out a tiny bay in the bank right into the base of the trees, leaving their roots under a thin mortar of salty dried mud. They look greyish and gappy, like old teeth. And other stones, dragged in from the sea on the high winter currents and dropped there, are daily pulled and rolled up the beach by the methodical tide into an arrangement of ridges, the boulders lodged farthest up, a scree of stones you can walk on, and little pebbles and broken seashells shirring to and fro at the water's edge.

Here is where I sit most often to think about you, close in by the trees in the deepest part of the curve and hidden from Ron or Anna-bel, who might just be (though seldom are) strolling along the river from the bridge or from the cabin. Here is where I began, without knowing that was what I was doing, to build.

One day I saw two stones side by side not far from where I sat, and it so happened I noticed them in a spell of numbness when I was nei-ther talking aloud to you, nor crying. In fact I was caught off guard, when I was not thinking of anything at all. Of these two stones, one was large and dark and squarish and had a ribbon of quartz running through it. The other was pale and much smaller, and its rounded surface sparkled with dots of mica. It was touching the other one in a way that made me think of a person whose forehead was resting against the chest of someone bigger. They leaned towards each other, joined and motionless, arrested in the moment just before they would embrace. That was the remarkable thing, that their absolute stillness held within it an intimation of a movement yet to happen. Father and child. I moved closer, my eyes travelling across every line and plane, gauging the shape of the empty space around them, measuring the distance between. And as I gazed at the point where the two stones tilted and met – the touching of forehead to chest – I felt the world shrink around me. This was surprising, because what I was looking at were, after all, lumps of stone.

Yet I wanted them kept exactly this way, leaning together, and I wanted to be able to find them again the next time I came. So I got up and gathered together a lot of the biggest stones I could lift and I set them, one by one, in a wide circle around my stones (and they were certainly, after my concentrated attention to them, mine, as if I had sculpted every angle myself). Then I saw that one of the large stones I'd placed in the circle was crusted with dead strands of waterweed, blackened and brittle from the sun. This displeased me. I carried it down to the river and cleaned it and set it back in its place.

Now inside their circle, my pair of stones looked diminished and without distinction. So I began clearing the space between them and the circle, lifting away pebbles and digging my stones in with my hands to fix them precisely, so elaborating, without changing it, their relationship to each other. My mind was absolutely clear about how these two figures should look. Yes, they were now *figures*. When I had finished, they stood proud on a flat bed of shingle within the low ring of stones.

After that, every time I came there I set to work, adding a few more stones to the circle. To protect the figures, I told myself. I went up and down finding shards of slate and flat stones to keep the ring stable as it grew, then I added bulky stones again, for height. I made mistakes and learned as I went. As the circle rose up around the figures, there were collapses to deal with; I had to build, dismantle and rebuild. I needed to use smaller and smaller stones as it went higher, and I don't know why I didn't abandon the whole thing when it became irksome to go searching for just the right stone to keep going. Instead, feeling very clever, I started to bring Ron's hammers with me so I could break stones to the size I wanted. Nor did I know, when I loved the sight of my father-and-child stones, why I went on with a task that was going to conceal them from me. Because by then I had recognized that the ring of stones was a wall going up around my beloved ones.

After a few weeks, and almost imperceptibly at first, the wall began to incline inwards upon itself. At last I could see what was happening. With much trial and error, and slow and careful chipping, I fashioned long pieces of stone and slate and devised a way of laying them so they overlapped and evolved, finally, into a dome-like roof over the figures underneath. I had built a tomb.

I stayed away for a while after that, afraid that I would be too restless to let it alone, afraid I might take the whole thing down. But I drifted back, because now that you have a memorial, there are repairs to attend to, most days. I like to sit under the trees, to sit near you, the figures of you, invisible but close by and in the shadow of the trees. I like to be here at the time of the incoming current and watch the black rock disappear under the river until there is nothing to see except a patch of silver on the surface, strangely glassy and unrippled amid the running waters of the flood tide.

On the evening after the visit to the doctor in Inverness, Silva was full of a hard, snappy energy. Only six weeks to go, and was she the only one who was concerned? Six weeks! Her impatience, her air of unspoken superiority (what did either of them know about childbirth?) made Ron feel he had been lackadaisical in some way, while Annabel was simply worn out. While she dozed and half-listened, he watched, startled, as Silva talked, words flying from her mouth, about the new plans they now had to make. Though in fact she had made them already.

Annabel handed over her mobile phone, not used since the first night she'd turned up at the trailer. The next day Ron went after work to Inverness and bought a new charger for it, and that evening when it was working again Silva entered her own and Ron's numbers and explained once more how the system was going to work.

"We have phones switched on all the time, all day, OK? You don't go anywhere without phone, not even two minutes to the jetty," she told Annabel. "You're so heavy now, and what do you do if you fall? You take your phone in your pocket everywhere. Then, so, if I am along the river and there is a problem, if the pains come, straight away first you call me. Straight away, OK? Me first."

Annabel smiled and nodded from the sofa bed where she lay every evening now, her bare feet on two pillows. By the end of the day her ankles were swollen and her shoes tight.

"Then, if the pains are coming, I call you," Silva said to Ron. "So same for you, you keep your phone on. I call you and straight away you come to us here, straight in the boat. You bring her in the boat to the bridge, then we take her up to the Land Rover and we all go to hospital."

Ron nodded, too. Earlier that day, on Silva's orders, he had warned Mr Sturrock he might need to take some hours off at short notice.

"Or I might not, it depends," he'd said, not sure what mood Mr Sturrock was in. "I'm on standby. To take a... someone to hospital. She's having a baby soon."

"Fuck's sake. You having a wean? Congratulations in order, eh?" Mr Sturrock had said.

Immediately Ron not only corrected him but had an elaborate lie ready. No, he wasn't the father, in fact he hardly knew her, she was the partner of a friend of his. She wasn't due until the middle of October, but the friend was working on the rigs, putting in all the hours right through till the end of September, and they'd just moved and she had no family here. The friend could get off the rig in under three hours if the baby came early, but his partner was nervous. Ron was the backup to take her to hospital in case he was delayed. Almost certainly wouldn't be. It was just for her peace of mind.

Mr Sturrock had grumbled a little, then told him to inform the office if he had to go off-site and to keep his time sheet straight – oh, and be grateful he worked for a fool ready to let him away at the drop of a hat to be a fucking ambulance service.

Afterwards Ron wondered why he had lied at all, never mind so extravagantly. There had been no need to pretend that the mother was almost a stranger, he could have said that she and the baby were close to him without going into the peculiarity of their arrangement. Why, when every part of him wished he could be the child's father, was he so afraid that someone might suppose he was? Because he didn't deserve to be, that was it. What he deserved was what he most dreaded, to be found out for what he was instead: a man who had killed children. If that happened, Mr Sturrock – everybody – would turn on him, outraged that he was trying to pass himself off as fit to take care of anyone ever again. What he deserved was to feel like a monster for the rest of his life.

He and Annabel continued to bow under Silva's dictatorship. It was the price they paid to have her reanimated and back with them. It was lovely, they said to each other privately, to see her looking forward so much to the baby. A new life is a healing thing.

One day at low tide Silva untied the partly submerged white boat from the jetty and dragged it up onto the shore. Ron hadn't looked at it in months, but now she wanted it fixed up.

"Suppose the baby starts coming and we can't get hold of you?" she said.

She bailed out the rainwater and tipped the boat over, and Ron cleaned off enough of the clinging green weed to inspect the hull. It was sound, but the boat was barely eight feet long and made of a light plastic. A rowlock was hanging loose, and one of the oars was split at the handle end; although the paddle was in one piece, it would be difficult to use.

"We can mend it. Or we'll get another one," Silva decreed.

Ron laughed and chucked the broken oar on the ground. It would make a few sticks of kindling. "You can't go out in a thing that size, not even with two oars," he told her. "It's going nowhere, not without an outboard. Look at it. It'd be just about all right on a duck pond."

"But someone here before us must have gone out in it. Fishing, maybe."

Ron shrugged. "Probably brought it down here and realized it was useless in more than a breath of wind. Anyway, look at your arms.

You couldn't row three feet with Annabel on board. You'd never make it down to the bridge."

"I can row a boat all right," Silva said. "I want it ready, just in case."

He shook his head. "You wouldn't be safe," he said, and started back to the cabin, away from her objections. "There's no need, anyway," he said. "I'll be straight up in the launch when the time comes. It's all arranged."

In September, the weather suddenly turned colder. The cabin floors were damp all the time, and Ron began to wonder how he could put in a decent layer of insulation that wouldn't involve hours of disruption and threaten Annabel's calm. He thought carefully about her calm, and how to keep her cheerful. Lately, though she hadn't the will to withstand Silva, she was often tetchy with her. She complained of being bossed about, and being uncomfortable and bored. Silva was, by turns, impatient and morose, and she was also constantly watchful, like an investor with a stake in a dumb but valuable animal. Ron was struck by the simplicity of his function in it all, which was to move between the two women as a force dedicated to both of them equally, no matter how wayward or unaccountable either of them became.

Draughts whistled in through the windows and walls, and they had to keep the stove alight all day. He set to work on getting in a log supply for the months to come, but pine wood burned up fast, and he was having to go farther and farther into the forest to find dead trunks he could drag back for cutting. But it occurred to him over and over that secretly he was delighted all these obstacles had presented themselves, otherwise where else would he be now, what would he be doing?

More and more was being required of him, and it was exhausting, but also exhilarating. He loved how the land was sodden and chill and how the sky lowered; he hoped for a dramatic, freezing winter. All day long he walked around trying to keep his gratitude hidden.

The cranes and concrete pourers were at work; dull cranking sounds vibrated around the small group assembled on the jetty. Even after several months, the bridge talk was still an ordeal in public speaking for Mr Sturrock. He could not look at even familiar faces as if he had seen them before; he stared over his audience's heads for fear of making eye contact, and called above the noise.

"As you can see, the last segment has been brought along the new roadbed and the crane will lift it into position within the next forty-eight hours. This represents" – a gull streaked past him, shrieking – "a significant achievement, and not a little way ahead of schedule. Thank you for your attention, ladies and gentlemen," he added with a formal smile as he folded his speech back into his pocket.

The tiny group nodded. They had been expecting all this, because they had been on several bridge walks already. This was the very last one, and numbers had tailed off to just three; the bridge would be re-opening in a few weeks. Ron recognized every face, and so did Rhona and Mr Sturrock. Two of the three were a couple whose interest had become for some reason obsessive. Each time they made a day of it: after the tour they would drive up to Netherloch for lunch and in the afternoon walk through the forest to the top of the Netherloch Falls. There they would take photographs of the river snaking from the far end of the loch and widening into the distance as far as the bridge, and on the next bridge walk, after Mr Sturrock had finished, they would pass the new pictures around in a way that seemed to Ron strangely agitated and boastful, as if the gap between the broken bridge ends were being closed under their personal supervision. Today as usual the woman produced some new photographs, but apart from himself, Mr Sturrock and Rhona (who all saw the bridge every day), there was only Colin, the third member of the audience, to show them to. He took them reluctantly. The woman would not permit his indifference. She pointed out this and that detail, eager for him to show more pleasure. Not that she didn't understand that the restored bridge was no compensation for his loss, of course not, but still, a new bridge. That was something positive, wasn't it, something that would help everybody move on? Colin's big face worked away with an expression of polite interest. Handing back the last of the photographs, he sighed.

Rhona stepped forwards. As this was the final bridge talk, she said, she was sure the group would want to take this opportunity to join her in thanking Mr Sturrock. A thin, clacking round of applause rose and died. One by one the three shook Rhona's and Mr Sturrock's hands and then one another's, and they drifted away, pulling off their hard hats and depositing them on the ground at Rhona's feet. Colin lingered. It was four weeks since his tribute to the victims and his dead wife. Since then, he had been quieter than ever. He looked as if he might have wanted to speak, but instead nodded to Ron and turned away.

Rhona was applying something glittery to her lips and shaking out her hair. She grinned at Ron, who knew what was about to happen; she'd let him in on it two weeks ago, apologizing that she couldn't include him, too.

"And now, John," she said playfully, turning to Mr Sturrock. "I am spiriting you away. I'm taking you for lunch at the Royal Highland Hotel. I hope you're hungry?"

"What? Steady on, now. Lunch? The Royal Highland?" Sturrock said.

"It's on us. Just a wee thank-you from Forward Voice PR." She beamed. "As I shall put in my evaluation, your talks have helped us deliver a key campaign objective, rolling out the message to our community stakeholders."

He stared at her. "Fuck me. I can't just go off having *lunch*. I need to get back over the other side." He turned to Ron. "You need to get back over yourself, eh?"

"I'll be here when you're ready," Ron said, smiling.

"It's all arranged," Rhona said. "Our managing director Malcolm's going to join us, and so is Mrs Sturrock, so there you go. Table's booked. See you later, Ron. Thanks a lot for waiting."

Mr Sturrock was now pleasantly bewildered. "Christ, you in on it, too?" he said to Ron. "Well, thanks a bunch, son."

After they left, Ron picked up the hats and packed them in the boat, then walked over to get his own lunch at the service station. There were at least two hours to kill, and when he caught sight of Colin there, hunched at the same table as last time, for a moment he considered slipping away. But Colin looked up and saw him, so he bought sandwiches and tea and joined him at the table. From Colin's face, it was obvious there was no right thing Ron could say, but it wasn't possible to say nothing at all.

"So. That's the last of the bridge walks. That's it, now," he offered, hoping Colin would pick up on the idea of their finality. What else could the man do? It *was* the last; there was nothing more to be said or done. Ron knew he was being lazy about Colin's suffering, but he couldn't enter into it. He didn't really like him. While Colin certainly had ample cause to suffer, Ron suspected he was in any case inclined to self-pity.

"If you're about to say something about moving on, don't bother," Colin said. He pulled his pudgy fingers across his face before he spoke again. "That woman with her fucking photos."

Ron shrugged. "Yeah, sorry, mate. It's still tough going, is it?"

"Her, everybody. People at work. The number of people that say it. *Moving on*. They say maybe it's a blessing I didn't know her that long, like that makes it better."

"Aren't they just trying to help?"

"They think I should be getting over it. Some people tell me I'm lucky, I should be glad I wasn't in the car with her."

He blew his nose into a rag of used paper handkerchief with an embarrassing, piteous honk that blasted little wisps of tissue across his chin and cheeks.

"So, anyway, that's the last of the bridge walks," Ron said. "No more trailing up and down from Huddersfield. You'll be getting your weekends back, a bit of time to yourself. Any plans?"

Colin glared at him. "I'll still be coming. Why would I not still come? She's still here."

"Oh. OK. Sorry, I didn't mean—"

"You know the worst thing people say? They say I should be glad we weren't married long enough to have kids. Because imagine what that'd be like, they'd have lost their mother and I'd be left to cope on my own."

Ron knew how this line of thinking went: grief for loss of what you did have, beside grief for loss of what you did not but might have had, is a lesser grief. He also knew this thinking for what it was, the well-meaning, ill-contrived and fatuous condolence of outsiders, people uninitiated in loss.

"It's not like that," he says.

"No," Colin says, his voice faltering. "They don't know how stupid it is. They don't know how cruel."

"They don't mean to be cruel. Nobody understands what it's like to lose somebody until it happens to them."

"I don't mean that," Colin said. Then his face collapsed and his shoulders started to shudder. The used tissue went up to his eyes, but huge, splattery tears were already dropping on the front of his clothes. Ron watched them roll like raindrops down his barrel chest. "I mean don't they think I'd be glad if there was a kid? Don't they think I'd *want* to bring it up? I'd do it now if I could, I'd do it right, by both of them. I wish she knew that. I wish we'd had the kid. But we didn't, and now it's too late."

"The kid?" Ron says. "You mean you lost one, you lost a baby? I'm really sorry. That's really tough."

Colin nodded and cried noisily into his hands. "I never thought I'd want them both so much. They've both gone and it's my fault. Nobody knows. Nobody knows."

"It's not your fault, mate. Listen, it happens. Miscarriages happen. Nobody's to blame." Ron now wanted to offer comfort to this large, off-putting man, but his words were having no effect. "Here," he said, pushing Colin's mug towards him. "Here, go on, take a swig of that. You need to calm down."

To his surprise, Colin meekly swallowed some tea, then took another mouthful.

"No point falling apart, is there," Ron said. "Doesn't get you anywhere."

"Sorry. Gets to me, that's all." Colin drew a hand over his face.

"Nobody's to blame," Ron said again. "Miscarriages aren't anybody's fault."

Colin drank more of his tea in silence. After a while, he said in a flat voice, "She was pregnant. I didn't tell the police. Nobody knew but me."

"Why not? Why make a secret of it?"

Colin let out a massive sigh. "I felt guilty. Ashamed. Too ashamed to say."

Ron was confused. "I'm telling you, a miscarriage isn't anybody's fault, mate."

Colin sighed again and took a deep breath. "I'm trying to tell you. There wasn't a miscarriage. She was pregnant. What happened, see, I told her to get rid of it. The day before she died I told her she couldn't have a kid and me as well, I said I'd leave."

Ron stared at him. Colin's face was pulpy and unwell-looking; his eyes had an off-centre, uneven way of blinking. It occurred to Ron that remorse was, literally, a sickness. Colin was so sick, so unbalanced by it, he looked in danger of falling apart.

"She was my wife. She was going to be the mother of my kid, and I said that to her. I can't believe I said that to her," Colin said. "And now there is not one single reason I don't want that kid. I want them both, and there's nothing I can do about it."

Ron said quietly, "Do you have a photo of her?"

"No. To be honest, I can't stand to see her face. Only had a few pictures, anyway." Colin tapped his head. "She's in my mind. I see her face in my mind. But only here, I only see her when I come here. She hated Huddersfield, she didn't like the house. I didn't really listen. I should've done a lot of things different."

Ron let his breath out slowly. "We could all say that, mate."

I think a lot about Col, lying here. Not any more in the panicky, guilty way of a few months ago, but with a strand of regret I follow right back to the day I chose to disappear, a day I now perceive as marked as much by regret as by catastrophe. Not that Col will be feeling that. I'm certain he is back sympathetically engrossed in the caregivers' chat room, untroubled by ever having known me.

I think of our early days together, how to begin with I did not feel very much at all except embarrassment at living with a near stranger. But now I'm almost nostalgic for that early awkwardness: our misdirected attempts at endearments, my pursuit of some improved neatness in the arrangements of the house, his wordless, ritualized moves in bed. It touches me to remember the way every night he launched himself at me without speaking, his efforts to please, his mountainous heavings on and off. I forgive myself my mute acquiescence (I thought it sophisticated to have nothing to say at such times), which matched his lack of words. I can imagine the conversations we should have had, the conversations we lay so self-consciously *not* having afterwards, in the dark, but our silence strikes me now as more like generosity tongue-tied than disappointment throttling itself before it can cry out.

Anyway, it will surely happen one day that I'll be called upon to give some account to my child of its father, and by then words will have come to me and I shall have them waiting, as if written down and placed in an envelope, sealed and put by. I do not have them ready at present, but it will be years before I need them. When the time comes I will know what to say, surely.

Ron comes into the cabin scraping his feet, and dumps a heap of damp wood by the stove. This is what he does every evening; after he's tied up the boat he collects an armful of logs from the pile by the sawhorse he's set up between the jetty and the cabin and trudges up with it and adds it to our store. He'll make several more trips over the evening; against the thin cabin wall, on either side of the stove, an inner wall of logs is building up. It is shoulder-high already and rising in an uneven wave, and Silva keeps telling him not to make it much higher as we can't stand on chairs to get logs down every time we need to stoke the fire.

"How are you doing today?" he asks me routinely, as he starts to stack the new batch of logs.

Silva appears from the kitchen with a knife in her hand. "She got too tired," she answers for me. It so happens she is wrong; I was out of doors and out of her sight for over an hour, that's all that *too tired* means. But I don't contradict her, I just smile.

"I'm fine," I tell him. "I went for a nice long stroll. I sat down and rested every five minutes," I add, before Silva can lecture me again about drawing blood away from the baby.

She gives a snort. "Look at the colour of her, she's white like a sheet of paper. Ugh, don't put that one on, it's filthy. Don't make it any higher there, the whole thing will fall over." She returns to the kitchen, and Ron continues to stack.

When I'm resting here and watching him, I like to conjure animal faces out of the rings and whorls of the newly sawn log ends he puts in place: one looks like an owl, another is a baboon, yet another is a cat wearing spectacles. When this wall's complete, Ron intends to start on the adjoining wall, and once that's done he'll replenish our stocks as they go down. Not only will we have good, dry fuel all the time, he says, but double wooden walls provide excellent insulation. It's what they do in Norway, and there's not much you can teach a Norwegian about insulation. I'm sure this is true, but of course as the wall goes up our room grows smaller. You might even say it's closing in on us; it does smell blocked and earthy, with an end-of-year whiff that carries a note of decay. And the new wall is full of trapped, trembling insects. Whenever I lift a log to put on the stove, it comes away from the pile with a gauzy trail of tearing spider webs, gritty with rotting bark and mould and sawdust. Silva says mice will move in, and Ron laughs and says even mice need to live somewhere, and at least the wood will stay dry enough to burn.

"So you are all right?" he asks, as he's putting the last logs in place.

"Yes, I'm fine. I'm so lazy, I'm too heavy to do anything much," I say.

"He was there again today, that bloke from Huddersfield. Colin. The bloke whose wife died."

I pick up my knitting from the floor and fiddle with it. "How is he? Did he speak to you?"

"He says he's going to keep coming. Every weekend."

"What's the point in that now the walks are finished? He should stay away."

"There's a point in it for him. They still haven't found her. Have you ever been to Huddersfield?"

"No, never." I haul myself up till I'm sitting on the sofa bed, and I start on a row of knitting. "If I go for it, I think I could get this sleeve finished by bedtime."

"Annabel, where is it you're from?" Ron asks. He is breaking the rule. No matter that the rule is unstated, it has held us together for months. The rule is that the three of us ended up here by ways and means we don't have to explain. Ron knows that.

"What does it matter?" I say. "I don't ask you questions like that. I don't have the right. There's no need for me to know. And what about her?" I nod towards the kitchen, where the radio is blaring music. "Are you going to start asking her that kind of question? She'll run a mile. You shouldn't—"

Just then Silva walks in again, carrying a plate of bread. She looks tired in a way only a much older person should look. I can't be sure what she heard or didn't hear. She waits for me to finish what I was saying.

"You shouldn't stack the logs so high. Silva's right." I put the knitting aside and get up. "I need to stretch my legs," I tell them, and leave.

It's too cold to stay out without another sweater, and in fact I am too tired to walk far. I go down to the jetty and look back at the cabin, its windows glowing with firelight, squares of soft yellow in the grainy, grey dusk. The baby's weight makes me breathless. All I want is to go back inside, all I want is to carry on living by the rules that have served us well enough, but what awaits me in the yellow light is altered now. The door opens and Ron steps out. I turn away and stare at the river, listening to his footsteps on the shingle coming nearer and then the hard clump as he walks along the jetty and stands next to me. I am too angry to say anything.

He sighs, lifts a hand and strokes my hair. He is crying.

"He wants you back" is all he says before he unties the boat and climbs in, starts the motor and moves off into the tide flowing down towards the bridge. I wait until I'm shivering before I go back to the cabin. Silva is coming out of the kitchen with three plates, and when I tell her Ron has left she thinks it is because she spoke sharply to him about the logs. She is peeved and difficult all evening. In truth she exhausts me. Later I go to bed, and although the baby kicks and kicks I fall asleep. I'm glad I'm too tired to dwell on the strange truth that now that Ron may know who I am, I feel more unknown than ever.

She lies there. She lies there breathing with her mouth open while the stove burns low and the knitting comes apart in her hands, because her hands feel nothing, not the metal knitting needles that are hot from the fire or the stitches slipping off past her fat finger ends or the unravelling wool settling over the creases at her wrist. The hands don't move. The fingers look boneless, like stuffed tubes, her nails are sunk into the tips like flat baby buttons pushed into dough. She's on her back like a sleeping sow, her breath whistling in her throat, eyelashes twitching on her pink face. Her chest moves up and down, her breasts lift and collapse over her bulging stomach. Her giant bare feet look too lumpy to walk on. They still bear semicircular ridges across the fronts where the swollen flesh has bulged from her over-tight shoes, which lie splayed and distorted on the floor beside her.

I watch her for more than an hour.

"I told you you were too tired," I say in a loud voice, and I go to the table and make a noise clearing our plates and taking them to the kitchen. Her phone is also on the table and I clear that away to the kitchen, too. I have to do everything. Every evening I check that it's charged and working. She can't be trusted to.

When I come back she is awake and sitting up with the knitting in her lap, trying to push her feet into her shoes.

"You'll split them," I tell her. "You can't get them on any more. They don't fit."

"I know they don't," she says calmly. "But it's not worth getting new ones now. They'll fit me again as soon as the baby's born." She smoothes a hand over her belly and picks up the knitting, frowning at it.

"Oh dear, you shouldn't have let me fall asleep," she says, yawning, picking at the yarn with the needles. "Look at this mess."

"Don't blame me," I say. "I told you you were too tired."

She pauses with the knitting and looks at me, and then gets up, sighing. "I'm not blaming you, Silva. I'm going to bed."

"I suppose I'll clear up, then," I say.

Another sigh. "I'm happy to do it in the morning, but I'm very tired now. Please leave everything. I'll do it in the morning."

"Leave everything dirty all night? No. That's not how I am. You can go to bed if you like."

"Just leave it, Silva, it won't matter. I'll do it in the morning. Good night."

She shambles off without another word, bent over with her hands on the small of her back, her fat feet half out of her shoes. She doesn't walk like that when Ron is here. I want to tell her I know about them. Does she think I'm stupid? I see their faces, I know they whisper away together. I heard them at it this evening, and when I appeared she pretended she was talking about the logs. I want to tell her Ron is as much mine for the taking as hers, I could have him if I chose to. Then it would be me he gives whatever I ask for on a plate, it would be me he's ready to drop everything for, take anywhere I want. She has everything, and she deserves nothing.

She must be making all her plans. She must be feeling very clever. I am so angry I am going to have to cry. But I can't bear to go to my room, where I have nothing of you but your photographs, while she lies on the other side of the wall stroking that belly of hers, thinking of that baby, smiling to herself. I go back to the kitchen and pick up her phone. I check it, and it's just as I suppose: she's got it on silent. That will be so she can carry on text conversations with him all day, even while I'm around. Making all their plans for after the baby. How and when they are going to leave me.

I look at the Inbox and yes, of course there's a message from Ron, and in the Sent box is her reply.

HELD UP IN QUEUE. SEE YOU CAR PARK 4.30. DID YOU GET BANDAGE FOR S?

THX OK. YES. ALSO GETTING SAVLON + AFTERSUN.

Both messages are from a Sunday in late August, not long after she tried to see the doctor in Inverness and I'd made her start carrying her phone again. On the Sunday morning I'd cut my hand with a chisel, chipping stones for your memorial. It was a baking-hot afternoon, and I came back to the cabin with my shoulders and nose red and sore and my hand wrapped in the bloodied folds of my skirt. Annabel patched me up using small bandages and tissues and asked Ron to take her to the chemist in Netherloch. Ron said he needed some white spirit anyway, so they went, and she bought bandages and also lotion for my shoulders.

When they got back she cleaned the cut and dressed it, then she dabbed the sunburn lotion on me. She put the bottle in the fridge so it would be extra cold and soothing for the next time I needed it. She thought I was crying because my skin was sore, but I was crying for her kindness and how cared-for I felt. How long ago that is.

There are no other text messages from Ron since then, and only three or four from me. That means the ones they've been sending each other since she's been deleting as she goes, in case I find them. If she's doing that, I must be right to worry. Maybe it started longer ago than I think. Suddenly I recall the day in July when Ron brought the paper with the photographs of your chain and Anna's giraffe. They sat up that night together, waiting for me to sleep. Was that when they began to say to each other they would be better off without me? How long have those looks between them being going on, those conversations that stop the moment I come into the room?

There is nothing on voicemail. Now I scroll through the call records and between late August and now, there are no numbers either received or dialled except mine. Scrolling back, I find there is nothing at all between late August and February.

But on the eighteenth of February she called another number. On the nineteenth, she missed and received calls from the same number. It's a number so familiar to me, but so out of place and time, that at first I don't believe what I'm seeing. I get my own phone and look. Of course I know I am right, I am merely putting off the moment of acceptance. For a time I look from one number to the other, a phone in the palm of each hand, checking every digit, until I cannot deny it.

The person who called her on the nineteenth of February was you. Were you replying to her calls to you on the eighteenth? There are none before that and, of course, none since. My mouth is dry, and a kind of creak comes from my throat. Something is robbing me of the strength to call out. I drink a cup of water, and another.

Less than three hours before you and Anna were thrown off the bridge in a car rented by a woman whose body has never been found, you spoke to Annabel. This Annabel who lies in the next room, who that night wandered the choked roads with nowhere to go and came knocking on our trailer door. Annabel who collapsed sick and helpless in front of me the next morning and after that never left, and has never said who she is. She attached herself to me as if her arrival did not need explaining, and by the time I thought to ask her about it, she told me that she stayed with me to help me. If I shook her awake now she would say the same thing, in her flat, lazy way. She says she found the trailer by accident. But the trailer was not in a place she could have found by accident. I calculate quickly.

I'll never know all the small twists in the story that brought you to be in her car, but I can work out enough of it. I know her dates. Did she pick you up when you were working in the White Hart, over New Year? Was she there for the holidays, with the husband? There was a row with the husband, is that it? Then she comes on to you and you're drunk and angry with me, angry enough to give her what she asks for, a fuck against the wall? That's what happened. I know what you can be like. That's why she came back in February, it's why she's been hiding from the husband who can't keep away from the bridge. She came back to get you for herself, and when she couldn't, she made you give her money instead. The money she's so generous with is our money. Maybe you took her car, left her stranded somewhere, I don't care. You wouldn't have been in it at all but for her. What happened is her doing. She killed you, and she killed our daughter. She left me with nothing. And she is carrying your child.

Now there is a wet, smug snoring coming from her room. This fat and greedy taker of all the space and air and all my careful provisioning in this place also took you from me. My legs shake, and vomit rises from my stomach. My baby girl in that car, you twisting and trying to reach her, the pocket of air bubbling away while you push at the door against the weight of the river, the dense water swallowing you. You were too late to hold my baby in your arms.

There's a cough, the bed creaks. She's heaving the great bulk of her body around, shifting the living flesh of your child inside her. My child is dead, and this one is alive. It kicks and squirms and presses down on her; she whispers to it, she pats it, she tells it she loves it.

I stand in the kitchen and think of the times you and I sat by the river and spoke of the next child we would have and, God willing, the children after that. We talked of Anna being a big sister to them all, how they would go to school and squabble and play and grow up. Now this woman who stole my child lies with another in her belly. It, too, is a child stolen from me, and from you.

I remember all the other nights when Ron was here, the soft shufflings at Annabel's door, their voices, a needle of candlelight gleaming through a split in the partition wall. They must think I am stupid. Then utter darkness and stillness within the cabin, and outside, the river under the moon running silently seaward on the ebb tide.

On Sunday, Ron was on call for extra transport runs. Two weeks ahead of the bridge's completion date, more workers were being brought in to work more shifts, seven days a week. He was pleased to have a real reason not to see Annabel that day; he needed some time to think. He sent her a text message to explain why he could not come. Then he sent another one saying he would no longer be able to come to the cabin every evening, but he would be there whenever he could. There was no reply. He sent another message reassuring her that he would still go off-duty the moment he was needed, to get her to hospital. She or Silva had only to call, and he'd be at the cabin within minutes. Even from the farthest point on the opposite bank, it would take him less than half an hour to reach her. He ended the message with "Hope you're OK. Don't worry about anything."

She didn't reply. He called her number. Silva answered and said that Annabel was resting. An hour later he got a text message from her: "Missed yr call sorry. If evenings busy no problem don't come. Will call you when it's time for hospital. I'm fine. A."

On Monday, Silva called him. "She's fine, but she's got to that stage she doesn't really want a man around her. She doesn't want anyone to see her, she doesn't want to go out. It makes her feel awkward. It's how women are, just before. She needs to be with other women. When the labour starts, that's when she'll need you."

It was the natural way of things, Ron believed, that no man was capable of understanding this fully, and it would be pointless for him to try; it was important only that he accept it. This was a time for Annabel, for any woman, to be as fickle as she chose. The only proper response was to hope for nothing more than to be of service to her, on her terms, when the time came. He had never before been so close to this most female and ancient mystery, and was, in fact, a little afraid of it; the secrecy surrounding a woman soon to give birth both entranced and repelled him. He understood now, he felt, the sentimentality and awe of fertility worship. Though Annabel with her slatternly ways was unlikely goddess material, he was not really surprised to find that he was ready to do absolutely anything for her.

"I can still come," he said to Silva, "just not so often. I'll talk to her and see what she wants."

"No. She said she doesn't want to tell you herself, she doesn't want to hurt your feelings. But she definitely just wants me around, for the last few weeks. Maybe it's because I'm a mother."

"Well, but what will you do for food? You'll need to go shopping."

"We're fine. I can get up to the road and into Netherloch. I'll let you know if we need anything."

"Well, OK. I'm on call for anything, all right? Tell her that. Tell her she can call any time, just for a chat. Or text. And if she changes her mind—"

"I'll tell her. Must go, bye," Silva said, and hung up.

I have no shoes.

I got up late and couldn't find them, even though I knew I'd taken them off sitting on my bed, as usual. I must have kicked them underneath, I thought, and the size I am now I couldn't go scrabbling about hunting for them, so I went on bare feet to the cabin door, which was open. From there I smelled burning and I saw Silva a little way down the shore poking at a fire in the barbecue, and I yelled at her I'd lost my shoes and would she come and help me find them. She turned away, took the tongs and lifted one of my shoes out of the fire. She was laughing. She held it up high to show me. Flames were licking through the rope sole and canvas. Ashy shreds and melting drops of rubber were falling off it.

Even though it was really too late to save it, I had to get down there to stop her. But I couldn't get farther than the concrete at the doorway. The stones surrounding it were sharp and cold, and slippery. I yelped and stepped back and burst into tears. "What are you doing? Those are my only shoes!"

"They don't fit you," Silva called. "And they stink!"

She dropped the shoe she was holding back in the fire and lifted the other. There was less than half of it left, only a blackened piece of the sole with a rag of burnt fabric attached.

"You're mad! What am I supposed to wear?"

She dropped it, too, and stirred the fire around, then put down the tongs and walked calmly back. "They're not worth crying over. They were bad for your feet. And you lie around all day, you don't need shoes," she said, walking past me.

"Of course I need shoes! I can't go out without shoes!"

"Well, there might be flip-flops in Netherloch. I'll get you some. If I go."

That was four days ago, and she hasn't been anywhere except to her place along the river. I've put my phone somewhere, and I can't find it, so I asked her to call Ron and get him to buy trainers or something for me and bring them next time he comes. But he hasn't come.

"Where's Ron? When is he coming, did he say?" I ask.

Apart from anything else, my feet are cold most of the time, and I can hardly reach my toes to rub them. There were some thick socks of Ron's around somewhere, but I can't find them now, either.

"He's busy, he said. There's a lot going on to get the bridge ready in time."

"But he hasn't been here all week. He never misses more than a day. Ask him when he's coming."

"He's extra busy. He'll come when he can."

"I'm going to find my bloody phone and call him and see if he's all right. It must be somewhere. Have you seen it?"

"I haven't seen it for days."

I look for it again all morning but I don't find it. These days everything's in a muddle and things do go astray. It's somewhere around, no doubt. But Silva's never far away, so it's not essential for me to have it to hand. I ask her to send Ron another message, asking him to come as soon as he can, with some shoes.

"I still can't find my phone. And I do need shoes," I tell her when we have lunch, which is pasta again, with something out of a tin. "I have to get out. I'm supposed to walk every day! Please ask him if he can get something size forty."

"I'll ask him," she tells me. "There's no need to get upset. You're getting yourself in a state."

"No wonder! I haven't been able to get farther than the door!"

"It's quite normal to feel restless at this stage. But you should be doing less, not more."

"And ask if he can bring some apples or something. Or oranges. Tomatoes, anything fresh."

"I'll ask him. But he's very busy. Go and rest."

This is how it goes every day now. She's always telling me I'm too restless, and probably I am, but never for long. After a while a terrible listlessness will creep over me and I have to give in to it. I lose things and get annoyed with myself (the phone still hasn't turned up), and I'll try to settle to some knitting or tidying, but very often I just sit or lie looking at the ceiling. My back aches all the time.

I miss Ron. He has told Silva he'll be here any day, but still he doesn't come. She feeds me in the middle of the day now, big, hot platefuls of spaghetti with tomato sauce, or macaroni cheese, and I eat from boredom, not knowing where I have room to put so much food. Afterwards I'm even more sleepy. When I've rested I often feel bloated and itchy, so I'll go out and stand on the freezing damp concrete for a few moments to breathe in cool air and look at the river. The scent of pine from the forest has turned brackish, and every day the sky is full of geese, circling in wide, fluttering arrows, preparing to migrate. If it's not raining, I drag a chair to the doorway and sit and watch them for a while, wretchedly sluggish, wondering if even after the birth my distended, straining body will ever feel or look like mine again. But my feet are always freezing, and it's too cold to stay there, even wrapped up, and anyway soon Silva complains I'm letting cold air in, or blocking her way.

Ron went back to sleeping every night in the mobile unit with the other men. His reappearance went without comment, because neither his presence to begin with nor his many later absences had been noticed particularly; the unit was a place where the men went just to sleep, and there was a high turnover of occupants as shift patterns became more complex.

In the canteen a row erupted over all the extra men Jackson the cook was now expected to cater for; he stormed out and was replaced by a young man called O'Dowd, who went through his working day saying as little as possible. His sullenness spread, somehow, or maybe it was just a deeper concentration now that the end of the project was in sight, or maybe it was simple fatigue that had set in among the men. In any case, there was less banter, and that suited Ron. He felt some of the old knack return to him, acquired after his release from prison, of concentrating only on what was in front of him, on the immediate task in hand, no matter how trivial. He made himself notice frivolous details: the tiny *whoosh* of a cascade of sugar from the packet into a mug of tea, the smell of rain on concrete, the colour of toothpaste. He moved from job to job in this way, trying not to think about Annabel, refusing to bring to mind Colin's face and voice, and still less his words. Suppose he was wrong about it all? Suppose Annabel wasn't the missing wife? Why had he interfered? If she was his wife, and she wanted to keep away from him, why shouldn't she?

It was none of his business. Yet the thought of it – a father grieving unnecessarily for his unborn baby and its mother – nagged at him.

He couldn't stop himself sending Annabel messages every day to tell her he'd come as soon as she wanted him to. Only occasional, meaninglessly breezy answers came back. He called her a number of times, but she never picked up. He tried Silva several times also, and she answered once. Her reassurance that all was well was terse. He wasn't wanted. He decided to go on forcing the small things to absorb him, immersing himself in a private world deliberately shrunk to leave little room for hurt.

Do you remember Anna's birth? I never saw you so scared, before or since. I can still see your face, and I can hear her first squeezed-out, mewly cry. I hardly remember the pain.

I'm watching Annabel carefully, but not in the way she thinks. She can't think, actually. She's lost the power of thought. She's had only three contractions and it's nearly two hours since the first one, but she's been fretting and hefting herself around as if she's got a bucking bull in there. Weeping, now.

"Try him again! Why isn't he answering? He promised, oh, he promised," she wails.

"Don't worry," I say. "Don't worry, you've got hours and hours yet. I'm sure he's still busy and can't pick up his voicemails, that's all. He must be busy at the bridge. It reopened today, you know."

She does, of course, know. We watched it all from here. The bridge reopened at noon, and traffic has been streaming along it for four hours. Now the afternoon is fading and the bridge lights sparkle in strings in the sky across the river. Headlamps are gleaming through the dusk, and again the constant groan of traffic is in the air. The last time I remember hearing that, I was in the trailer, lying with your arm around me, and Anna asleep between us.

I'm making a show of timing the contractions. Thirty minutes. I'll keep her thinking they're at thirty minutes even as they gradually crowd together and come at her every twenty-five, twenty. I don't want her to panic. We have to spin this out for hours. I do want the child born alive, and her alive to see it.

"Why not go and make sure all your things are together?" I say. "It helps if you move around. I'll make a cup of tea and try Ron again."

She has packed and repacked her overnight bag a number of times already, but at least doing that occupies her. She gnaws her bottom lip, nods and hauls herself to her feet.

In the kitchen I put on the kettle, and while she wanders around picking things up and putting them down, I stand in the doorway and say loudly, with the phone at my ear, "Hi Ron, me again. You got my other messages? It's coming, she's started, it's all going fine. But will you get here as quick as possible? Can you call me back? We're OK, but we need you here now. She really needs to be in hospital soon, OK? Call me back, OK? Soon as possible!"

Annabel appears from her room, looking brave. She pulls in a long, deep breath and lets it out slowly. She thinks I dialled Ron's number before I spoke.

"He'll be on his way the minute he hears that," she says, trying to keep her voice smooth. "Won't he, Silva? Nothing to be worried about. Is there? And it's all going fine! It takes hours, doesn't it?" She glances at the door. "I heard something! I heard the boat! I'm sure it's him, go down and see! Go and wave, make him hurry!"

I pretend excitement. "Maybe you're right! Quick, come on!"

We go outside. While she dances at the doorway on her bare feet, I run down to the jetty and scan the water. There's a heavy drizzle falling, and the river and sky are the same grey. Of course it's not the boat. It was probably a lorry on the bridge. I haven't spoken to Ron for days and days. I've replied to maybe one in ten of the messages he sends to Annabel's phone. Anyway, he thinks the baby's not due for another two weeks.

But for several minutes I wait there gazing across, allowing her to think it might be him. Of course it's cruel. But she deserves cruelty. Don't you know what she did to you and Anna? I walk back to the cabin shaking my head. Oh dear, it wasn't the boat.

Out here in the fading light, her face is blotchy. She's shivering and sweating and trying very hard not to cry again. Naturally I'm moved by her distress, but I resist any wish to take her in my arms by remembering exactly why it is she's in all this trouble. Why she is in even more trouble than she understands yet. Of course it's cruel, but has she not been cruel, is she not being cruel even now? She let her husband believe her dead in the river, she lets him go on believing it. Every day since the bridge went down she makes him suffer for the loss of her, as I suffer my loss of you. What is happening, what is about to happen, are what she deserves.

We drink our tea. I make another show of calling Ron, and we wait by the light of the stove. Then the contractions stop. We wait. She shifts about, complains of backache, of wind, goes to pee. We wait for an hour, and still no more contractions. Then she goes to lie down. When she gets up, it's quite dark. She announces she is hungry and starts foraging in the kitchen. She comes back with a plate of crackers and cheese and, for God's sake, beetroot.

"Aren't you hungry?"

I shake my head and turn away from the sound of crunching and the sight of her tongue licking crumbs from the corners of her mouth. She is joking now, while she shoves the food in and chews. Her gusts of laughter smell of vinegar. She says the baby was just having a practice, keeping her on her toes, she's heard this can happen several times, up to three weeks before the birth. I have to agree this is possible, and then I find I have nothing more to say. The thought of this not being her time depresses me unbearably. I sit staring at the stove with my arms tight around myself. I have no taste for what I must do,

I simply want to get it over with. If it becomes any more drawn-out than this, I am afraid I may be unable to go through with it.

She slumps back to the kitchen with her empty plate, and it's when she is calling out to me to let Ron know it was a false alarm that she has another contraction, one that stops her breath in her throat and produces a long, quiet moan. I wait, pretending I haven't heard. After a quarter of an hour, she reappears.

There's a look on her face now that wasn't there before, a steadiness. She is going into battle. When the next contraction comes, nineteen minutes later, she's ready for it, and for the next one, another nineteen minutes later. In between, she walks up and down and gibbers on about Ron, will he bring her some shoes when he comes, because without them how will she get to the jetty? After another hour and three more contractions, I tell her it's time to forget about him. He must have lost his phone or something. The contractions are getting stronger and we have to work this out by ourselves. I remind her about the little white boat. I tell her we'll take it downriver, keeping close to our side of the bank, and moor it at the bridge jetty. Ron won't be far away, but even if he can't be found, somebody there will call an ambulance and it'll come straight away now that the bridge is open. It will get her over to hospital in Inverness within minutes.

"And you've got at least twelve more hours to go," I say. "Plenty of time."

She looks at me in terror. "We can't go on the river in that boat! You know what Ron says, it's not safe. And it's pitch-dark!"

"Then you'll have to have the baby here," I tell her. "You couldn't walk along the bank to the bridge jetty now, even with shoes. You can't climb up through the trees to the road. Do you want to have it here? I'm not a midwife."

"I can't even make it down to our jetty like this, in bare feet," she cries.

"Of course you can," I say. "Come on, I'll help you."

I can't offer her my arm, can I, because I'm carrying her bag in one hand and the oars (which I brought into the cabin weeks ago to keep dry) in the other. She'll have to manage. It's a drizzly night, but a fuzzy three-quarter moon shines down through the cloud. This is helpful, because I haven't thought to bring a torch. Annabel hesitates. She peers through the dark to find an easy way down to the jetty, but there isn't one. I shout at her to hurry up. Soon she is sliding around on clumps of wet, warty seaweed and sharp stones, falling and cutting her feet and hands, gasping with pain. Every step is treacherous. After half an hour she is not even halfway, and she screams at me that she's going back. I shout at her not to be stupid. She has no choice. On she goes, yowling louder as she treads on lacerated feet through freezing saltwater puddles. When another contraction comes, she stops and moans and struggles to stay upright. I walk ahead, listening to her as she snivels and stumbles behind me.

I turn and watch her. She slips again, falls sideways and lands heavily on her hip. "Get down on your hands and knees," I call out. "Safer for the baby."

Down she gets, lifting her backside high as the next contraction comes. When it has passed, she begins to move forwards, sobbing, lumbering on all fours and her belly hanging to the ground. I turn and keep walking to the boat. I wait for her there, watching her crawl after me.

When she gets to the jetty she takes fright again at the size of the boat and how strong the river is, until I ask her if she wants to go back up to the cabin. Just as I get her in, she falls forwards onto her hands and knees and nearly tips the boat over. Slowly she turns herself around and sits down in the stern. The boat is so low in the water it wouldn't take a very big wave to capsize us. I hope I've timed this right. The river is at its lowest ebb, the flow tide is just starting to come in. It will be at its highest and strongest in about six hours.

I manage the rowing quite well, although we are going against the incoming tide. We don't speak, to begin with. I'm busy keeping an even stroke, and she's groaning and rolling about, almost hysterical. I tell her it's dangerous to throw herself about like that, and she'll slow us down.

"But it hurts! Oh, God it hurts, it fucking hurts!" she sobs, rocking herself to and fro.

"Breathe the way you're supposed to and keep still," I tell her. I'm already exhausted. My arms are aching and my heart is pounding, and the bad thing is we have slowed down. Though the wind is blowing hard down the estuary, in our favour, we are going against the tide, and it is stronger than I expected. This is going to take much, much longer than I thought.

Out of my mouth comes a little cry, more of surprise than pain. It's nothing sharp or stabbing. It's like cramp, as if I'm being grabbed around the middle and squeezed by a great pair of toothless jaws that crush but don't bite. I'm standing over a pan of water in the kitchen that I'm heating up for something or other, and suddenly I can't remember what. Low down in my belly a hardening begins, the grab tightens. I wait, watching the trembling surface of the water in the saucepan with concentrated interest: a miniature ocean, wraiths of steam wafting off it, tiny waves beating themselves out against the side. Taking a deep breath isn't as easy as it should be. Suddenly I can picture my lungs hanging in my chest, two wrinkled, complaining old bellows pushing for room. Next I realize the floor is wet, my feet are wet from fluid that's trickling down my legs. Another band tightens around me, squeezes, and lets go just in the split second before I'm going to cry out, this time in fear. Instead, I breathe. It is so absolutely simple. And I am so afraid.

I hurry to find Silva and blurt out that it's starting, and she takes in what I'm saying with a level look, staring me in the eyes. She doesn't glance even once at my stomach. She's dismissive, in fact, and I try to absorb some of her calm, but at the same time her composure unsettles me. When she calls Ron he doesn't answer, and if this surprises her she doesn't show it. She leaves him a message and tells me there are hours and hours to go yet. The one thing we've got is plenty of time, she assures me, and I force myself to understand she is right. But although the gripping in my belly has subsided, my fear rises. The cabin is tiny and hot, and even with just the two of us, crowded. I never did find my phone, so I have to pester Silva to keep trying Ron on hers. I get more and more afraid. I can't keep track of time, either. There is no clock.

The next contraction comes a long time after the first, and once it passes, my fingers and legs feel hopelessly weak, and it's hard to swallow. The evening is drawing in, and the day is turning lopsided. The light from the stove, the only light in the room, thrums with a bluish, fluttery gleam. I have to get away from here, and I can't.

But Silva's right. There is plenty of time. There are more contractions, at long intervals. Then they stop. Some more time passes, and I wonder if they were contractions at all. It could have been my stomach playing up, a confusion of the body brought on by not much more than heavy food and anxiety. Whatever it was, it's stopped, thank God. And I'm glad I've gone through this, because when it happens for real, in a week or two, I'll be more prepared. By then we will have seen Ron and I'll be sure there won't be any difficulty reaching him next time. I've worn myself out with silly fretting. Silva has withdrawn into one of her moods; she would like to disappear off down the river as she usually does but can't, I suppose, because of me. The air between us reminds me of a sky before a storm, charged with pent lightning. I'm still a little out of breath. I make excuses and go to my room.

Later I get up with the intention of making Silva more cheerful, but she has retreated too far. She isn't hungry, she doesn't want to talk, she's too bored even to listen to anything I might say. And it turns out there is little time to spare for bringing her round, anyway, because it begins again, it really does begin.

There is no doubting it this time. The contraction is painful, and I tense myself against it, squeezing my eyes and mouth tight. The next one comes and I do the same, clenching all my muscles until it passes, and then I realize how tiring that is, and how futile. I cannot hold them away. I am going to be seized by another, and another, and many more, and worse, and I will not win any struggle to prevent them hurting me any more than, if I were walking into the sea, I could by force of will not be drenched by waves breaking over my head. It will be a case not of staying dry, but of not drowning. I must adjust my expectations: I have to be delivered of this baby, and we both must stay alive, but I will not escape injury. With this clear in my mind, I inform Silva that my labour has begun.

I am measuring time in spaces between the pains, and in waiting for Ron. My legs are shaking, and there's a tinny taste in my mouth. Silva moves around quietly, talking to me about breathing. It must be her way of hiding her own anxiety, but her voice seems to have hardened. She is completely unhurried and practical. Still Ron doesn't come, and when she announces we have to give up on him and go downriver by ourselves in the rowing boat, she becomes almost brusque. I daren't think about the possibility that she is as frightened as I am, for I am in pain – worse than I ever imagined – and so I try to concentrate instead on what I must do to get away from here. I need to find people who can do something about the pain. I am not so out of my wits that I do not grasp that in order to do that, though it terrifies me, I will first have to cross the broken shingle and slippery rocks in the dark. Then I will have to go in the tiny rowing boat onto the rushing black river. But however I get there, I have to get to a hospital.

By the time we reach the place, the tide is rising. I lift the oars, and we drift until the wind pushes us over close to the bank opposite the flat rock in the river. Annabel has been sitting hunched up with her eyes tight shut and doesn't see what's happening until the boat starts bumping against the half-submerged boulders close to the shore. I make a way through the maze of rocks while she gasps and peers around in the dark.

"What are you doing? Where are we?" she asks.

"Be quiet," I say.

When I'm close enough to the shore, I jump out and try to haul the boat up. With her in it, I can't get it more than halfway out of the water.

"Get out," I say.

"Silva, please!" She's crying and clutching her belly. "What's going on, where are we? We're not at the bridge, this isn't the jetty!"

"Get *out*," I say.

She does as I tell her, protesting the whole time, and straight away topples into the water. She starts to sink in the mud. When I haul her to her feet she's soaking wet and shivering. There's weed sticking to her face. As soon as she has enough breath to speak, she starts on at me again. I tell her she's getting hysterical, and give her a good slap.

She follows me quietly enough after that, up the scree of stones to the place where the trees meet the shore. I sit down, and she collapses beside me on the ground a few yards from your memorial.

"Silva, please! Why are we here? Silva, please, what's going on? Silva, listen! I've got to get to hospital—"

"Do you see that?" I say quietly, pointing.

"What? The stones? That pile of stones? What about it?"

"Pile of stones?" I reach over and grab a handful of her hair and turn her head. "Look at it. A pile of stones? Those stones, they are for Stefan and Anna. The people you killed. *They* are why you're here."

"Killed? I didn't kill anyone! What are you talking about? Oh, *God*!" She grits her teeth and pulls away as the next spasm starts in her belly. I let go of her hair and stand up. She rolls with the pain, holding herself tight. She draws in her legs, moaning. When the contraction is over, she sits herself up. She begs me to take her to hospital, she tells me to calm myself. She tries to talk to me about the baby. Please, think of the baby, she pleads. For the baby's sake, she has to get to hospital.

"The baby's sake? Your baby?" I take her mobile phone from my pocket and fling it at her. It lands on a rock, and the casing splits. She scrabbles for it, picks it up and another bit breaks off in her hand.

"Why have you got my phone? Where did you find it? Silva, what is going on!"

"My Stefan. You're having his baby, aren't you? My husband's baby. That's why he gave you our money."

"What? Silva, no! No, I swear! It's not his, of course it's not!"

"You spoke to him before he died. It's your fault they were in that car."

"Oh God, no! Silva, listen. Listen, yes, I spoke to him, I met him. But only once. Please—"

"It's because of you they're dead. And you think that baby's yours?"

"Silva, listen! The car, and the money. I needed money. I wanted to tell you—"

I step forwards and, making sure not to miss, I kick the phone out of her hand. As she screams, the phone flies away and lands somewhere in the dark behind us. She cradles her hurt hand in the other one and sits sobbing, pushing herself to and fro, telling me I have to believe her. The next contraction will be coming very soon. I wander away some distance and find a place where I will be out of the wind. Then I sit down to wait.

It's very cold. As the hours pass, she calls out for me, urgently at first, with a note of hope in her voice that I might really come to her. Later she cries out in pure desperation. I hear her vomit. She tries to get up and come to me, but collapses again and again. I grow used to the raging, gurgling cries and the teeth-gritted roars. The sound carries over the water and is lost on the wind. On and on it goes. I sit and watch the tide.

The struggle approaches its end, as it must. When I finally go to her, she's on her back with her knees drawn up, and between her legs she's split and bloodied and gaping, like a half-skinned animal. I lean down, and she clutches my wrist and won't let it go. She's babbling, and on her face is a look of disbelief and outrage. She is panting and straining down mindlessly, and eventually from between her legs there appears a glistening mound. She writhes and pushes, digging her fingers deep into my arm. I wrench my arm away, and with the next push she lets out a scream, and now the baby's head bulges out and wobbles in my hand, and as she screams again one shoulder and then the other come slithering bumpily out of her, and then its flailing stick arms appear, and all the rest, all the warm, bloodied tangle of it. There's so much of it, now the unfolding legs and the feet trailing strings of stained slime and wet twisted cord and, also, a surprising amount of dark blood. I let all of it slide into my hands. I cup the back of the baby's head and rub its scrunched face and then comes a crackle of mucus from its open mouth and a rush of air, a splutter and a wheezing cry. Annabel's hands reach out. She's crying. I am, too, as I draw the child into my own arms. Its head lolls, it turns its face to my chest. Annabel strains forwards but can't get up.

"Let me see! Oh, let me see! Is it all right?" she cries. "Let me see! Give it to me! What is it?"

"I have to wrap him up," I tell her. "He's shivering. It's a boy."

And to you I whisper – though there is no need to whisper, for she does not understand a word – that we have a son.

I pull a towel and a cardigan from her bag and wrap the baby up and lay him on the ground. She falls back, exhausted. I wait until the cord stops pulsating, and then I cut it using the string and scissors I brought. The child is now separate from her.

"Please. Please let me have him," she croaks. But before I can answer she cries out and gasps. "Oh, God! Oh God, what's happening? I'm bleeding! Help me, I'm bleeding! What's happening?"

Sure enough, blood is pouring from her, along with ropes of steaming membrane.

"It's the afterbirth," I tell her. "Push." She obeys, still moaning to be given the child, and eventually the flabby, dark, veined sac is delivered. She tries to wriggle away from it, leaving a heap of shining pulp and a slippery trail behind her on the stones. The air is thick with the smell of blood.

"Give him to me, please," she weeps. She is shuddering with cold and shock. "Let me have him."

I did not expect this to be the hardest part of all. I imagined myself with a lot to say. How jealous I was that she was carrying her child after mine was lost, that I didn't know what I would do when it was born and she took it away, when she left me to be with Ron and the child for ever. That I dreamed of stealing it. That for a while stealing it was all I dreamed of.

Then how I was shown that it would not be stealing, but only taking what is mine. I thought I had those words ready, too. How I forgive *you* for the existence of this child, but I will never forgive her, how unthinkable it is that she should have it to love and keep for herself when she killed the child who was mine and yours. I was going to tell her how I promise every day to come back to you, that I have stayed alive just so that I can take this newborn baby with me out onto the black rock and wait there until the tide rises and carries us both back to you. I want to tell her that she is going to watch her child disappear under the river, and when she does she ought to remember that that is what she did to my Anna. She is going to know my sorrow.

My love, I know you are with Anna, waiting for me and the baby boy, and when the flow tide sweeps over the rock, we won't struggle. I shall let it bear us down to the riverbed, and we shall all be together.

But when I try to say any of this, the words sheer off and crumble against my chattering teeth and I feel myself getting dizzy, falling and breaking apart. It's like demolishing a wall and discovering I also am the wall. Every blow I inflict I also take. I'm made of it, I'm a part of it. I get to my feet and walk away towards the river with the little thing in my arms, taking Annabel's bag with me. The screams that follow me now are more agonized and urgent even than the sounds she made when he was forcing her body to open and expel him, and now his fists beat the air and from his mouth come wave upon wave of a bleating cry that answers his mother's.

All this while the river has been rising and the boat is now afloat. I wade in, place him on the bottom, and push off into the current. The rock is almost half under the water, so I will be able to climb onto it. But it will be difficult, as there is nowhere to attach the boat. I bring it alongside and wedge the prow in one of the rock's jutting angles. But it won't stay there long. I have to find a place where I can grab hold and get out of the boat and onto the rock. I will need both hands, so I sling the bag over my shoulder and pull the child in under my clothes, against my bare chest, and bind him to me using a sweater from Annabel's bag, tying him close with the sleeves. From the shore she is screaming at me to come back. I want her to be watching, but knowing that she is makes me feel sick and empty.

I use one oar to steady the boat as best as I can in the current, then I count to three, drop the oar and throw myself at the rock. I land on all fours and hang on until I am able, carefully, to move one foot, then a hand, then the other foot. I crawl forwards. It's slippery, and I struggle to keep hold but not cling too close, lest I crush the child. I crawl to the middle of the rock and lie on my back for several minutes before sitting up and unwrapping him.

His head drops back on his flimsy neck, his eyes are closed. I feel his face with the back of my hand. It's cold. I cradle his head and wail. I intended to take him with me when I drown, but now he's dead, and his death pierces me to the heart. I clasp him to me, and from the riverbank Annabel screams again. Then he stirs, and before I know what I am doing I am weeping, and laughing and covering the top of his head with kisses. The little thing was asleep! He fell asleep against my breast, his face bloody and gluey with birth slime stuck fast to my skin. I wrap him up warm again and hold him close, and rock him back and forth. His mouth turns to my nipple, and he latches on and sucks. After a moment he tugs himself away from me, his mouth opens again and he screams. I hear Annabel's voice calling back to him. I have failed him, for of course my breast is dry. I do not understand why it distresses me that I have nothing to give him. Just then a high wave hits the edge of the rock and rolls like a cold wet cloth over it, soaking my legs. I do not understand why I lift him clear, taking care to keep him dry.

Behind me there's a scraping noise, and I turn just in time to see the tide nudge the prow of the little white boat clear of the rock. It clunks two or three times as it goes, then spins free and is borne away upriver. From the shore, Annabel pleads for her baby. Holding him tightly to me with one arm, I use my free hand to reach into my pocket for my phone. Another freezing wave slides over the rock, and he cries and cries for his mother while the wind cuts into my back.

Colin had called Ron and asked if they could meet up in the evening of the day the bridge reopened. He had something to show him. Something he was doing for his wife and the baby.

"What is it?" said Ron.

"Tell you when I see you," Colin said. "It's nothing spectacular. Just want to show somebody, if that's OK."

Ron agreed. He had no idea what, if anything, he might tell Colin about Annabel. *I know a pregnant woman, that's a coincidence, isn't it? I know a pregnant woman, she turned up after the bridge fell down, maybe it's your wife?* Even supposing – *supposing* – Annabel *was* Colin's wife, she must have good reasons to stay away from him. What right did Ron have to interfere? And what would be the point, when the body of Colin's wife was probably a clean skeleton at the bottom of the river, the boneless embryo of Colin's child long disintegrated? That was what Colin – and he – had to accept. There was nothing he could say about Annabel that would not do more harm than good.

He trudged down from the sleeper unit through the mud towards the jetty and the new walkway leading under the bridge. The construction site had been emptying for days and was now deserted and almost cleared; the casting sheds downriver had already been dismantled and removed, and massive criss-crossed ruts and divots of earth marked the departure of the heavy plant. Only a few huts remained, a dozen skips were filling up. The sleeper unit was due to be removed on Monday, and then Ron would be fending for himself again, bedding down in the back of the Land Rover, waiting for the baby's birth. He was still needed for a while to run the boat, for inspectors checking the new sections of the bridge, and for journalists, but soon he would be gone himself. Where to, he had no idea. He could form no picture of a future for himself that did not include Annabel and the baby and, if necessary, he quite willingly supposed, Silva too.

The ground for the memorial garden, reached by the walkway under the bridge and stretching for an acre beyond it, had been pushed into a succession of improbable hollows and mounds and phoney undulations. In the moonlight, it lay bare, whimsical and miniaturized; stone walls only inches high curved around elliptical flower beds full of bark mulch, and a path of crazy paving wound in and out, connecting places where the ground swelled randomly into small circles of cobbles. It ended in a large and still unpaved circle overlooking the river. Nothing was finished and nothing had been planted yet. The landscaping ended abruptly next to a padlocked and fenced enclosure full of upright saplings, their roots wrapped in sacking, and stacks of stone slabs and bags of sand. Ron turned and walked back the way he had come. He waited for Colin by the railings, where a flight of stone steps set into the wall led down to a small landing stage; it was intended that visitors would be able to travel to the garden by boat from Inverness.

The strobing headlamps of cars on the bridge above him hurt his eyes; below the railings, the night wind chopped the surface of the incoming tide. From this angle, almost under the bridge, he could barely see the service station across the river, but the place would be full. There was a reception going on there to mark the reopening. High sodium lights over its car park and petrol pumps cast an orange haze into the sky.

Colin appeared, hands in pockets, and greeted Ron without a smile. "Hiya. Something going on over there, all right. I thought there would've been people over here, too," he said.

"Not much to see, yet," Ron answered.

"No," Colin said, looking round. "You can see it better on the website. Come on."

Ron followed Colin back into the garden.

"Here," Colin said. They were at one of the places where the path became a circle before leading out and away again around the curve of another artificial hillock. "Here's where it's going," he said. "Right here. I'm getting a memorial bench. She's going to have a memorial bench with her name on it. What about that?"

"That's a great idea," Ron said.

"Sustainable hardwood, three hundred pounds," Colin said proudly. "Expensive item. They bolt them to the ground. Fifty for the plaque. And I'm sponsoring a rosebush for the baby, that's another forty. Then fifty pounds a year after that for four years. All proceeds will go towards the upkeep of the garden."

"And you'll be able to come in the summer and sit here."

"Yeah. Won't bring them back, though."

"But it's a nice thing to do."

There seemed little else to say after that. The sounds of the bridge reached them as a rushing noise, like approaching weather; the bare, unplanted earth and the briny estuary smelled of winter. They wandered back to the river and leaned on the railing. Ron wanted to get away, and he wanted to get Colin away, too. A vandal-proof bench surrounded by a furze of low-maintenance municipal shrubs; even with a wife's name on it, just how was that "a nice thing to do"?

"Your wife. Suppose she, if she—" Ron began, then hesitated. He nodded back towards the garden. "Never mind. It's a very nice thing to do."

Colin blinked and sucked in a deep breath. "Thanks, mate. Fancy a pint, if you're not too busy?" he asked, with so much hope that Ron couldn't refuse. They were on their way up to the Land Rover when Ron's phone rang. It hadn't rung for days.

"Silva? What's the matter?" He listened for a moment. "Christ, no. Oh, Christ! Silva!" He ended the call and began running back down towards the jetty.

"Come on! Hurry up!" he shouted to Colin over his shoulder. "Come on!"

When they got to the boat, Ron set Colin at the prow with a torch. Then he turned the launch upriver towards the cabin, straight into the flow of the still incoming tide.

When I try to move, blood gushes from me. It's hot and thick, and there is far, far too much of it. My eyes are streaming with tears, so I can hardly see her, but she's sitting on the rock with my baby bundled to her, and she's got her head tipped towards the sky as if she's looking up at the bridge. Lights streak across it, white in one direction, red in the other. My throat is raw with screaming. I can see the white rowing boat out on the water bright in the moonlight, a little silver thing rocking in the black and silver river. Then I see a wave wash it loose from the rock, and now it is spinning away with the rising tide. Now my child is trapped. My child is screaming for me, but when I try to raise myself to stand up, my head swims and I fall back. My heart thumps all through my body, and there is another gush of blood. I scream again and roll myself over, and crawl down to the shore. The blood pours. Though I'm almost down on the ground, it tilts up, turns black, and hits my face.

I open my eyes and manage to raise my head and spit some of the freezing grit out of my mouth. I hear a boat, a boat coming nearer and nearer, with the tide. There's a darting light on the water. I know the sound of Ron's boat. I hear his voice and want to call back, but with every breath I feel dizzy, and he wouldn't hear me above the engine noise. He's shouting to Silva. The river is swirling under me now as I lie on the shore. Somehow I drag myself to my feet and try to take a step forwards. I scream and fall again, into deeper water.

The stinging cold steadies me, and I scream out again. Ron's boat is on the far side of the rock now, and I can't see it, but he is on the rock, crouching down to her. She's sitting in a flow of water, and he is taking the bundle from her arms. Another wave breaks over the rock and pushes at them. Silva slides away. I can't see Ron clearly any more. The boat's engine surges wildly. I struggle to my feet again, ankle-deep in water now, but I slip in the mud and can't get up. I scream out again, and there comes another surge of the engine, almost out of control, and then the boat appears from around the rock, making for the shore. Ron is standing on the rock, and he has got Silva to her feet somehow and is holding on to her. The boat's engine stalls. Then it stops.

In the sudden silence, the light on the boat turns a giddy half circle as the tide catches the prow and spins the boat upriver. I watch it drift away from me, the light bobbing and fading. I glance back at the bare rock. A wave washes over it. Ron and Silva have gone. With the next wave, the rock will vanish under the tide.

Then the engine coughs and roars, and the boat makes a crazy turn into a heavy wave. The light beam sways across the river and onto the shore. I close my eyes. For several moments, everything is quiet but for the chug of the boat and the running river. Blood warms the water lapping between my legs. The boat engine stops. I can't scream, and I can't open my eyes. I do not believe I shall open them again. I hear the splash of slow, wading steps coming towards me. I hear my baby's cry, and I hear Col's voice, calling out my name in the dark.

Acknowledgements

My thanks are due to Elisabetta Minervini and Alessandro Gallenzi, the owners of Alma Books; I am very proud to be published in Britain by one of the UK's newest, most successful and innovative stars in the firmament of independent, literary publishing houses. I'm grateful, specifically, to Alessandro for his meticulous editing and to Elisabetta for masterminding the promotion of this novel.

I also owe an immense debt of gratitude to Kate Miciak at Random House, New York for her unfailing encouragement and brilliant editorship of this novel for its original USA publication.

I thank also my two wonderful agents, Jean Naggar of the Jean V. Naggar Literary Agency in New York and Maggie Phillips at Ed Victor Ltd in London, for all their support, guidance and skill.

Dr Nina Biehal kindly gave permission to print extracts from her work (with co-authors Fiona Mitchell and Jim Wade) *Lost From View: A Study of Missing Persons in the UK*. Thank you.

Dr Stafford Craig, who designs bridges all over the world, found time to check some of the technical details of the bridge in this novel. Thank you. Any errors are, of course, mine alone.

While I worked on this novel I was a writer-in-residence at the Heinrich Böll Cottage on Achill Island, County Mayo, Ireland. I offer my sincere thanks to the Achill Heinrich Böll Association for awarding me the residency, and to the hospitable Achill islanders who made my time there so much fun.

And most of all, I'm grateful to my lovely daughter Hannah who, whenever she's around, makes me laugh and makes me lunch.